Alexandra Adornetto famously wrote her first novel *The Shadow Thief* when she was thirteen, and with her second series Halo went on to become a *New York Times* bestselling author. She now lives in Hollywood with all of the other misfits — and her miniature Yorkie called Boo Radley.

You can find her online at
facebook.com/AlexandraAdornetto
and follow her on Twitter: @MissAllyGrace

Also by Alexandra Adornetto

Halo
Hades
Heaven

Ghost House
(also published as *Lament*)

HAUNTED

ALEXANDRA ADORNETTO

Angus&Robertson
An imprint of HarperCollins*Publishers*

Angus&Robertson

An imprint of HarperCollins*Publishers*, Australia

First published in Australia in 2017
by HarperCollins*Publishers* Australia Pty Limited
ABN 36 009 913 517
harpercollins.com.au

HarperCollins*Publishers*
Level 13, 201 Elizabeth Street, Sydney NSW 2000, Australia
Unit D1, 63 Apollo Drive, Rosedale, Auckland 0632, New Zealand
A 53, Sector 57, Noida, UP, India
1 London Bridge Street, London SE1 9GF, United Kingdom
2 Bloor Street East, 20th floor, Toronto, Ontario M4W 1A8, Canada
195 Broadway, New York NY 10007, USA

National Library of Australia Cataloguing-in-Publication data:

Adornetto, Alexandra, author.
  Haunted / Alexandra Adornetto.
  ISBN: 978 0 7322 9934 7 (paperback)
  ISBN: 978 1 4607 0310 6 (ebook)
  Ages 12+
  Ghost stories.
  Apparitions—Juvenile fiction.
  Interpersonal relations—Juvenile fiction.
A823.4

Cover design by Darren Holt, HarperCollins Design Studio
Cover images: Girl by Jessica Truscott; Los Angeles Orphanage by University of
Southern California
Author photograph © Julian Dolman 2017
Typeset in Bembo Std Regular by Kirby Jones

To Neil Salvano,
with love

Awake and sing, ye that dwell in dust: for thy dew is as the dew
of herbs, and the earth shall cast out the dead.

ISAIAH 26:19, KING JAMES BIBLE

Cold in the earth — and the deep snow piled above thee,
Far, far removed, cold in the dreary grave!
Have I forgot, my only Love, to love thee,
Severed at last by Time's all-severing wave?

Now, when alone, do my thoughts no longer hover
Over the mountains, on that northern shore,
Resting their wings where heath and fern-leaves cover
Thy noble heart for ever, ever more?

Cold in the earth — and fifteen wild Decembers
From those brown hills have melted into spring:
Faithful, indeed, is the spirit that remembers
After such years of change and suffering!

Sweet Love of youth, forgive, if I forget thee,
While the world's tide is bearing me along;
Other desires and other hopes beset me,
Hopes which obscure, but cannot do thee wrong!

No later light has lightened up my heaven,
No second morn has ever shone for me;
All my life's bliss from thy dear life was given,
All my life's bliss is in the grave with thee.

But when the days of golden dreams had perished,
And even Despair was powerless to destroy;
Then did I learn how existence could be cherished,
Strengthened and fed without the aid of joy.

Then did I check the tears of useless passion —
Weaned my young soul from yearning after thine;
Sternly denied its burning wish to hasten
Down to that tomb already more than mine.

And, even yet, I dare not let it languish,
Dare not indulge in memory's rapturous pain;
Once drinking deep of that divinest anguish,
How could I seek the empty world again?

EMILY BRONTË, "REMEMBRANCE"

CHAPTER ONE

The tray slipped from my fingers, hitting the cafeteria floor with a resounding crash. My hands remained frozen in place as the world seemed to slow. I watched a cascade of soda rise and fall again, drenching my feet as dozens of eyes automatically swivelled in my direction. I might have felt the sting of embarrassment had it not been for the numbness pervading my entire body. Instead, I felt disconnected, like a spectator on the outskirts of life.

My eyes fixed on the linoleum floor, now sloppy with food and drink, until I became aware of voices reaching me as if from a great distance.

"Chloe? Are you okay? What's going on?"

The trance broke, shattered by the barrage of questions from Sam and Natalie who flanked me. I was reluctant to meet their eyes, knowing that an explanation would be required of me and I had none to offer. Somehow I doubted *oops, butterfingers* was going to cut it.

The feeling of disconnection passed, overshadowed by sickening confusion. Surely I'd misheard. Alexander Reade ... here, at Sycamore High? The idea was too absurd to even contemplate. Only a few weeks ago I'd watched Alex's spirit disappear from this world, sucked into a black void where I knew I'd never find it again. At least not in this lifetime. And even if by some impossibility his spirit *had* managed to slip through the cracks of eternity and find its way back, Alex wasn't free to wander at will. His spirit was bound to Grange Hall, the house my grandmother ran as a B&B in England, where my brother Rory and I had been relegated for the summer after the sudden loss of our mom. Alex had told me himself that he'd wandered the grounds for over one hundred and fifty years. So the odds of him crossing the Atlantic Ocean and making his way to Southern California were zero to none.

No ... there had to be some mistake.

For goodness sake, get a grip, I told myself. This was the year things were supposed to get back to normal. This was the year I was going to take all the crazy, lock it in a box and throw away the key. Up until this moment I hadn't done too badly.

"Need some help?"

I looked up to find Zac Green standing in front of me. In the crowded cafeteria, he was the only person to come forward instead of simply gawping.

Sam and Natalie waited for him to acknowledge them, but he seemed oblivious to their presence. Sam blinked rapidly, the way she always did when irritated, her heavily mascaraed lashes almost dusting her cheeks.

"Chloe?" Looking concerned, Zac snapped his fingers under my nose.

I swallowed; my throat was as dry as old parchment. "Sorry," I croaked. "Did you say something?"

"I think maybe you should sit down."

"She's fine." Sam put a possessive arm around my shoulders,

as if to reinforce that external help wasn't necessary. I'd noticed before that when a guy failed to show interest in her, it always made her a little peevish. "*We're* taking care of her."

"Evidently," Zac replied, his eyes never leaving my face. "Well, I'm here if you need anything, Chloe."

I managed a grateful nod.

Only when he'd retreated to a safe distance did Sam release me. "Okay, what the hell just happened?" she demanded. "You totally zoned out on us!"

"It was nothing," I lied. "Just a dizzy spell."

"Maybe you should go see the nurse," Natalie weighed in. "You don't want to be the person who passes out in class. You'll never live that down."

It was amusing how she was more troubled by me losing status in the school community rather than any potential health issues I might be battling.

I waved my hands at them. "Don't worry. It's over now."

I felt a small stab of guilt for cutting them out instead of confiding in them like I would have ordinarily. But as far as I could see, I didn't exactly have a choice in the matter. There was no way I could explain what was happening without sounding like a total basket case. Besides, I wasn't sure myself what was happening.

"Are you sure?" Sam peered at me inquisitively. "You were like a zombie for a minute there. It was supes scary."

"Supes?" I repeated dubiously. "Come again?"

"It's like super," she explained, like she was imparting classified White House information. "Only now we say supes instead. It'll be trending in a few months, but by then we probably won't use it any more. It's more fun to say, don't you think?"

"Uh, I don't really get it ..."

"That's because you're behind the times now, Chloe." Natalie shook her head gravely. "It's very important to stay ahead of the game."

"What game?" I asked.

Sam gave up. "Don't worry. We'll try and bring you up to speed before anybody notices."

They were behaving as if I'd been gone a lifetime when in fact it had only been a matter of weeks. Although so much had happened in that short space of time, it felt more like years. I had to admit, this once-familiar place was now utterly foreign to me. It was like I didn't belong any more, like my true home was somewhere light years away. Both my mother's death (which I was still struggling to accept) and then my separation from Alex had left me with a cavernous metaphorical hole in my chest.

It was lucky my friends had short attention spans. They had already delved into a new topic of conversation, chattering away like monkeys, my weird episode all but forgotten. I grabbed some paper napkins and bent to mop up the mess. The task offered a momentary reprieve in which to gather my thoughts.

As soon as my mind returned to Alex, my heart began fluttering like a caged bird against my ribs. It couldn't be him. Of course, it wasn't him. But then who was this person claiming to be Alexander Reade? Was it some cruel supernatural prank? Or just a hideous coincidence? I had no idea, but I knew I wouldn't calm down until I found the answer.

Despite doing my best to keep a level head, I couldn't quash the little voice of hope that sprang up in my mind: *Perhaps our connection ran so deep, not even death could separate us.*

It was a wildly romantic idea, but there was a small part of me that wanted desperately to believe it was true. Okay, a large part. Ugh, I sounded like a moony teenager who'd read one too many romance novels. Besides, deep down I knew I was only setting myself up for more heartache. When "Alexander Reade" turned out to be some random guy who'd moved here from Montana, I'd be devastated.

I heard a rattling sound and looked up to find the school janitor, Miguel, wheeling his clunky yellow cart in my direction. Miguel was a sweetheart. He had a shaky grasp of the English language and most of the students treated him as if he were invisible, yet he wore a permanent smile from ear to ear. I wondered if cleaning up after hundreds of entitled teenagers was what he'd had in mind when he came to America, the land of opportunity? I immediately felt bad for adding to his daily workload.

"It's okay," I said once he was close. "It's my mess, I can clean it up."

"No, no." He shook his head firmly, gently swatting my hands away. "My job. You no worry, Miss Chloe."

I was touched to discover he knew my name, but it wasn't altogether surprising. Miguel was one of those people who said little but observed much.

"Thank you," I said, before my friends each took an arm and steered me away from the prying eyes of the cafeteria.

"I have an idea!" Natalie declared once we reached the privacy of the hall. "Why don't we ditch fourth period and all go to lunch in West Hollywood instead?"

Sam snorted. "On the first day of our last semester of senior year? We'll never get away with it. Right, Chloe?"

"What did he look like?" I blurted. I'd been planning to work up to that, but it slipped out before I could stop it. Alex's face was flooding my thoughts, leaving little room for much else.

"Who?" They fixed me with matching blank stares.

"The new guy, the one you saw this morning. I think I might know him from somewhere."

"I don't think so," Natalie said dismissively. She was already on her phone looking up the best West Hollywood hot spots. "If we don't know him, I doubt you would. Besides, he looked a little creepy."

"What? No way!" Sam protested. "He was sexy, in a bad boy kind of way."

"More like a serial killer kind of way. His skin's so pale it's like he's never seen the sun before."

Sam shrugged. "Whatever. I liked him and I wanted to talk to him."

"We *did* talk to him," Natalie snapped back. "He didn't seem that interested in talking to us so quit your whining."

"What did he say?" I fought to keep my voice casual.

"Nothing much," Sam replied. "Actually, I can't remember anything he said — I was too distracted by that voice. My God, he talks just like a prince! You know British accents are my one weakness."

Natalie laughed. "Any male with a heartbeat is your weakness."

"Shut up!" Sam elbowed her good-naturedly and they descended once again into a conversation that didn't require my input.

It was a good thing since I'd forgotten how to breathe.

A pale-skinned guy named Alexander Reade with a British accent had just showed up out of nowhere? That was no coincidence. But what the hell was going on? If Alexander was really here, it could only mean one of two things: that he was now alive, or I was dead. But he couldn't be alive. And I was pretty sure I hadn't died because that would mean Sycamore High was the afterlife, which would be the worst afterlife of all time. Imagine all that good behaviour only to end up relegated to high school for the rest of eternity? I'd opt for hellfire and damnation any day.

"What is up with you?" Sam peered into my face. "You're doing it again — going all weird and spacey."

"I have to go," I said, ducking my head to escape her scrutinising gaze.

"What? Why?"

I went with the first thing that popped into my head. "I'm sick. Rory's got that stomach flu that's been going around. I must have caught it from him. I better go home before I pass it on to you guys."

I hurried away before they could argue or fire off any more questions.

"Chloe!" Natalie yelled after me. "At least call us later, okay? *Okay?*"

I barely heard her. Adrenaline was buzzing through me, making my ears ring and my face flush like I was riding a Tilt-A-Whirl. I had to find Alex … or at least the impostor masquerading as Alex. The only problem was I had no idea where to look.

I decided a systematic approach made the most sense so I worked my way through the main building, starting with an extensive search of the science wing. This basically involved me creeping along and peering through classroom windows, leaping out of view every time I was at risk of being seen by a teacher. It was definitely the kind of behaviour to spark attention so I was surprised when no one spotted me. When it was obvious Alex wasn't in the science wing, I moved on to the library, then the infirmary, the gym, the assembly hall and everything in between. Along the way I stole surreptitious glances at every long-haired boy who passed me, hoping that one of them might look back at me with those crystalline blue eyes that I only saw in my dreams now.

By the time the final bell chimed, I was out of ideas. I'd looked everywhere and Alex was nowhere to be found. This was hardly what I'd had in mind for my first day back at school, and part of me wondered if I shouldn't just get in my car and go home. Perhaps tomorrow would bring the fresh start I so desperately desired.

But standing alone in an empty hallway, I realised it wasn't desire I felt or even frustration. It was anger. It seemed the universe was messing with me on purpose. It was playing a little game, only I didn't know the rules. It was just so … *unfair*. I hated that word, it sounded so whiny, but I couldn't think of anything more fitting. Hadn't I been through enough? The loss of my mom was sudden and unexpected. Maybe that was what made it so much more devastating. It shouldn't have happened. She left for work one morning complaining of a slight headache and never came home. A blood vessel burst in her brain, flooding it and causing irreparable damage. Up until then I hadn't even heard of a cerebral aneurysm. She was in her forties and I'd never known her to have so much as a cold. Researching via internet forums is never a smart idea, but I couldn't help myself. I was looking for signs we might have missed, a concrete reason that might make the loss a little more bearable. But it was only meeting and falling in love with Alex that lessened the grief a little. The fact that he had long departed this world made him the only person who could really understand. Now it felt like old wounds were about to re-open. Couldn't something, *anything*, in my life go according to plan just once?

I'd spent the last weeks trying to erase Alex's memory from my mind and finally I'd felt like I was making headway. My return from England had hardly been smooth sailing; in fact, it had been downright agonising, but with every passing day I told myself I was moving forward. Now I felt like some invisible force had seized me by the throat and flung me right back where I'd started. To add insult to injury, I would now be in trouble for not attending classes on the first day of semester. But I'd have to deal with that later.

I wished I could say that since coming home, Alexander Reade had never crossed my mind. But that would be an epic lie. I'd thought about him every day, more than I cared to admit. I knew it was a problem, but I could see no simple solution. Before I fell for Alex, I'd never known what it felt like to miss someone the second they left a room. I'd never understood the idea of trusting someone so implicitly that my innermost thoughts were no longer private; or that true intimacy wasn't physical, but a merging of souls. What if I never found that again? What if I spent the rest of my life in a fruitless search for something that never came close to what we'd shared?

If there was any truth to the theory that humans had only one soul mate, I'd met and lost mine in the space of a few weeks. Now didn't that seem a little unfair?

As I made my way to the parking lot, the sound of laughter distracted me from my gloom. A group of senior hipsters were swaggering toward me, headed for the theatre. Had rehearsals for the school play started up again already? They sure weren't wasting any time.

I knew Rory had a swim meet after school, and my dad was always working late these days, so I decided to follow the group. I didn't have the strength to face an empty house.

I slipped into the theatre just before the door swung shut behind the last student. It was cool inside, with that airless musky scent of velvet. This was the oldest part of the school, still awaiting renovation, so the acoustics weren't great. On the stage a jumble of kids were swigging from soda cans and making a general racket. A few of the younger ones had raided the prop chest and were playing catch with a dented old skull, until the drama teacher, Mr Helton, marched onto the stage and confiscated it.

"I don't remember seeing you before," Mr Helton said to me as he stomped back to his seat in the front row. "I have no room for idlers in my theatre."

"Actually … I'm the stagehand," I said without thinking.

What a dumb move. I watched his eyes light up.

"I didn't think anybody had signed up for that, but better late than never! I have a long list of things I need you to do. Wait right there."

I made for the exit as soon as his back was turned. The

play was at the end of the week and if I didn't get out quick, I'd be working flat out till opening night.

In the split second before pushing open the door, I glanced up into the balcony … and there he was, Alexander Reade, sitting in shadow, his body completely still as he watched the figures onstage. I couldn't see his features clearly, but I recognised the planes of his face and the locks of hair falling around his shoulders and over his eyes.

There was no question. Alex *was* here. In fact, he was right above me, just a few feet away in a place I'd never thought to look.

Although my first instinct was to bolt upstairs and fling myself into his arms, I decided to show a little restraint. I made my way cautiously up the carpeted steps until I reached the gallery. I could see him more clearly now and the urge to run to him was overpowering. Yet something held me back. Something wasn't right.

At first I couldn't figure out what. Then it hit me. Was Alex dressed in jeans? Yes, he was. Black jeans, and a black T-shirt with what appeared to be a band logo on the front. What had happened to his tailcoat and riding boots? And it wasn't just his clothes that were different. Every time I'd seen him at Grange Hall, he always looked the same; from one day to the next his face, his hair, his clothes, remained unchanged. That was how it worked: ghosts weren't meant to change. Except now Alex had. His hair was dishevelled and there were deep, dark shadows under his eyes. Even though he was sitting stock-still, there was an uncharacteristic nervous energy surrounding him.

I wasn't sure how to approach him. Should I announce my presence with a discreet cough? Should I rush over?

Or tap him politely on the shoulder like I would a stranger? There was no correct etiquette for this unique situation.

I deliberated for a moment before deciding to tiptoe up behind him. I wanted to reach out and touch the back of his head first, just to make sure he was real, but my hands remained leaden at my sides.

Instead, I whispered his name so softly it was barely audible.

I half-expected him not to hear me. I was scared that if he moved even an inch, he might crumble to dust or fade away into nothingness. But he heard me alright because he turned around.

As our eyes met, a swarm of butterflies took flight in my stomach, making my whole body break out in goosebumps. His face was as composed as a painting, exactly how I remembered him. His features were refined, light emanating from his eyes even in the dimness of the theatre. The loose strands of hair framing his face were the colour of burnished brass. I felt a leap of elation. He might be dressed differently, but he was still Alex. My Alex. And now he'd come back for me.

"Alex? Is it really you?" The tears of relief stinging the corners of my eyes were immediately followed by confusion. "How the hell did you get here?"

If I was expecting some big emotional reunion, I was about to be bitterly disappointed. There was a long, drawn-out pause while he frowned and searched my face. I stood there feeling like a specimen in a jar, waiting for the awkwardness to subside. *Any minute now*, I thought, *we'll fall into an embrace and never let go. He'll tell me what happened, and we'll both marvel at how we managed to beat Fate and vow to never let anything come between us again.*

But that didn't happen. In fact, nothing could have prepared me for what happened next. It was worse than my worst nightmare; worse than any scenario I could have imagined.

Alexander's frown deepened and his eyes narrowed. "Are we acquainted?"

It felt like all my organs had travelled south at the speed of light, stopping abruptly at my toes and leaving me reeling. Alex stared at me without a glimmer of recognition. His eyes were completely blank. In fact, it felt like he wished I'd go away and leave him in peace.

My mind spiralled back to our first meeting on the wooded path on the outskirts of Grange Hall. He had looked at me with the same confusion then, when he realised I was the first living person able to see him. But things were different now, or at least they were supposed to be. Alex and I shared a history; my memories of him were precious. But he was watching me with an expression of complete indifference mingled with mild curiosity.

One thing was as clear as day: to him I was no one.

CHAPTER TWO

"How do you know my name?" he asked finally. His voice was a little raspy, like an unused instrument clogged with dust.

I felt awkward and conspicuous — feelings that had never existed between us in the past. A long pause followed as I scrambled to compose my thoughts.

"Don't … don't you recognise me?" I asked, unsure if I was ready to hear the answer.

"Should I?" His voice was blunt, but he softened a little when he saw the hurt in my eyes. "I apologise. I do not mean to offend."

"We were together only a few weeks ago," I said slowly. "We were … there was … It's *me*, Chloe."

"I think you have mistaken me for someone else," he replied.

"But I haven't!" A note of anguish crept into my voice and I quickly tried to calm myself before he got the wrong idea and pegged me as some kind of deranged stalker. "I was staying with my grandmother at Grange Hall. Grandma Fee, remember? We met on a walk and then …"

There was no reasonable way to finish that sentence. *Then your crazy dead ex-lover tried to murder me so we banished her to the afterlife. But you went too — only that part wasn't supposed to happen.*

Alex was regarding me with some suspicion and I imagined how loopy I must seem to him. Grange Hall felt like a million years ago, as if I'd quite possibly dreamed up the entire thing. I had so many questions I wanted to ask but couldn't. Apparently I was a stranger, and strangers didn't enjoy the privilege of asking personal questions.

I mustered what composure I had left, forced a smile and extended my hand. "Let's start over. I'm Chloe Kennedy. It's nice to meet you."

"Chloe Kennedy?"

For a second I thought I saw a flash of something in his eyes. Recognition perhaps? He frowned, as if trying to grasp a memory floating just out of reach. A second later the wistful look was gone and his eyes darkened again, filled with thinly veiled mistrust. He cautiously returned my handshake.

The moment our skin connected, I felt an electrifying jolt in my belly. I thought he must have felt it too because he quickly pulled away and wiped his palm on the leg of his jeans. That stung, but this time I was careful not to show it.

"So you're new here?" I asked, a little too brightly.

"In a manner of speaking," he replied, his gaze drifting back to the stage where rehearsal was now in full swing. "I mean *yes*. Yes, I am."

He was a bad liar. He was hiding something, any idiot could see that. But not in a deceitful way. This was not the confident Alex I knew. He was behaving like a little boy who'd lost his way but was reluctant to speak for fear of stranger danger. Beneath his feigned calm I could see that he needed help. I just had to figure out a few things before deciding how best to offer it.

I pulled my phone from my pocket and held it out to him. "Why don't you put your number in here?" I suggested. "Then if you need help with anything you can just ask. I've been at this school for years and I'd be happy to show you around."

Sam and Natalie would have cringed on my behalf, and under normal circumstances I'd never be this forward. But this was no time for playing it cool.

He looked at the phone defensively, like he wanted to touch it but wasn't convinced that it wouldn't grow jaws and bite him.

"I do not carry one of those instruments," he said, then added under his breath, "Lord knows, I keep seeing them everywhere."

Well, that was one question down. Alex might have been dressed like a normal, everyday guy, but on the inside nothing had changed. He didn't know the first thing about technology despite his poor attempt at masking it. Inside, he was still Alexander Reade and the world he knew was Victorian England.

But we had a bigger hurdle than cell phones to conquer. It seemed Alex had no memory of me, of what we meant to each other. How could that have happened? Had he been in some kind of accident and wound up with a bad case of ghost amnesia? Could ghosts even get into accidents?

Unless he had somehow become ... *human*. Was that even possible? No way. People didn't just come back to life after more than one hundred and fifty years of being dead.

Did he remember Isobel, his ghostly ex-lover, and Grange Hall, or had the slate been wiped completely clean? I wished I could ask him, but I didn't want to make him more uncomfortable when he was already wary and on edge.

By the same token, I couldn't very well let him wander off on his own. He clearly wasn't okay or he wouldn't have spent the day sitting alone in the theatre. He didn't know anything about how this world worked, which meant it was dangerous for him out there.

I needed time to figure out how this bizarre sequence of events had unfolded. But first I had to get Alex to trust me. I appraised him discreetly. Even in jeans and a T-shirt, he still looked out of place. He wouldn't survive here … not on his own anyway. It was funny how the tables had turned, I thought, recalling all those times he'd come to my rescue at Grange Hall. He'd been a stranger to me at first, but I'd trusted him anyway. Now he was going to have to trust me.

It wasn't easy keeping my emotions in check when all I wanted was to take his hand, bury my face in his neck and tell him how much I'd missed him. But that would have to wait. The situation needed careful handling: he was giving off a restless energy now that made me wonder if he was a flight risk. I needed to show superhuman patience and focus all my attention on delivering the best performance of my life.

I gave my idea of a flippant laugh. "I'm so sorry! You're right — I mixed you up with someone who happens to look a whole lot like you. I hope I didn't freak you out."

He gave me a quizzical look that felt like a laser cutting through my bullshit. For a moment I almost panicked.

I wasn't a great liar either; in fact, I was crappy at it. I'd never been able to pull off a poker face no matter how hard I tried. Already I could feel my hands starting to sweat the way they always did when I was under pressure.

"You have not answered my first question," Alex said. His eyes travelled down to my feet, which were tapping in a nervous rhythm.

"Huh? What question?"

"How did you know my name?"

"Oh, that." My stomach did a somersault. "Well, you're the new guy so obviously everyone is talking about you ..."

"But you said you thought I was someone else."

Was he trying to catch me out? Unlike Sam and Natalie, I hadn't built up experience from years of lying to my parents. The longest I'd ever kept a secret from my mom was exactly eight minutes and forty-two seconds before I cracked and told her after trying my first cigarette.

"His name happens to be Alex too," I said weakly. "Funny coincidence, right?"

"Indeed," he replied in an acerbic voice that told me he doubted every word that was coming out of my mouth.

"I'm Chloe by the way," I said, realising my mistake a second too late. "But I think I told you that already ..."

"You did."

My cheeks flushed and I knew I was about to start babbling. Awkward silences always gave me a bad case of word vomit.

Thankfully, Alex spoke first. "A pretty name."

I was sure he felt obliged to say something complimentary. Maybe he was starting to feel sorry for the crazy girl with no friends and too much time on her hands.

"Thanks. It comes from some Greek goddess. At least that's what my mom told me."

He nodded. "The Olympian goddess Demeter, mother of Persephone and Queen of the Harvest."

"When I was little I wished I was named after someone cooler, y'know? Like goddess of the stars or of passion or something. The harvest seems a bit lame."

"On the contrary," Alex replied with no hint of humour in his eyes, "the harvest maintains the cycle of life. It gives sustenance to the earth and all who dwell upon it."

Damn, he was good. He had me completely floored to the point that I didn't know what to say next.

"I never thought of it that way," I mumbled.

I realised I was looking at him the way I used to back at Grange Hall; a look that blatantly screamed, *You're the love of my life. We're meant to be together. Nothing can come between us.* Only Alex didn't know any of that, which meant I probably looked like some sad Bridget Jones character about to run home and doodle his name all over my diary.

"I must leave you," he said. "It was nice to meet you, Chloe."

The distance in his voice had me on the verge of tears, but I tried not to take it personally.

He was already making his way to the stairs. Where was he planning on going? I knew if I let him walk away now, I might never find him again. He could easily wander off and be lost forever in the great state of California. I pictured him as a hitchhiker on the highway to Las Vegas, or lost in a sea of tourists at the Walk of Fame, or combing the beaches and desert scrub of Malibu. But a more likely scenario was that, not knowing how to function in the modern world, he'd end up getting into some kind of trouble, maybe even committed. It was only a matter of time before people realised he was *different*.

My hand flew out automatically to grab his arm. "Wait! Do you live around here?"

My action took us both by surprise and I released him as fast as if I'd just touched the handle of a scalding saucepan. I cringed inside, knowing how pushy and desperate I must seem. But I needed to keep this conversation going. I needed to make sure Alex was safe.

"Not far away," he said, deliberately vague.

It might have been my imagination but I sensed he was happy to be detained. Like he knew he needed my help but wasn't sure how to ask for it.

"Hey, me too!" I said, embracing the part of "that girl who just can't take a hint". "Why don't you come over to my house and I can help you get the lay of the land. If you have time to kill, that is …"

Alex gazed into the middle distance as if a sudden thought had captured his imagination. "That is an interesting expression," he murmured. "The idea that people may kill time, when in fact the very opposite is true."

"Right now I'm just *wasting* time," I said lightly as an idea occurred to me. I needed to move this along and couldn't afford to delve into a philosophical conversation with him. "I'm supposed to be at home working on an essay on Shakespearean sonnets. Only problem is, those sonnets are almost impossible to decipher. I have quite a laborious task ahead of me."

I thought I'd done a good job of subtly dropping the hint, but it backfired immediately.

"I find it difficult to believe that a girl who uses the word *laborious* cannot decipher a sonnet," he said.

I'd forgotten how perceptive Alex was. He'd always had the ability to see right through me.

"Anyone can read a thesaurus!" I gave a clumsy, clueless shrug. "Do you know much about Shakespeare?" I offered a hopeful smile.

"I am familiar with his work."

"Do you think you could help me work on the essay?" I pressed on, despite the hesitation in his face. "I mean, I *really* don't want to flunk and have to do summer school. My dad will kill me."

"Very well," he said reluctantly.

"Super!" The ditzy, oblivious act seemed to be working in my favour so I ran with it. "Do you have a car?"

A look of confusion flitted across his face. "I am afraid not," he answered in a tone that blatantly said *don't ask me any more questions*.

"No problem," I said. "We can take mine."

Before Alex could change his mind, I beckoned for him to follow me and headed quickly out of the theatre. I didn't have a plan worked out for the rest of the afternoon. In fact, I hadn't planned further than getting him into the car. So far, I wasn't the smoothest operator. It had only been twenty minutes and there were already a dozen things I regretted saying.

"Which of these vehicles belongs to you?" he asked when we reached the parking lot.

"That one." I pointed to the maroon Volvo parked neatly in its usual spot. "The colour's pretty gross, I know."

"Indeed," he said. "It is rather unsightly."

I smiled to myself. It was the first uncensored thing he'd said to me and I caught a hint of the Alex I knew so well. It made me relax a little.

"It used to be my mom's when she was alive."

The surge of guilt was evident on his face as he took in my use of the past tense. "My apologies, Chloe, I was unaware ..."

"Don't worry about it," I said, laughing. "She used to make fun of it all the time. She'd say we were driving around town in a giant yam."

I waited for him to join in the laughter, but he didn't. Instead he was peering into the back seat of my car with a look of alarm on his face.

"Who is your passenger?" he asked.

"What are you talking about?" I replied. "There's no ..."

Only there was. A young child was seated in the back of my Volvo, hunched over and staring through the windshield, her eyes wide with terror. For a second I thought she must be a junior drama student in costume, but a second look confirmed that something was very wrong. The girl's dress was blackened with scorch marks, as was the exposed skin on her body. Her hair was frazzled and clumping together. She turned her head and gazed wordlessly at us for a moment and I saw tongues of flame reflected in her irises. Then suddenly she began to scream. "Help! Help!" Her mouth became a terrible cavity and her clenched fists pummelled the windows. She clutched her throat, spluttering violently, and we saw that the skin on her hands was scorched and bubbling. The invisible burn crept up her body, until her face became stretched and distorted. One eye closed over with red welts and the other drooped grotesquely. Bile rose in my throat as the flesh of her cheeks ran down into her jaw like melting rubber.

"Please!" she screamed with what was left of her mouth. "Somebody … anybody … help me!"

I managed to stifle my own scream as Alex leapt forward and grappled with the door handle. But it was locked … they all were. Upturning my bag on the asphalt, I fumbled for the keys. My trembling hands sent items rolling in all directions — lip balm, stray mints, tampons — but in that moment I couldn't care less.

I found the keys and snatched them up, furiously hitting the unlock button. Nothing happened. It seemed the battery had died. The girl remained trapped in the car with all four doors locked fast. The car alarm began to wail and the high beams flashed like strobes. I felt the child's intense panic resonate in my own body and knew Alex felt it too.

"What do we do?" I cried over the noise, wondering fleetingly why no one had come to see what all the commotion was about. It didn't cross my mind that perhaps we two were the only ones witnessing the tragic scene.

Inside the car, a thick smoky vapour rose from the dashboard, snaking over the windows and obscuring the girl from view.

"There is nothing else for it," Alex replied. "We must break the glass!"

I looked around and grabbed the first thing my eyes fell on: an avocado-sized rock in a nearby garden bed. I didn't even think about it, I just drew back my arm and swung.

The side window shattered, spraying glass at my feet and across the back seat of the car where the girl was being burned alive. Then everything fell silent. The alarm stopped, the lights went out and the fog dissipated to reveal an empty car. The child was nowhere to be seen.

I heard a soft click as the locks were released and the doors flung open of their own accord. Diving in, I searched every inch of the car from the hood to the trunk, but there wasn't so much as a hint to suggest anyone had been there.

I glanced around the empty parking lot. The sun hung like a blistering ball in the cloudless sky, and glossy palm trees swayed in the afternoon breeze. My little high school in the valley was the most non-threatening environment you could imagine. Strange happenings were non-existent here. Until today, Sycamore High had felt like a safe haven for me; a place where petty teenage dilemmas such as failing calculus or not scoring a cute prom date were the worst things you could imagine. Now that world had shattered before my eyes.

I turned to Alex, who was staring with a nauseated expression at the place where the child had been. "Okay, I'll say it." My voice was a little hoarse. "What the *hell* was that?"

"I … I do not know," he murmured, pushing away the damp hair clinging to his forehead.

It was such a *human* thing to do. I'd seen Alex wrestle with a wild spirit and not break a sweat.

When he spoke again, his voice was concerned. "Chloe, you are bleeding! We must find a doctor."

I looked down to see a small triangle of glass wedged into the flesh of my palm. I hadn't even noticed. "It's no big deal," I said, inserting a fingernail under the rough edge and wiggling the glass out. The blood flow intensified, but the wound wasn't serious enough to warrant stitches. "I just need a temporary bandage. There's a scarf in the trunk. Could you open it for me?"

One look at his face told me that "trunk" was foreign terminology. "Never mind." I pulled it open with my good hand and wound the scarf tightly around the wound.

Alex didn't look satisfied. "Are you sure you are not in pain?"

"Physically I'm fine," I said. "Emotionally, I may need therapy for the next ten to twenty years. That was pretty horrifying. Do you have any idea who that little girl could be? Where do you think she disappeared to?"

"I have no answer, but I think we should leave this place." Alex looked around uneasily. "It is not wise to linger."

I had to agree with him, although … "I *really* don't want to get in that car."

"I am not eager to do so either," he said. "Do you live far from here?"

"About ten minutes on a clear run." Alex frowned but rather than explain I slid behind the wheel and leaned over to open the passenger door so he'd know where to sit.

"That seems a tolerable length of time," he said, trying to look casual as he got in. "Then we shall be able to discuss the matter in private." I let out an involuntary shudder recalling the vision of the trapped and burning child.

"Alright," I sighed. "Let's get this over with."

CHAPTER THREE

As I drove, Alex stared tensely at the lights and knobs on the dashboard. His discomfort over the burning child seemed to be replaced by concern over my driving. I supposed car travel was nerve-racking for someone who was experiencing it for the first time.

"You should put your seatbelt on," I instructed. "And there's no need to look so worried."

"I am not worried," he said a little too quickly. "And what should I put on?"

There was nothing he could do to conceal his ignorance here. Alex was in over his head and the modern world was running circles around him. I decided to brush over the moment; there was no point making him feel even more like an outsider. Besides, I was working on a strategy and I wasn't about to blow it.

"This." I reached around his waist and fastened the belt, very aware of my shoulder brushing momentarily against his chest. I couldn't help noticing that he smelled exactly as I remembered: like sandalwood mingled with understated notes of something both spicy and sweet. I clicked the seatbelt into place. "See? It's for safety."

He held my gaze for a moment, before dropping his eyes and clearing his throat. "Thank you."

We drove the rest of the way in silence. Each time I glanced in the rear-view mirror I wondered if our friend would decide on an encore performance. Every "back-seat car attack" scene I'd ever seen in a movie came back to me. I wanted to believe I'd be calm if the girl did show up again, but in reality I'd probably run the car off the road. Who was she? Why had she shown up now and what did she want from us?

I exhaled loudly, unable to hold back my relief as we pulled into the driveway of my house. I wasted no time cutting the engine.

"So this is where I live," I said as we climbed out.

Although I'd been to, and in fact lived in, Alex's home, I never thought I'd see the day when I'd be showing him around mine. *Bringing the boyfriend home to meet the family*, I thought, swallowing back a bitter lump that sprang into my throat. How apple-pie normal it sounded. Only Alex wasn't my boyfriend, I no longer had a functioning family, and nothing about this situation could begin to pass for normal. Alex didn't even know who I was. Hell, I wasn't sure he knew who *he* was.

From outside, our Cape Cod-style home looked warm and welcoming with its white shutters and dormer windows. Inside, it was a slightly different story. The silence was the first thing to hit you. It wasn't a peaceful silence, like you might find in a library or a church. It was *too* quiet; the sort of stillness in a horror flick when the protagonist comes home to a strangely silent house to find his whole family murdered at the dinner table. Okay, maybe it wasn't that bad, but there was definitely the sense of something amiss.

It was never like this when my mom was alive. There was always noise and bustle of some sort. I remembered complaining about how I could never find a moment of peace, but now I realised that noise had signified life. I missed the rattle of pots and pans in the kitchen, the reedy twang of Rory's clarinet from the den, or the sound of Frank Sinatra spinning on Dad's old record player. I'd never taken much notice of those things before, but I sure noticed their absence now. The house smelled different too; like air freshener and the chemicals used by the cleaning lady Dad had hired. It used to smell like Mom's favourite cinnamon candle or pie baking in the oven.

Once inside I called out to Dad and Rory as a formality. No one answered, and the resounding silence seemed more aggressive than usual, like it was trying to drive home a point: *Alone. Alone. Alone.* I hadn't expected anything different. My family was falling apart at the seams. The three of us might live under the same roof, but we were more like roommates than relatives. At the start of every day we retreated into our own private worlds and didn't surface unless it was absolutely necessary. We didn't even eat together any more; we just shared a communal kitchen. Rory was probably still at his swim meet, and as for my dad — he kept such irregular hours I never knew where he was any more. But I did know one thing: when they eventually showed up, they'd be hungry. My brother had been living off cereal lately and Dad barely ate anything at all. I pulled a frozen lasagne out of the freezer and punched some buttons on the oven.

Alex watched me with fascination, but his expression quickly reverted to neutral when he noticed me noticing him.

I set the oven timer and grabbed a couple of cold drinks from the fridge. "Come on," I said, and ushered him out to the yard. "We can talk by the pool."

Our backyard was still peaceful — at least that hadn't changed — with crystal-blue water in the heated pool and the canvas sails over the pergola rippling gently in the breeze. I dragged two sunbeds to the edge of the pool and sat down. Darcy, our chocolate Lab, bounded over to us as soon as we stepped outside. Normally social around people, he behaved oddly with Alex. He sniffed him warily at first and then began barking so vociferously that I ended up having to lock him in the pool house before I sat down.

"Sorry about that; he's usually pretty friendly."

"Dogs are more intuitive than people," Alex replied. "I confused him."

Alex remained standing, surveying his surroundings with a frown. "Is it always so warm here?" he asked, squinting at the sun like he was willing it to disappear.

"Pretty much. We get a handful of cooler days but not many. Would you rather go inside?"

"No, this will be fine." He sat down on the other sunbed.

Small talk wasn't going to help us solve this mystery. I decided to jump right in. "So what do you think is going on?"

"I think that's perfectly obvious," he replied with a level stare. "Your school is haunted."

"It can't be," I answered automatically. "I've been at Sycamore High since the ninth grade. Of all people I would know if it was haunted."

"Why do you say that?"

"Well …" I hesitated, trying to figure out the best way to explain myself. It felt strange having to reveal myself all over again. He was watching me curiously. "The thing is … I can sometimes see ghosts … people who haven't moved on. It's a little quirk I've had since I was a kid."

I tried to gauge his reaction, but his face was inscrutable. I noticed that detached look in his eyes again, like he wasn't fully present.

"Seeing the dead is an unfortunate affliction," he said eventually. "I would not call it a quirk." His tone was formal and gave nothing away.

I decided to try a different angle. "So how old are you?"

"Twenty-three."

"Aren't you a bit old for high school?"

My lame attempt to lighten the mood didn't help. Alex examined me with those penetrating eyes of his; a look so intense I didn't know what to do with myself. Eventually I couldn't take it any more and was forced to shift my gaze.

He pressed his lips together, as if having an internal debate, then said, "There is something I must tell you, Chloe. And I am only telling you because you do not seem entirely normal."

"Thank you?" I replied. I was torn between feeling embarrassed that he thought of me as a nutcase, but also pleased with the outcome. I really needed him to confide in me, so the reason why he was didn't matter. If he did, we just might have a chance of getting somewhere.

"What I meant to say is, you do not seem alarmed by things that are … shall we say, out of the ordinary."

"That's true," I said with a smile. "I'm the queen of weird. You couldn't out-weird me if you tried."

Again, he failed to share in my humour. "First I must be sure I may trust you with what I am about to say."

"It will never reach another pair of ears," I assured him. "You have my word."

He looked away, as if readying himself to spit it out, then dropped his voice to a tightly controlled whisper. "I believe I have been in some kind of accident."

"What accident?"

"I am not entirely sure. But I have no memory of how I came to be here. Where am I? What is this place?"

"You're in California," I told him. "The Golden State."

"The golden state," he mused softly. "Do they call it that because of the perennial sunshine?"

"I think it's because of some gold rush in 1849." I saw something flash across his face at the mention of a past era and seized the opportunity. "Why don't you tell me the last thing you remember? It might help."

Alex didn't answer immediately. Instead he stood up and stared at the soft ripples on the surface of the pool. But he seemed to be looking through them into some other time and place.

"Alright," he agreed finally. "I was at home. I was arguing with my brother. Then everything went black and I felt as if I were falling from a great height. For a time there was only darkness. Then a blinding light woke me and I found myself here."

"Where exactly?"

"At your school. It was already night when I arrived and I had nowhere to go. So I sat on a bench and waited till morning. People began to arrive and I thought someone might help me. But when they all looked so different I realised something was terribly wrong; I was not in my own world. Yesterday it was 1853 and I was at home at Grange Hall. Today I am here, in this place I cannot make sense of."

What did he mean that yesterday it was 1853? An unpleasant feeling stirred inside me.

"Alex," I said slowly, "I need you to tell me *everything* you remember before you woke up here."

He looked at me like he hoped I might have the answers. He was going to be bitterly disappointed when he found out I was as much in the dark as he was.

"Very well, although my mind is still cloudy." He fixed his eyes on the ground as he struggled to dredge up the memories. Seconds passed before he spoke again. "I was in the library and Carter — my brother — was shouting at me. I could tell he had been drinking. His wife, Isobel, was growing agitated so I tried to calm them both. My infant son — I mean my nephew — was sleeping upstairs. He is like a son to me, you see, and I was concerned that Carter might wake him. I believe I said as much, which caused Carter to laugh in a crazed fashion. Then he said something and Isobel ran from the library, and a few seconds later I heard her footsteps flying across the upstairs landing. I was confused. What had happened? I turned back to my brother and that is when I felt the strange sensation — all went black, as if ink were slowly flooding my vision. I felt a pain in my chest, but it eased quickly. The last thing I remember with any clarity was Isobel's screaming ..."

"You must miss your old life," I whispered into the silence.

"I do miss my nephew." His eyes became tender. "His name is James and he is but eight months old. I must go back to him. He needs me."

My heart was suddenly a deadweight in my chest. This was far worse than I could have imagined. Alexander had no idea of the fate that had befallen him all those years ago. I had seen for myself the scene he'd described: the fatal moment when his brother had put a bullet in his chest; and later, Isobel sinking into the icy lake with the body of their dead son in her arms. But Alex didn't know any of that. His memory had been wiped clean.

"I suppose there is only one explanation for it," he said, more to himself than to me.

"What's that?" I asked tentatively.

"Somehow … by some dark magic … I must have travelled through time. I know such a thing is impossible, but I cannot think of any other explanation."

"Time travel?" I couldn't keep the scepticism from my voice.

"I know how ridiculous it must sound, but I do not know what else to think. Unless all of this is an exceptionally long and detailed dream from which I cannot wake. I need to go home, and you, Chloe, are my only hope. If you can see what others cannot, surely you must be the one to help me?"

A wave of nausea welled up inside me. Alex wanted to go home, but he had no home any more. He hadn't had one for over one hundred and fifty years. How could I help him? How could I break the truth to him?

He was silent, waiting for me to say something, but words eluded me. I could only focus on the questions that kept playing over and over in my head.

How do you tell someone they'll never go home again?

How do you tell someone they're dead?

The sound of my dad's BMW pulling up outside drew our attention. I couldn't say I much looked forward to seeing my father these days, but right now he was a welcome distraction. What I had to tell Alex wasn't something that could simply be blurted out. News like that had to be handled carefully, with kid gloves. For all I knew, learning the truth could send him into a full-blown meltdown. It might be like dying all over again.

And what if he couldn't handle it? It wasn't exactly an easy truth to accept. What if the same madness that had consumed Isobel in the afterlife now took hold of him? I couldn't bear to see him suffer, especially if I was the cause.

I never thought I'd see Alexander Reade again until the day I died. Now that he'd come back, I had no intention of letting him go. His memory of us would come back, I was sure of it. He just needed time. Didn't Rochester's sight return once he was reunited with Jane Eyre? Although my life was not a Brontë novel I was fully convinced that true soul mates had a way of making miracles happen.

"Okay, listen," I told Alex, trying to sound like a gal with a plan. "I'm going to help you figure this out. You have my word. But my father just got home from work and he can't know about any of this. We have to keep it between us, okay? I really can't stress that enough."

"Is your father not to be trusted?" Alex asked.

"It's not that. Try thinking of it like Frodo and the ring — he has to keep it secret to keep it safe."

"Is this Frodo a friend of yours?"

I bit my lip. Sam and Natalie had put a non-negotiable ban on all my *Lord of the Rings* references, but they still slipped out from time to time.

"Never mind, it's just a story," I told Alex. "But I meant what I said about keeping this a secret. Other people might not understand. So let me do the talking, okay?"

He agreed, and we headed into the kitchen, where my dad was already opening a bottle of wine and pouring himself a generous glass. That seemed to be his custom these days, and by the end of the night the bottle was invariably empty.

My dad was a partner at a top accounting firm in the city, but he'd never really enjoyed his job. The first thing he used to do when he got home was kick off his shiny shoes, throw on a Bobby Darin record and start telling stories about all the hotshot d-bags he'd had to deal with that day. Now he seemed to live for work. It was all he had time to think about. Since getting back from England, he hadn't once set foot in his workshop and all the pieces of furniture he once worked on so lovingly were abandoned like dusty skeletons. To be honest, he didn't even look like my dad any more. He didn't bother changing when he got home, he just stayed in that stupid starched shirt and tie all night. What happened to the man who used to laugh and talk about his old Pendleton jacket like it was his best friend? That man seemed to have died alongside my mother, replaced by some cold corporate cut-out who was more or less a stranger to Rory and me.

"Hi, Chloe," he said without looking up. "What happened to your car?"

"No idea," I said flatly. What else could I say?

"Well, get it fixed. If you get pulled over, you'll be fined." If only a fine were the worst of my worries right now, I thought.

"I'll take care of it," I replied. "This is my friend Alex."

Dad turned around. "Oh, I'm sorry. I didn't realise we had company. It's very nice to meet you, Alex."

They shook hands and my father introduced himself, but Alex didn't say a word in response. I realised he was taking my *let me do the talking* instructions literally.

"So are you two in school together?" my dad went on.

He asked the question in a perfunctory manner, like he was a news reporter on a routine assignment he couldn't care less about. Every time he spoke to us now, it felt like he was checking the basics off some mental list, like he'd much rather be someplace else. Are you eating properly? Are your grades decent? Did you remember to take out the trash? I thought it ironic that he expected us to eat properly yet never actually ate with us to make sure we were. He wanted us to work hard at school, but I'd bet fifty bucks he had no idea what classes we were taking. He kept using the word *responsible*. "Be responsible, Chloe" he'd tell me on a weekly basis. *Really, Dad, that's the only gem of paternal wisdom you've got to impart?* I could be shooting up in my closet or facilitating orgies on a Friday night for all he knew, but apparently use of the phrase *be responsible* concluded his parental responsibility. It was like the real challenges of parenting were beyond him.

"Actually Alex is new to the area," I said. "I'm showing him around."

"That's nice." Dad was about to move away when Alex's appearance seemed to stop him. "So where do you hail from?" he asked.

For the first time it struck me how odd Alex must seem to someone who didn't know him. He had the pale skin of a vampire, the long hair of a drifter and the shadowy eyes of a war survivor. He was still beautiful but in a very tortured way. In other words, he looked like trouble — not a father's first pick for his vulnerable teenage daughter.

Alex, who seemed to have gone completely mute, looked at me in alarm. It was my fault: I shouldn't have told him not to speak. But I hadn't expected his improvisation skills to be so underdeveloped. We were going to have to work on that.

"From the other side of the pond, actually," I said, choosing an expression I never used. Perhaps I thought it would better explain his strangeness. "Alex is British."

Dad smiled as if that did indeed explain everything. "I see you've found a way to bring England to America, Chloe."

"You have no idea," I replied, although Alex resurfacing in my life was not a result of anything I'd done.

"I was just about to order some food," my dad told us, failing to notice the lasagne almost ready in the oven. He turned to Alex. "You're more than welcome to stay."

"Thanks, he'd love to," I piped up.

"For God's sake, Chloe, I'm sure the young man can speak for himself. Do you like Chinese, Alex?"

Alex blinked, clearly confused by the question. Was he being asked about the Chinese language, or the Chinese people? He settled on the safest answer. "Yes. I do."

"Great."

"Why don't you wait for me upstairs?" I took Alex's arm and propelled him through the doorway. "My room is first on the right, and the sonnets are on the top shelf. Maybe we can get started on that essay? I'll be up in just a second."

Okay, so the execution was artless, but I needed to get Alex out of there before Dad started asking more probing questions. I could tell he was gearing up to delve deeper than food preferences.

Alex obliged, glancing back at me from the foot of the stairs. His expression was so miserable and misplaced, I felt a pang just looking at him. I tried to give him my most reassuring smile but wasn't sure I pulled it off.

"So," Dad said once Alex was gone, "doing homework together?"

"Yeah ... why?"

"That's interesting."

"It's really not."

"Is he a friend or more of a *friend*?" He waggled his eyebrows suggestively.

"Don't do that," I snapped, although I wasn't surprised by his sudden interest. When was the last time I'd brought a guy home? That would be never.

Mom even tried to have a talk with me about it once. "You don't have to like boys, Chloe. People are people, you can like anyone you want."

"I don't think I'm gay, Mom, but I appreciate the sentiment."

"Well, we love you whatever you do, honey."

Truth be told, before I fell for Alex I'd actually come to the conclusion that I was asexual. I just didn't *notice* people that way. Sam could look at a guy and be seized by a burning desire to tear his clothes off. That never happened with me, no matter how sculpted his abs were. It wasn't really that way with Alex either. Of course I appreciated his physical beauty, but I didn't think of him as *hot* or *sexy* or *cute* or any of those banal words that didn't mean anything. He was utterly bewitching in every sense of the word. I didn't just love him, I *adored* him. I knew that now. He'd only been back in my life for a few hours and already everything I felt for him was rushing back, hitting me like a tidal wave. But I couldn't afford to let that show. Not yet anyway.

"Just don't give him a hard time, alright?" I said to Dad. "Try and be cool."

"In case you haven't noticed, I'm the epitome of cool," he replied breezily.

"That is definitely not true, and I'm serious. He's really private. Don't ask him personal questions."

"Yes, sergeant. Anything else?"

"No jokes. Under any circumstances."

"He doesn't like jokes?" My father got that old cheeky twinkle in his eye. For a split second I saw a glimmer of his old self that made me miss our playful banter.

"He's British," I reinforced.

That excuse seemed to work for everything because my dad nodded. "Don't worry, I'll be on my best behaviour."

"Thanks. Can you pull the lasagne out when the timer goes off?"

"What lasagne?"

I just rolled my eyes and headed for the stairs. I wanted to get up to my room before Alex did anything like wander off. Then it occurred to me that I had no idea what I was going to do with him after dinner. He couldn't stay here.

Despite his jesting, my dad would never allow that. Yet I couldn't let Alex go off by himself either. He needed protection until he remembered who he was. There were all sorts of dangers that could befall him out there and it made me nervous just thinking about them. Maybe I could hide him someplace and make him promise to stay put. But he wasn't some trinket I could lock in a drawer for safekeeping.

When I reached my bedroom I was surprised to find the door closed. I knocked out of habit, because my mom taught me never to barge in on someone. "You never know what you might barge in on," she used to say, and I figured the rule still applied here even if the room I was walking into was my own.

There was no answer so I knocked again, louder this time. Nothing.

I turned the handle and burst in to find my bedroom empty.

CHAPTER FOUR

My heart sank. I could have kicked myself for leaving Alex alone. He was still disoriented and confused by what had happened; I should have known he'd go straight for the front door. But as I looked around, it seemed that he had been in my room after all. The items on my desk had shifted slightly, and the book of sonnets lay open on my bed as if he'd been reading them only moments ago. There was even an indentation on my duvet where he must have been sitting.

What could have scared him off like that? And why didn't I pass him in the hall? The only other way out was through the window. But that was a two-storey jump, and besides I could see the window lock hadn't been opened.

I ran back to the landing, whispering his name. "Alex! Alex, where are you? Can you hear me?" Even though my gut told me not to expect an answer, I couldn't help hoping.

I forced myself to walk calmly through the house checking every room. This was my second Alex-related search of the day and the stress was beginning to take its toll. Where the hell had he disappeared to? Why hadn't he said anything? Just when I thought he was starting to trust me …

The TV was blaring in the den and I wondered if Alex had found his way in there and become mesmerised by modern technology. But it was only Rory, back from his swim meet and glued to a cartoon show. He was sharing a bowl of Lucky Charms with Darcy.

"Hey!" he yelled when I switched off the television and marched out of the room still holding the remote. He spent too many hours sprawled on the couch these days, but I would save that lecture for later.

"Do your homework," I called over my shoulder. "And stop ruining your appetite. There's lasagne in the oven."

Wherever Alex had gone, he certainly hadn't left by the front door as he would have passed right by the kitchen where Dad and I had been talking. Where was he? What if he got lost? What if something bad happened to him? I'd never felt more protective of anyone, except maybe my little brother, and it was causing a slippery feeling in my stomach.

Stop it, I told myself. *Alex is a grown man, not some puppy stranded on the highway.*

So why didn't I trust that he'd be safe out there? Maybe it was because of the alarm bells ringing so loudly in my head I could barely think.

Ten minutes later, I'd concluded my second loop through the house and also searched the backyard. Circling around to the front porch, I realised I'd been holding my breath and my lungs were now aching for air.

I was surprised to find my dad sitting on the front steps, lighting up a cigarette. As I watched him blow smoke at the amethyst-streaked sky, I couldn't help wondering what my mother would say if she could see him. She was a health nut and thought smoking was the most irresponsible thing in the world. She called cigarettes *cancer sticks* and Dad supported her all the way. But stress could do strange things to people and Dad had had more than his share over the past six months. Was it really fair of me to sit in judgment?

"I didn't know you'd taken up smoking," I said. I sat beside him and picked up the packet. "Camel Crush, huh? That's what Natalie smokes."

"I guess I have teenage-girl tastes," he replied. "I know it's a disgusting habit."

"Disgusting," I agreed as I slid out a cigarette, put it to my lips and lit up. I guess I wanted to test whether he'd let me get away with it … whether he still cared enough to object.

"What do you think you're doing?" he asked.

"Hey, I'm stressed too."

But Dad shook his head, snatched the cigarette from my lips and stomped it out under his heel. "Don't do that again, Chloe. My bad habits are my own. Your mother would never forgive me if I let you smoke. Now what happened to your friend?"

"He had to leave," I said, trying to sound nonchalant. For some reason I didn't want my dad to know I cared.

"I'm sorry."

"Don't be. It's not like that." The last thing I wanted was pity from my father. "He had a family emergency."

"Well, that's a shame. He seemed nice. A little out of it maybe, but nice. He wasn't high, was he?"

"No, Dad, he's just shy."

"If you say so. Oh, by the way, a package came for you today."

"Really?"

I hardly ever got mail of any kind. I'd complained about it once to my mom and she'd assured me that when I was older and had bills to pay, I would miss the days of no mail.

"It's from your grandmother," Dad said. "When she phoned last week she mentioned she was sending you something. I think she really misses having you and Rory around."

I smiled. "I miss her too. Good old Hurricane Fiona."

Gran's package was a welcome relief as it provided me with something concrete to do so I didn't obsess over Alex. It wasn't like I could text or call him to find out where he was. I had no choice but to wait. So I went inside to the hall table where Gran's brown-paper package was waiting for me. It looked very official with its stamp that read *Royal Mail*.

I went upstairs to my room where I knew I wouldn't be interrupted and could open it in private. As I settled on my patchwork duvet, I couldn't help sneaking glances at the window and door. Where was my self-control? But Alex had left so suddenly, how could I be sure he wouldn't reappear in the same abrupt fashion? Even though I seriously doubted he was going to come in through the window, I got up and threw it open anyway. Just in case he decided to stage a Peter Pan-inspired reappearance.

I could focus better with the window open and the cool breeze hitting the back of my neck. I tore off the brown paper. Inside were two smaller parcels and a vanilla-coloured envelope. I opened the envelope first. It was so lovely, I wished we had a letter opener so I could avoid tearing it. But this was California; I didn't know anyone who would even know what to do with a letter opener. I took out the creamy letter paper and held it for a moment, marvelling at the fact that someone had actually taken the time to sit down and write to me. Grandma Fee's graceful cursive script filled the page that felt like velvet beneath my fingertips and smelled faintly of rosewater. Besides the odd birthday card from distant relatives, this was the first handwritten letter I'd ever received.

It read as follows:

Dearest Chloe,

I hope you are happy and healthy and staying out of the Californian sun. You know how punishing it can be on the skin! I wish I could have kept you and Rory here with me forever, but I know you both have lives to get back to. You were only at Grange Hall for a short while, but I watched you change in that time and saw glimpses of the woman you will grow up to be. You demonstrated courage and a trueness of self that made me very proud to be your grandmother. I will always look back on our time together with the fondest of memories.

You will be pleased to hear that Joe Parrish is almost fully recovered and has now gone back to school. He cannot work with the horses just yet, but he still visits the stables at weekends and asks after you every time.

I know this is a big year for you, Chloe, with graduation only a few months away. My goodness, how time flies! I've already spoken with your father and I will be flying out to watch you graduate in June. Even if you are sick of me, I wouldn't miss it for the world.

I don't know if you recall the old outhouse by the lake, but for some time now I have been wanting to convert it into something more useful. I'm pleased to announce that my plans are finally in motion and renovations are underway to turn it into a day spa for my guests. Perhaps this will be an enticement for you to visit again in the future?

Before the workmen arrived, Harry and I spent a few days clearing out the space. It was mostly full of junk — dusty old portraits and moth-eaten furniture that shall be discarded or donated to the local charity shop. But I did keep a few souvenirs that looked too special to part with, one of which I have enclosed for you. I do hope you like it. It's a valuable antique so perhaps don't wear it every day, but take it out whenever you are missing Grange Hall, and know that you will always have a home here.

Give Rory a hug from me.

Your loving grandmother.

I folded the letter carefully and put it away in the drawer of my nightstand. Since returning home I'd tried hard to keep my mind off Grange Hall, but Gran's letter had plunged me right back into the life of the old house and I realised it would always have a hold on me, even with thousands of miles between us. It was in that house that I'd fallen in love with Alex, a troubled nineteenth-century ghost whose mad ex-lover had tried to murder me, Joe Parrish and a whole bunch of other innocent teenagers. Now Alex was back, only neither of us knew why or how it had happened.

Mark Twain was right, I thought: *Truth is stranger than fiction, but it is because fiction is obliged to stick to possibilities; truth isn't.*

I turned to the parcels to distract myself. Inside the first was an old edition of Jane Austen's *Mansfield Park* with a cloth cover and fraying spine. The fragile yellowed pages were covered in neat, almost minuscule print, the letters pressed so tightly together it gave me a headache to look at them. It smelled the way all old books do, of cut grass and worn leather.

The second parcel contained something small and hard swaddled in tissue paper. It was a faded felt-covered box, and inside was a swirling moonstone brooch in the shape of a flower. It looked too delicate for my world, like it didn't belong here. I turned it over in my hands, marvelling at its perfect shape. The central milky stone was set in a frame of silver studded with tiny pearls. The brooch was tarnished with age though still beautiful.

As I admired it, turning it over in my hand, a sudden wave of drowsiness came over me. Soon I could barely keep my eyes open. Perhaps the strain of the day was finally catching up with me.

Alex will be fine, a voice in my head reassured me. *What's the worst that could happen? Everything will look different in the morning.*

I was too exhausted to argue, so I curled up on top of my duvet, the brooch still in my hand, to close my eyes for just a few minutes. But the moment my head hit the pillow, a wave of sleep washed over me so heavy that I was powerless against it.

I stand in the dark listening to the sound of my laboured breathing. It takes me a moment to realise my eyes are closed, and when I open them I blink in the white winter sunlight. I'm standing on the doorstep of Grange Hall with the bell only inches from my nose.

I stagger back a few steps to take in the vast grey manor. Its looming facade soars skyward. The air smells fresh and I see droplets of dew gathered on the petals of lightly perfumed roses. A short distance away, fog rolls at the edge of the woods.

I shiver and watch my breath unfurl like a wreath of smoke in the frosty air. I glance down to see that I'm wearing a flimsy dress made from a fabric that offers all the warmth of a paper bag. When I lift my hands to my face to warm them with my breath, I notice my fingernails are cut neat and short and some cuticles are ragged. These aren't my hands. I'm not sure who I am exactly, but I know I'm not myself. These thoughts don't belong to me. But they are too powerful to ignore and soon Chloe is pushed further and further away until my mind belongs to someone else. I know this is a dream so I decide to go with it, offering no resistance.

At my feet is a battered old trunk that contains all my worldly possessions. I kneel down and unclasp the latches. There is not much inside: a few items of clothing, a shawl made by my mother, a leather-bound journal, and a letter from my baby sister, Eileen. She was terribly upset to discover I was going away. But we always knew this day would come, right after my fourteenth birthday. Still I do not feel prepared, although I had no other choice. With our father not working, who else will take care of the family if not I, the eldest child?

The wind hits me from behind, blowing a tumble of rust-coloured curls over my shoulder. Eager to get out of the cold, I ring the brass bell. Its chimes echo through the house. I wait patiently, but the place remains as still as a morgue. I wonder if I have made a mistake about the time and date, but then I hear the brusque rattle of keys in the lock.

The door swings open and a plump housekeeper stands before me, hands on hips, cheeks like two bright red apples. "You must be the new housemaid," she says. "Rebecca Burns, is it not?"

I open my mouth to answer but find I am racked by nerves. It has been a long time since anybody has called me by my full name. At home, I am always Becky. I nod meekly and stare at my shoes, knowing I have already made a poor impression.

"Don't just stand there like a stunned rabbit, child," she continues. "Come inside out of the cold."

She ushers me through the doorway and I step into the grand foyer of Grange Hall. It is draughty, with vaulted ceilings and rich furniture I cannot imagine ever sitting upon. Suddenly I feel very shabby, even though my mother hemmed my dress meticulously and polished my shoes until her arms ached.

"Leave your trunk outside," the housekeeper instructs. "I shall have it taken up to your room later this morning. I'm Mrs Baxter. If you need anything, you're to come to me. Don't go bothering anyone else, do you understand?"

"Yes."

"Yes, Mrs Baxter," she corrects, her bushy brows arching with disapproval. "Come along then."

I scurry after her, up a vast staircase lined with family portraits. I spy one which I assume depicts the master of the house. He is quite a handsome man, although his features are severe and his eyes seem to glower at me. I notice the banister rail is so polished I can see my own reflection. I drop my hand immediately so as not to leave fingerprints.

"I know it's a lot to take in," Mrs Baxter says without turning to look at me. "But if you go about your chores quietly, show respect for your superiors and refrain from gossip, we shall get along just fine."

"Will I be meeting the lady of the house today?" I ask.

"I hardly think so," she replies, as if I've said something amusing. "The mistress has more important things to do than meet the servants. You've heard talk about her, I suppose?"

"Oh, yes! She is admired by all the girls in the village. Although nobody has seen her more than once or twice."

Images click through my mind: a veiled face at the window of a luxurious carriage as it sails by, the swish of a silk hem sweeping dusty cobbled streets, a white-gloved hand being kissed by a man on bended knee. I can still hear the girls speaking in hushed tones whenever Mrs Reade's carriage passed by: "I hear she's a Spanish noblewoman!" "Mr Reade claims he never met a young woman so accomplished." "Do you suppose it's true she has a dress made of emeralds to match her eyes?"

Mrs Baxter's voice brings me back to the present. "The mistress rarely goes out these days." She offers no explanation as to why.

On the upstairs landing she veers onto a narrower, darker flight of steps that leads to an attic. Once my eyes adjust to the gloom, I look around to see three narrow beds crammed under the sloping ceiling. The room is clean enough but spartan, with very little by way of furnishing. Other than the beds with their flimsy coverlets, there are three rickety bedside tables, each holding a Bible; a cupboard and a washstand. I am merely observing, not complaining. Work is work and I am lucky to have it. It is more than I can say for some of my friends in the village. What will become of them, I wonder, when their fathers are gone and there is no one left to put bread on the table? At Grange Hall, I shall have a roof over my head, a bed of my own and food in my belly every night. I cannot ask for more than that.

"Here you are." Mrs Baxter points out the bed that is to be mine. Linen is folded neatly on top of the single lumpy pillow.

I notice a row of wooden hooks with a maid's uniform dangling from one peg. "Is that for me, Mrs Baxter?"

"Don't ask foolish questions," she tells me. "Who else might it be for? Now get changed quickly, then come and meet me in the drawing room. I shall expect you there in precisely ten minutes."

She is gone before I can tell her I don't have the faintest idea where the drawing room is.

I hurriedly wash my face and change, fixing my mob-cap so my unruly curls are well concealed. I fold my dress and place it neatly at the end of the bed. My cheeks are hot despite the chill in the room, so I splash a handful of icy water on my face. Then I scamper downstairs, coming to a breathless halt in front of Mrs Baxter, who is in the foyer holding a tea tray.

She clicks her tongue and glares at me. "No running in the house! The master won't stand for it."

"I'm sorry, Mrs Baxter," I mumble. "It won't happen again."

"See that it doesn't." She pushes the tray into my hands. It is heavier than it looks. "Take this tea into the parlour. The master and mistress are taking their breakfast and we must not keep them waiting any longer."

"You want me to do it?" I stammer. "But I thought I was not meeting the mistress today?"

Mrs Baxter makes a clicking sound with her tongue. "You are not meeting the mistress, you are serving her."

I can hardly believe it. Just an hour ago, I was at home in our three-room cottage. Now I am about to be thrust in front of the most noble people I shall ever encounter in my lifetime. I take a deep breath, trying to compose myself, but Mrs Baxter's hand is on my back, prodding me toward a door on the far left. Before I can say a word, she opens it and propels me inside. It is all I can do not to drop the tray!

The parlour is bright and inviting, with sunlight spilling through the tall windows and reflecting off a crystal bowl filled with freshly cut roses. They are outshone in beauty only by the young woman sitting in front of them. She cannot be much older than twenty and I think she must be the most elegant creature I have ever laid eyes on. I feel remarkably plain and coarse in comparison.

Mrs Reade's lustrous dark locks are piled atop her head and held in place by delicate pearl-studded combs. The sweep of her hair draws attention to her pale, swanlike neck. Her skin is flawless

51

and the pink bloom on her cheeks so perfect it could be the work of an artist's paintbrush. I cannot tell the colour of her wide, almond-shaped eyes; only that they seem to glitter when the sun catches them. It is little wonder she is the envy of every woman in the county. Her beauty quite literally takes my breath away, although I cannot fail to notice the glum expression on her face. She is gazing out the window at the rainclouds inching their way toward the sun.

"I simply cannot bear another day of rain!" she declares. Although she is complaining, her voice has the cadence of music. "I wish to go walking or to ride in the woods. It is wretched to be always indoors."

Opposite her, Mr Reade is generously buttering a crumpet and studying the newspaper with a grave expression. He cannot yet be thirty, but he seems much older. He is undoubtedly handsome, but fierce-looking. Something warns me to stay out of his way.

"Sadly, my dear, the weather is beyond the scope of my influence," he says with a hint of annoyance. "I am not a wizard to command the clouds at will."

"Why must you always mock me?" Mrs Reade asks.

I feel obliged to make my presence known lest I be accused of eavesdropping. I softly clear my throat and they both turn to look at me. I dare not speak, so I offer a wobbly curtsey and begin to unload the tray onto the table.

Mrs Reade resumes the conversation, seeming to look right through me. "Must you leave for London today?" She pouts as she daintily stirs a lump of sugar into her gold-rimmed cup.

"I'm afraid so." Her husband turns the page of his newspaper without looking up. "I have business to attend to. Surely you can find something to entertain you while I am gone."

"I do not understand why you will not take me with you."

"Because I know you would find it tedious."

I can see Mrs Reade does not appreciate being dismissed like this. Her eyes narrow. "What then do you suggest I do with myself?"

"There is plenty to occupy the mistress of a house such as this. Mrs Baxter will let you know of matters requiring your attention."

Mr Reade's manner is so abrupt it is hard to believe they are newlyweds. His young wife seems to him more of an encumbrance than an asset despite her obvious beauty. I watch her face fall and almost feel sorry for her, until my mind conjures the careworn faces of the village girls I know. Their lives hold problems for which there are no ready solutions, and they will struggle and toil every day through rain or shine until the Lord calls them to Him. What can a woman in Mrs Reade's position have to complain about? She lives in the lap of luxury, and if her biggest problem is how to fill her day, I daresay she has never known real hardship.

Her head lifts suddenly and her gaze locks with mine as if she has heard my thoughts. Now I see that her eyes are the most exquisite gold and green, like light falling through a forest. I am acutely aware of my own muddy brown eyes.

I think I have lingered too long in the parlour. It is the duty of a maid to be unobtrusive; being noticed likely means you are doing something wrong. I make for the door, but unfortunately with too much keenness and accidentally bump Mr Reade's elbow. He gives a shout and I see with horror that I have caused him to spill hot tea all over his shirtfront.

The room goes deathly still and silent. Outside in the hall, the grandfather clock chimes the hour ...

CHAPTER FIVE

The chime of the grandfather clock morphed jarringly into Wham's "Wake Me Up Before You Go-Go". It took me a second to realise my alarm clock was going off. Heart pounding, I slammed my fist down on it, hoping to recapture the scene I'd just been jolted from.

The cosy parlour was gone, but the livid look in Carter Reade's eyes remained emblazoned on my memory. Even though it was just a dream, I felt afraid for Becky and the fate that might befall her. But even more strangely, I felt afraid for myself. I sensed that somehow our lives were inextricably linked, although I had no idea how.

I lay there for a while longer until I was forced to accept that Grange Hall was gone, for the time being at least, and no amount of willing would bring it back. I couldn't deny it felt good to be there even in a dream. But the dream had been too vivid for comfort. Who was Rebecca Burns? Was she a figment of my imagination or was I somehow reliving the memories of a real person?

I noticed with surprise that it was light outside. How long had I been sleeping? I heard the shower running in the bathroom and the TV blaring from the den where Rory was probably *not* getting dressed for school and *not* eating any kind of acceptable breakfast. He'd taken to grabbing whatever was in the cupboard, which usually meant a Twinkie with a handful of Doritos.

I had a feeling I'd heard Rebecca Burns's name before, only I hadn't the faintest idea when or where. Alex had certainly never mentioned her, nor had Grandma Fee. But somebody had, I knew that much. The question niggled like a mild toothache at the back of my mind as I washed and changed quickly before going downstairs to pour some cereal. But I was too distracted to eat more than a few mouthfuls. Instead I sat there absorbed in my own thoughts until I felt sure I would drown in them, just like my Cheerios drowned in the milk. I tossed the remnants down the sink and checked my watch to find I was late for school. It wasn't even eight o'clock and I already felt tired.

I was heading upstairs to my bedroom when it happened. The moment my hand connected with the banister, the memory came flooding back: *"My baby, Becky! He's not breathing!"* The voice was Isobel's and I'd heard her cry those words in a haunting vision I'd had at Grange Hall. I remembered it like it was yesterday. With a stricken face, she'd come flying down the stairs, clutching to her chest a bundle wrapped in white cloth. She was a mess of tangled hair and huge, glistening eyes. She'd looked past me at someone I couldn't see and asked for help from … Becky, the young housemaid.

Remembering the name didn't lessen my confusion. In fact, I was more confused than ever! Why was I dreaming about Rebecca Burns; or dreaming *as* her if that was even possible? I didn't know anything about this girl. It occurred to me that she might have been the person who found the bodies, but I quickly discarded that thought. I couldn't bear to be shown Alex's corpse lying there in the library at Grange Hall where he'd been fatally shot.

Speaking of which, where *was* Alex? I still had no leads about where he'd disappeared to. He could be in Canada for all I knew.

Outside, the sun was obnoxiously bright. That was the downside of living in California with its desert climate: when you were in a crappy mood, the sun seemed to make a mockery of you. Just for once it would be nice to have the weather reflect my emotions.

I made it to school in time for my first class of the day: French. It was my toughest subject by far because Madame Giles was one of those teachers who believed the entire world revolved around her subject. If you dared to show up even thirty seconds late, she left you tapping helplessly at the door while she pretended she couldn't hear you. Madame was always dressed in a tailored pantsuit, with her hair wound up so tight it made the prominent vein on her forehead throb. She had impossibly high standards and was a firm believer in the immersion method, which meant she'd banned all English in her classroom, no exceptions. If you needed to use the bathroom, you'd better be able to ask permission in French. If you'd just eaten a peanut and had a deathly allergy, you'd better be able to call the paramedics in French. If she caught anyone speaking English, she banished them to the library for the remainder of the lesson, where they had to write in French *Speaking French will make me fluent* one hundred times. Yeah, Madame Giles was a little archaic. But today she'd broken her own golden rule. She was almost ten minutes late.

I'd been in her French class for two years now and not once had anybody gotten to the classroom before her. Feeling unsettled, I flipped to a random page in my textbook and tried to distract myself by memorising its contents while the other students seized the opportunity to talk.

My concentration lasted about thirty seconds before my thoughts derailed like a freight train. I was worried about Alex, worried about my dream, worried about my family, and now worried about the fact that it was 8:50 am and our pedantically punctual teacher still hadn't arrived. It felt like everything in my world had been off-kilter since my mom died. With her gone, my world had crumbled and the things I'd thought important didn't seem so any more. And since Alex's disappearance last night, that coil in my chest had grown tighter by the second. Now I felt as if it was strangling my heart.

I was itching for the lesson to begin just so I'd have something else on which to focus my mind. *Finally*, I thought, when I heard the classroom door opening. But it wasn't Madame Giles who entered the room. It was our school principal, Mrs Kaplan, otherwise known as Kraplan by the entire student body. The room fell silent as her heels clacked across the floor. She was dressed in her customary grey garb, which looked about as comfortable as armour.

By her side was an older man with long silver hair and a regal air. It was funny, I thought, how men grew to be distinguished while women just grew older. He was wearing a tweed three-piece suit with a spotted bow tie, which made him something of an anomaly at our casual Californian school.

"I have good news and bad news," Mrs Kaplan announced. "The bad news is that Madame Giles has been involved in an unfortunate car accident which resulted in two broken legs. But don't worry, she is expected to make a full recovery, although we won't be seeing her back at school for the rest of the semester. Now for the good news. Everybody, allow me to introduce Doctor Ritter. He is here to take over this class and I can assure you that nobody comes more highly recommended."

Why was she telling us that? We didn't care about the credentials of our teachers. Maybe she was hoping we'd go home and feed that information back to our parents. Maybe she thought we actually talked to our parents.

Doctor Ritter, I noticed, had sunken cheeks and skin with a leathery sheen, like he was a well-preserved ancient relic. I watched his gaze sweep across the room, taking us all in. He lingered on me a fraction too long and jerked his head slightly as if he knew me from somewhere. I felt a shiver run down my spine. His whole demeanour reminded me of a predator. A great white shark perhaps? His eagle eyes were dark and strangely glossy, while the corners of his mouth turned up in a way that suggested both sneering and smiling. It was unnerving to say the least.

Mrs Kaplan's ruby-red lips stretched into a smile. "Alright then, I'll let you get on with it."

As she made her exit, Doctor Ritter set down his briefcase and settled on the edge of his desk, watching us all in silence. He picked a piece of invisible lint from his creaseless trousers and flicked it away.

"So this is how it's going to work," he said eventually,

his voice surprisingly reedy. I was expecting it to be low and commanding to match his silver fox exterior. "We are all adults here, aren't we? Therefore we all deserve to be treated with mutual respect. Do you concur?"

A few heads nodded and some voices mumbled their agreement.

"School need not feel like prison," he continued. "Believe it or not, I was young once and I know there is probably something other than French on your minds right now. For example: what are you going to wear to that party on Saturday night? Why hasn't he texted you back? Will you be picked for the football team and finally make your father proud? All perfectly valid concerns."

Hart Anderson, captain of the swim team, was sitting at the desk next to mine. He angled his face toward me and widened his eyes. I repeated the gesture, sharing his confusion. What was Doctor Ritter's deal? I didn't know what to make of him. Was he trying to be funny or disciplinary or was he just plain weird? It was hard to tell.

"Is something troubling you?" he asked.

He pronounced the letter "s" with a slight hiss like a snake. It distracted me and at first I didn't realise he was talking to me. Oh, great. Of course the heat would fall on me and not Hart, who was now frowning down at his textbook. I was not going to catch a break today, was I?

"No, sir," I answered. "Sorry about that. Everything's fine."

He accepted my apology and was turning away when his eye was caught by something just below my elbow. I followed his gaze to my jacket, which was hanging on the back of my chair. Pinned to the inside pocket was the brooch Grandma Fee had sent me. For some reason I hadn't wanted to leave it behind.

"That is a fine-looking piece," Doctor Ritter said, drawing closer to take a better look. "Is it genuine?"

"I think so; it's from my grandmother's estate in England."

"England?" he repeated. "How fascinating. Do you know what it is made of?"

"Um, I think it's some kind of gemstone."

"Actually it's moonstone, seed pearl and marcasite, circa 1850 if I'm not mistaken."

I was impressed. This dude really knew his way around antique jewellery.

"You really should have made a point of finding out, Miss Kennedy. It seems foolish to wear something without knowing its origin, don't you think?"

"I —"

He cut me off. "Yes, I suppose you have more important things to do with your time. Why bother discovering the history of an antique when Netflix awaits?"

Something came over me then that I couldn't explain. Maybe the stress of the last twenty-four hours made me reckless. I had a faultless record at Sycamore High; I'd never had so much as a detention. But instead of apologising again, I folded my arms across my chest and stared back at Doctor Ritter, uncowed by his authority. His jibe was unwarranted given that he knew nothing about me. Why should I let him get away with it because he was my superior and older than me? Alex was older than both of us put together and I wasn't afraid to speak my mind to him. *Afraid* — I was sick of that word. I was sick of over-thinking every little detail and feeling that tense, nervous knot in my stomach from the moment I woke up to the moment I went to bed.

"Do you think just because we're young, you can ridicule us and dismiss our problems?" I asked.

"Excuse me?"

My brain told me this was a good time to stop, but my mouth had other ideas. "Are you suggesting that girls are vacuous and boys only think about sports? I'm sure life would be much easier if we were as stereotypical as you see us, but we're a little more complex than that."

The Adam's apple in Doctor Ritter's tanned, taut throat bobbed around, the only sign of anger. His face betrayed nothing. "I'm going to ask you to leave my classroom, young lady."

"Fine." I pushed back my chair and stood up, feeling every pair of eyes on me, their expressions ranging from admiration to disbelief. I was trembling, but it felt more like adrenaline than fear.

I hastily collected my books and made sure to seal my departure by slamming the classroom door behind me. It was only when I reached the silence of the hallway that my indignation abated and I stopped to reflect. As I waited for my heartbeat to return to normal, a thought struck me. Doctor Ritter hadn't been at our school ten minutes so how did he know my name? Could he have memorised a class list with our photos attached? If so, he must have one hell of a photographic memory. But I wasn't sure any such list even existed. The admin department wasn't that organised.

I'd have plenty of opportunity to regret my outburst after Doctor Ritter reported me to Kraplan and she called my father. But in that moment I felt empowered, like I was capable of anything. *Bring it on, universe*, I thought.

The first thing on my to-do list for the day was to find Alex. I'd turn the school inside out if I had to, and then I was going to sit him down and tell him the truth. I needed to take control of this situation instead of letting it control me. It sounded like a cheesy line from a self-help book, but it was the only thing that made sense.

My new vigour gave shape to an idea that seemed so obvious I couldn't believe it hadn't occurred to me before. *The theatre.* I had been here yesterday, standing in almost exactly the same spot, thinking almost exactly the same thoughts. *Where was Alex? Where could he be hiding?* The anticipation proved too much and I broke into a run.

At this time of day the theatre was deserted, and so silent I became aware of my own breathing as I paused at the foot of the stairs to pull myself together. I might have to start going to Natalie's spin class if I was going to be chasing ghosts all over the city.

The stage was empty, with props from the last rehearsal stacked haphazardly into a corner. I ran up the stairs without looking at the balcony to see if Alex was there. Because there was a fifty-fifty chance he wouldn't be and then what?

My spirits dipped with doubt, but I refused to give in to negative thoughts. I liked the assertive Chloe better. She understood that the only way to deal with a situation like this was to go in guns blazing. You couldn't tiptoe around like some timid mouse. I would not be a timid mouse … at least not any more.

I straightened my shoulders and stepped onto the landing. He was there, sitting in exactly the same place as yesterday.

I wanted to laugh with relief, but I didn't. Instead I sauntered over to him and flopped down next to him in one of the faded folding seats. He didn't seem surprised to see me.

"Guess you're not the social type," I said drily.

"I prefer to stay in the shadows," he replied. "The sunlight is so harsh here; there is nowhere to hide."

"You don't need to hide. And you don't need to run away from my house without telling me. Irish goodbyes are not cool."

"I am not Irish," he said calmly. "Nor did I run away."

"What do you mean?"

"I was sitting on the bed waiting for you. Then darkness closed in and I found myself here again."

"What? How is that possible? Actually … never mind. I think we've clearly established that *anything* is possible right now. So you've been here the whole time?"

"Yes. I knew you would come to find me eventually."

I gave a faint smile. "Well, that makes sense. But before anything else happens, there's something I need to tell you. And if I don't tell you now, I never will, because it's not the easiest thing to tell someone."

"Very well." His brow furrowed. "What is it?"

"It's just … well … here's the thing …" My tongue felt awkward in my mouth, like there wasn't enough room for it. "How can I put this? You're not … you aren't exactly —"

"Chloe," he interrupted, "please, just tell me."

He was right. This wasn't a truth that could be sugar-coated. The only thing to do was lay it bare on the table.

I released a long whoosh of breath, steeling myself for the both of us.

"Alex," I said quietly, "you didn't travel through time."

"How can you know that?"

"Because I know something you don't. Believe me, I wish I didn't have to tell you this but ..." I trailed off again. It was just so difficult to put into words.

His eyes searched my face. "Chloe, for goodness sake, just —"

"Alex, you're dead!" I could see from the look on his face that my words cut deeper than any dagger. "You've been dead since 1853."

It didn't take long for the shock in Alex's eyes to be replaced by disbelief. He looked at me like I was a child declaring something outlandish to be fact. "I beg your pardon?"

"I know how strange this must sound. But I can explain everything if you'll let me."

"Has anyone ever told you that you have a macabre sense of humour?"

"I wish I *was* joking," I replied softly. "You have no idea how much."

That troubled look crossed his face again and I could see him struggling not to give in to fear.

"In that case you must be a very disturbed person," he said.

"I would think that too. But, please, just hear me out. Then if you still think I'm crazy you can leave and never speak to me again."

Alex didn't say a word. But he didn't turn his back on me either.

I took that as permission to continue. He was already on the defensive so I'd better choose my words carefully. I decided it was best to stick to the facts, keeping emotion out of it.

"I know about Isobel and Carter and the life you had together at Grange Hall," I said slowly. "I know that you and Isobel were having an affair, and that James was your son, not Carter's."

Alex threw an alarmed glance over his shoulder, as if worried someone might be spying on us. His voice dropped to an agitated whisper. "How could you possibly know such things?"

I pressed on, even though what I said next would devastate him. "I know because Grange Hall is owned by my grandmother now. Her name is Fiona Kennedy. She turned the place into a bed and breakfast —"

"How dare you," he interrupted, like I'd said something sacrilegious. "Grange Hall belongs to the Reade family and will continue to do so for many generations to come."

"It *did* belong to your family. But that was a long time ago. In fact, they haven't lived there in many decades."

"Stop." Alex's voice was icy. "I have heard quite enough from you." He got to his feet, eyeing me with outright distaste.

Before he could walk away, my hand shot out to grasp his. He seemed startled by the physical contact and pulled away like I was a leper.

"Can't you see I'm trying to help you?" I implored, only to receive a withering look.

"By inventing spurious stories about my family? I will not listen to another word."

"If I was making this up, how would I know that the second bedroom on the third floor used to be yours?" I blurted out. "How would I know that you painted Isobel's portrait in the summerhouse by the lake, but she would only sit still once you promised to take her riding? How would I know that Carter laughed at you for wanting to pursue a career in art? That he thought you'd wasted your time in Paris? How would I know that you offered to run away with Isobel, but she was too afraid of a life of poverty?"

What little colour there was in his face drained away and he seemed lost for words.

"The reason I knew your name yesterday wasn't because you reminded me of someone," I told him. "It was because you and I have met before ... even if you can't remember it."

"I thought I knew your face," he admitted in a hollow voice. "Although for the life of me I could not remember from where."

"Like I told you, I'm no stranger to seeing the dead. But you were the first person on the other side I've actually been able to talk to. It scared us both at first, but we got used to it. You told me yourself how your spirit had lingered at Grange Hall since 1853, the year of your death. You haven't travelled through time, Alex ... time just went on without you."

He met my gaze with a fierce look, as if willing me to retract everything I'd just said.

"I'm so sorry, but it's true."

"Why do I have no recollection of dying?" he asked with a slight tremor in his voice.

I could tell his thoughts were starting to shift, giving way to understanding.

"You know how the last thing you remember is fighting with Carter?" He nodded hesitantly. "Well, that fight ended very badly."

"What do you mean?"

The hardest part was coming. My heart felt like it was cracking in my chest.

"I mean that Carter shot you. That's how you died, and that's why you don't remember anything past that point."

Alex let out a sharp breath. "That is the most absurd thing you have said so far. Killed by my own brother? That's preposterous."

"Carter was outside the library that day." The words were spilling out faster now, like a wall inside me had been breached. "He came home early and was listening at the door. He heard everything you and Isobel said. You were right about one thing — he had been drinking. And when he discovered the truth, it drove him mad."

Panic rippled across Alex's face. "Isobel ... did he harm her?"

"No. But she died anyway." I pushed on, deciding it was better to get it all out in one go. "She drowned herself in the lake."

"*Isobel ...*" He whispered her name urgently, like he still believed he could save her. "Why would she do such a thing? How could she leave our child alone?"

As the truth sank in, I felt his pain as acutely as if it were my own. Alex was the last person in the world I wanted to hurt. It wasn't fair he should have to relive the deaths of the people he'd loved all over again. He had lived with that torment for so long already. Hadn't he suffered enough?

"She didn't leave him," I whispered. "James was already gone."

That knowledge brought such despair to his face that I had to look away. Part of me wanted to deny everything I'd just revealed, to declare it nothing more than a tasteless joke, even if it meant him despising me forever. That would be preferable to watching him go through this.

"But James was only an infant … what could have happened to him?"

I didn't want to answer, but having started this I knew I had to finish it. "Carter."

"What?" Alex cried, fury flashing in his eyes.

"Isobel found him in his crib. And with you already gone, she had nothing left to live for. Hers were the last screams you heard."

"And my brother?"

"Once Carter came to his senses and realised what he'd done, he hanged himself from the willow tree in the garden."

Alex's rage melted into a deep and bottomless sorrow. He stared fixedly into space, not bothering to wipe away the tears snaking down his ashen cheeks. There was nothing I could say to comfort him or even reach him through so much loss and despair. I knew he must be picturing his son. He thought he'd be around to watch James take his first steps. He'd imagined a lifetime of precious moments ahead of them. He thought he'd had all the time in the world to say *I love you*. But the child's life had been ended before it had even begun. Like a wisp, his soul had sailed in and out, leaving behind just the tiniest, faintest imprint on the world.

Even though I knew what it was like to lose someone you loved, I couldn't begin to comprehend what Alex must be feeling. I couldn't imagine what it must feel like to wake up one day to find that everyone you knew and loved was gone. They just weren't there any more, and the world was full of strangers. And to make matters worse, you weren't even alive to do anything about it like search for answers or seek justice.

Alex slumped forward, fingers scraping his temples like he wanted to rip what I'd told him from his head. All I could do was sit silently and watch his back rise and fall with grief.

When he finally looked up, his eyes were red. "I need to be alone." He rose purposefully to his feet even though it was clear he didn't have anywhere to go.

"Please don't disappear on me again," I said. "I understand this is painful, but it's not safe for you to be alone. At least not until we've figured out what's happening."

"That must wait. I need time to … to come to terms with everything you have said. Do not try to find me. When I am ready, I will come back."

There was nothing for it but to let him go. When my mom died, all I wanted to do was curl up in a ball and blot out the world. Contact with people was a physical strain, and time seemed to stretch like elastic, turning each minute into a lifetime. Alex had three deaths to come to terms with, *four* if he included his own, and as much as I wanted to help him through it, I knew he was better off alone.

I watched him walk away. I had no idea where he planned to go. I was pretty sure he didn't know either. But he'd said he would return when he was ready and I just had to trust him.

CHAPTER SIX

I made my way out of the theatre and back into the dazzling sunshine. When black splotches appeared in front of my eyes I realised I hadn't eaten properly in hours. My vivid dream hadn't left me with much of an appetite this morning.

It was already ten minutes into my science class and the decision to ditch it came easily. It wasn't like me, but then again I didn't really know what was "like me" these days. Who was Chloe Kennedy? A few months ago I would have given a definitive answer. Now, I was a work in progress and nothing was certain. It felt strangely liberating to admit that to myself. Too much had happened in the past twenty-four hours to pretend anything was normal, and it was a relief not to try. There were ghosts in my car, ghosts in my bedroom and ghosts in my dreams.

I immediately felt bad for lumping Alex in with the other strange happenings. He wasn't some fleeting apparition; we were part of one another. His presence here only reinforced my certainty about that, and sooner or later he would remember it too.

Despite how crazy everything seemed, I would always choose to have Alex in my life, even if he still thought of me as a stranger right now. There wasn't anything I wouldn't do for him, and I knew that not so long ago he did everything in his power to protect me against Isobel's vengeful spirit. Now it was my turn to look out for him, even if I hadn't quite figured out how.

I found myself wishing I could consult Mavis and May, the paranormal investigators from Baton Rouge who'd helped me out at Grange Hall. They'd written down their contact details for me, but somehow I'd lost the scrap of paper in transit. Perhaps I could ask Grandma Fee for their email address and see if they had any suggestions for curing post-mortem amnesia.

I didn't feel like heading home to eat in an empty house, so I drove to a diner to get myself a burger and fries. My plan was to keep busy until Alex resurfaced. Hopefully he'd come back with a plan, or at least a theory about what was going on.

I checked my phone to find a barrage of messages from Sam and Natalie. I knew they were only worried about me, but at the same time they'd never understood my need to be alone sometimes. I decided to ignore them for now and slipped my phone back into my bag.

Once I'd lingered as long as possible at the diner, I went back to my car and spent the next few hours aimlessly cruising the hills. I eventually ended up on Mulholland Drive, sitting on a ledge overlooking the valley. I thought about nothing and everything at the same time. Or perhaps I thought about everything for so long and with so much intensity that it broke down into nothing.

By the time I noticed the time, the sky was already streaked with fire and the city lights were beginning to glow. Dusk was the prettiest time in Los Angeles. The sky transformed into a watercolour painting, the peaches and cream light of the sun merging into cotton-candy pink and then bold purple. The shifting colours framed the silhouettes of the trees. I didn't want to leave, but it would soon be night and I wasn't keen on the idea of driving around these winding roads in the dark.

When I finally reached home, it was well after five and I wasn't surprised to see Sam's convertible parked in the driveway. I should've known my friends wouldn't be so easy to shake off. They knew me too well to not sense that something was up. But I was in no mood right now to fend off their questions and laugh along at their jokes. I didn't want to appear rude, but what I had to deal with was not something that could be explained. And in some ways it was safer to keep them in the dark.

"Oh my God, where have you been all day?" Natalie blurted the second I walked into the kitchen. "We looked everywhere for you."

"Where's my dad?" I asked quickly. "What did you tell him?"

"Nothing," Sam replied indignantly. "He's not home yet."

"Good. Don't say anything. I don't want him to worry — not that there's anything to worry about."

"So why weren't you at school?"

"How did you guys get in?"

"The front door was unlocked. Jeez, Chloe, what is your problem? We're your best friends. Or have you forgotten that?"

They both folded their arms, waiting for an apology I didn't feel I owed them. It was clear I didn't feel like talking, but they weren't willing to accept that. I was starting to squirm, feeling like a specimen under a microscope being examined by two clumsy teenagers. Thank God my brother walked in when he did.

"Rory!" I said. "There you are! Come and say hello."

"Hey." He gave Sam and Natalie an awkward wave and looked at me like I must have lost my mind. When had I ever invited him into my social life?

Ever since turning thirteen, he'd become increasingly self-conscious in the presence of girls, especially pretty ones. He barely used to notice them before, but I guessed my goofy kid brother was growing up.

"Hey, muppet," Sam said, affectionately tousling his hair. The nickname was from years ago, when Rory's curls were so long they'd completely obscured his vision.

Natalie joined in, giving him a hug and inadvertently pushing his cheek against her chest. "You're getting so tall! I can't believe we haven't seen you since you got back."

Rory turned bright red and grinned sheepishly.

"We were going to stop by last night, but *someone* didn't answer her phone," Sam said.

"That's because she was with her new boyfriend," Rory chimed in helpfully.

And *that's* why you don't hang out with thirteen-year-olds: they either don't say anything at all or they say way too much.

I shot my brother a warning glance, but it was too late. Sam and Natalie were staring at me, their perfect features twisted in expressions of shock and betrayal.

"What are you talking about?" I scoffed. "I don't have a boyfriend. You're not funny, Rory."

"Nice try," Sam said. "You've been holding out on us!"

"Tell us everything." Natalie settled comfortably against the kitchen counter.

"There's nothing to tell. I was just helping out a friend."

"Fine. Be cryptic then." She tossed her head. "Rory will tell us."

My brother looked hesitantly from her to me, but one flutter of Natalie's doe eyelashes and he folded like a cheap suit. "He's that English kid with the long hair," he blurted. I could practically see him clocking up brownie points in his head.

My laugh couldn't have sounded more forced. "And how would you know? You didn't even meet him."

"Dad told me." Rory had to know I was going to kill him later, but he was too busy lapping up the attention to care right now. "He said you guys went upstairs and then —"

"Don't you have homework to do?"

"It's all done." He grinned at me broadly. Having gained the attention of my friends, he wasn't about to relinquish it easily.

"Well, you better find more," I growled. "Before I tell Dad to check the search history on your computer."

That did the trick. Rory's eyes went wide and he edged out of the room.

I turned back to my friends.

"So you and the new guy, huh?" Natalie poked me in the side with all the maturity of a seventh grader. "Interesting. What is it they say about still waters?"

"No," I said, darting out of her reach. "Rory doesn't know what he's talking about."

74

"Why all the secrecy then? What happened upstairs, hmmm?"

"Nothing happened." I was impatient now. "If you must know, my night couldn't have been more boring. He left early and I spent all evening reading up on Shakespearean sonnets. Happy?"

Natalie shuddered. "That's worse than boring."

"So really … nothing happened?" Sam sighed, her disappointment evident.

I shook my head firmly. "Really."

"Did he at least ask you out? Was this supposed to be a first date or more of an impromptu hangout?"

"Of course it wasn't a date," Natalie cut in. "Dates involve dinner and candlelight."

"That's true. So what exactly did he say when —"

"Would you just drop it?" I snapped, and they both went silent, blinking in surprise. "I'm sorry, but it's not like that."

"Then what's it like?"

"I don't want to discuss it."

The girls exchanged looks.

"Why are you in such a bad mood lately?" Sam asked. "Are you PMSing?"

"Look, I have a lot of work to catch up on," I said. "I'll see you guys at school, alright?" I was already shepherding them into the hall.

"So you'll be there tomorrow?"

"With bells on."

"But we thought —"

"Okay, great, talk soon!"

I practically kicked them out, shut the door and put on the safety latch for good measure. I'd never felt so disconnected from my friends. Before my mom died, I used to consult them about pretty much everything. But back then I didn't know what a real problem was. Now I had a big one, and I was painfully aware that if I asked anybody for advice, they'd have nothing but disbelief to offer.

"Rory?" I called, and his face appeared from the den looking guilty as sin. "Well, thank you for that awesome display of loyalty. It's good to know I can always rely on my family."

"I'm sorry," he whined. "I just wanted them to like me! And Natalie is super persuasive."

"You mean her breasts are persuasive."

"What? I wasn't looking at her —"

"Spare me! Breasts are dangerous things, little brother. Try not to give all your worldly possessions to the first girl who shows you a pair."

He hung his head, embarrassed. "I feel bad."

"So you should. My life isn't a soap opera and you shouldn't treat it that way. There are some things I prefer to keep to myself. I wouldn't have done that to you, would I?"

"No," he said dejectedly. "Are you gonna tell Dad?"

"That depends. Have you learned your lesson?"

"Yeah." He nodded vigorously.

"Then I won't tell him. But only because I'm a loyal sister."

He charged at me and wrapped his skinny arms around my waist. "Thank you! I'll never do it again." He looked up at me. "I think I understand how you feel now."

"You do?" I felt a little spark of pride for imparting some older-sibling wisdom.

"Sure," said Rory matter-of-factly. "You're mad because you love him."

By eight o'clock Dad still hadn't shown up, so I threw two containers of frozen mac and cheese in the microwave. It wasn't the healthiest dinner, but I was too tired for anything more complicated. After taking one in to Rory, I went upstairs to my room. It was a bit depressing to eat alone, cross-legged on the bed. But not as depressing as the silent dinner table.

Besides, I was still feeling shaken by my brother's surprising astuteness. *You love him. You love him. You love him.* The words bounced around my brain. I didn't know why they bothered me so much. Maybe because I knew it was true?

I was reluctant to admit it, even to myself, because that would make it too real. And then all the very *real* problems associated with loving Alexander Reade would rear their heads. I would have to ask myself *how* it was possible to love a ghost and that wasn't a question I was ready to answer.

I opened my laptop to find several emails from disgruntled teachers demanding an explanation for my absence. Each one had an attachment of the material and homework I'd missed that day. I knew I should look at them, I knew how important senior year was in terms of my future prospects, but I simply couldn't bring myself to care.

"Life will teach you more than school ever can" — that's what my mom used to say. "Years of law school won't give you the same rush as riding through Spain in the summertime on the back of a motorcycle." Dad would usually jump in at that point to clarify that Rory and

I should go to college first and then proceed to bike around as many European countries as we liked.

It was funny how so much could change in such a short space of time. I was the girl who wanted to get into Cornell. I had no intention of betraying my West Coast roots and moving to New York, but I wanted to get in just to prove I could. At the back of my mind I'd always thought I'd go to Stanford, but at this rate I was heading for community college. I might as well start dropping off resumés at Applebee's. How had my life become such a mess? It felt like all the building blocks I'd put in place over the years had crumbled to rubble at my feet. And I wasn't even concerned about it.

I slid down on my bed, leaning back on a mountain of pillows. The conversation with Alex had left me physically and emotionally drained. Telling him the truth was one of the hardest things I'd ever had to do. I didn't doubt for a second that I'd made the right decision, but in breaking his heart I'd also broken my own. I wished I could be with him now. I wished I could help ease what must be a terrible grief. Mortal struggles were meant to come to an end in death, but death had not brought Alex any peace.

Waiting for his return was making me incredibly anxious. I wished I could go back to Grange Hall, back to the beginning when all we'd had to contend with was one vengeful spirit. Isobel's wrath was almost easier to handle than the tangled situation we now faced. How was I going to keep Alex both safe and in my life?

I instinctively reached for Grandma Fee's brooch, squeezing it in my hand and letting the sharp petals dig into my flesh. As had happened last time, I soon felt my eyelids grow heavy as a strange lethargy crept through my body.

I opened my palm and studied the brooch. It seemed to wink at me; a shining reminder of a time long gone. Already everything was blurring at the edges. I could have shoved the brooch into the back of a drawer and opened one of the emails from my teachers, but I didn't. I wanted to go where I knew the brooch would take me.

I am conscious of my steps through the gathering dusk, afraid of stumbling even though I have been sent on this errand a hundred times before. Thunder rumbles overhead and the skies are threatening. I pray the rain will hold off just a while longer. Once it starts, the path will grow slippery with mud and I am sure to fall, dirtying my dress and scraping my knees.

The golden lights of the alehouse glow up ahead. When I reach the door I hesitate to enter, even though no one bats an eye upon seeing me any more. This place has become my father's refuge, the place he favours over the company of his own family. I think seeing our hopeful, hungry faces every day reminds him too much of his shortcomings.

I love my father and always will, but he is not a man built for hard labour. He is a dangerous mix of charm and recklessness. He used to work as a tanner in the village until he gave it up to follow a fool's dream. Now he is a magician. Perhaps in London he might find work entertaining the upper classes, but his card and disappearing tricks are not so well received in Wistings. After a few ales, folk are content to watch but they will not part with more than a few pennies. The night wears on, the audience disperses and my father drinks himself into oblivion. When the last patron has staggered off home, he will still be there.

Mother has sent me to fetch him home before the storm. I am expecting a struggle, but he welcomes me cheerfully, throwing an arm around my shoulder.

"Becky!" he cries. "My little duckling. What are you doing here?"

"I've come to take you home."

"You've come for me? You're an angel! Isn't she an angel, Fernley?" He turns to the barkeeper, who nods and throws me a sympathetic glance. "Do I have time for one more pint?"

"No, Papa," I say. "It's getting late and it will be pouring rain any minute. We must go now."

"In that case, let us make haste!" he declares, losing his balance a little as he climbs off the stool.

Together we stagger home, weaving along the cobbled alleyways. I pray nobody will see us. I am tired of pretending not to notice their pitying looks.

As we near home, my father's legs grow leaden and he leans against me more heavily. I may be slight, but it is remarkable the strength one finds when one has no other choice.

Mother greets us at the door of our cottage and together we lug my father inside, just managing to get him to the bed. His eyes are shut before his head hits the pillow and he lets out a belch that reeks of liquor.

Mother looks down at him in despair, then shakes her head and returns to mending by the firelight. I watch her from the doorway. Her face is haggard with worry, her hands are calloused from hard work. I wish I could do more to ease her burden. The reason I can read and write is because my mother is an educated woman who once worked as a governess for a lord in London. But that was long ago, well before she met my father. She does not like to talk of those days, and tells me it is my job to go out into the world to make a decent life for myself.

Before I go to bed, she beckons me over and takes my face in her rough but familiar hands. "You are a blessing, Becky, my dear. What would I do without you?"

"You will never have to find out," I tell her.

I know Mother has high hopes for me. She says I have a sharp mind and must not be afraid to use it. I know the names of the ancient philosophers, and that the stars are made of dust. But I am a plain girl from a poor family. My chances of marrying well are not high, but that does not matter to me. I would rather have knowledge than a husband, and I do not care much for expensive trinkets or pretty dresses.

That is why I am leaving home to work as a maid at Grange Hall, the big house on the hill. Maids are seen and not heard and that suits me fine. Without my father's wages, there is nothing to support us, so I take my new responsibilities seriously. My sisters are only seven and ten; too young to go out to work. So it has fallen to me and I shall not let my family down.

My employer, Mr Reade, and his new bride are rarely seen in public. What I know of them comes from rumour. I know he spends much of his time in the city on business, and that his younger brother has come to stay after a sojourn in Paris. The girls in the village fall over themselves when they see him out riding. Granted, he is very handsome, with a softer disposition than his brother. I believe his name is Alexander and he is a painter or artist of some kind. Only the wealthy can afford to fritter their time away on art, but it is hard to resent the younger Mr Reade for it. His eyes are too kind and his manner too gentle. He is the only one of the family who ever comes into town and always converses pleasantly with the few girls bold enough to approach him.

They once tried to convince him to hold a ball at Grange Hall. It is the best, and perhaps only, way for girls in our position to associate with eligible gentlemen. But he only smiled at them and said, "I promise to put it to my brother." Then he gave a short bow, mounted his horse and rode away. The ball was never spoken of again.

It is odd to think that soon I shall see the Reade family every day. I have always wondered what secrets exist within the walls of Grange Hall. The family is guarded and mysterious. Why do they never go out? Why do guests never come to stay? What are they hiding?

I suppose I shall soon find out.

CHAPTER SEVEN

It was midnight when I woke. I lay sprawled across my bed and felt the kiss of cool air on my cheeks from the open window. I was still clutching the antique brooch and my fingers had stiffened around it. I wasn't surprised I'd dreamed of Becky again; it seemed the brooch was infused with some kind of supernatural power. It had a story to tell and had chosen me as the recipient. I wondered who it had belonged to and how it came to be connected to Becky. It didn't seem like the sort of thing she'd ever be able to afford given what I knew of her so far. Yet for some reason it insisted on transporting me back to her world.

Even though it was late, I couldn't get back to sleep, so I went downstairs in search of a midnight snack. I heard a soft rustling in the kitchen and found my father eating leftover Chinese out of the carton.

"Hey, kiddo," he said. "What are you doing up?"

"I fell asleep way too early and now I'm wide awake."

He offered me his carton. "Want some orange chicken? It's cold but still good."

"No, thanks." I went to the freezer and popped a couple of cinnamon waffles into the toaster.

"Good move. I lied. The chicken's not so great."

"When did you get in?" I asked, feeling more like the parent than the child.

"Around eleven thirty," he said, hearing the note of censure in my voice. "Sorry it was so late. I ... got held up."

"Were you working late again?"

"Not exactly." It was obvious he was avoiding the question, but what he said next took me completely by surprise. "I went out to dinner."

I raised my eyebrows. "Pretty late dinner."

"Well ... yeah, I lost track of time, I suppose. We had a few glasses of wine at this great little Italian restaurant, then went for a walk on the Santa Monica pier. I'll have to take you and Rory there one day."

"I've been to the Santa Monica pier," I told him frostily. "And what do you mean *we*?"

Silence fell. The only sound was the cheerful pop of my waffles as they shot out of the toaster. I made no move to claim them, still waiting on my father's answer. There was a nasty taste in my mouth as I watched him hesitate. I already knew what he was going to say and I'd completely lost my appetite.

He let out a heavy sigh. "There's no point beating around the bush. I was with a woman. Marcie."

"You mean like on a date?" I stared at him, dumbstruck.

"I wouldn't exactly call it that."

"What would you call it then?"

"I know this might come as a bit of a shock," he continued when it became clear I wasn't budging. "I didn't want to tell you just now because you have enough on your plate, so I thought ... Well, I don't know what I thought. But

Marcie's a lovely person. I think you'd like her. Please don't look at me like that, Chloe."

My face was frozen in a mask of disgust. I'd never hated my father more than I did in that moment. In fact, I barely even recognised him. He seemed like a stranger sitting in our kitchen and trying to hide the guilt in his eyes.

"You should be careful," I said coldly. "Chinese after Italian is asking for trouble." Then I dropped my waffles into the trash and walked away.

I was so outraged, I felt tears coursing down my cheeks. The only woman I'd ever imagined my dad with was my mom. Theirs was the kind of bond that was supposed to weather any storm. Was it possible he'd forgotten her so quickly when I was still reeling from the loss? There wasn't a day when I didn't come home from school expecting to hear her singing along to some golden oldie as she unpacked groceries, or out the back on her knees adding mulch to her prized herb garden, or in her gym gear coming back from her power walk with Darcy, who was flaked out and panting on the tiles.

All I wanted to do was punish my father somehow for what he'd done, for betraying my mother like this. I wanted to run to his room and cut up all his suits with scissors, or throw him out and change the locks. But of course I couldn't do either. Instead, I sat on the floor of my room where I could seethe in private.

I needed to connect with my mom so I opened the bottom drawer of my chest and pulled out my favourite photo of her, the one I'd packed and taken with me to England. I was still not ready to have it on display.

In it I'm just a toddler and Mom and I are on a windswept beach. Her hair is swept across her face and her expression is the most carefree I've ever seen it. Sometimes when things got too tough to handle I'd cradle this photo and pretend she was there in the room with me, that she could hear me rattle off all my problems. If I concentrated on the photo hard enough, I had the sensation of the scene coming to life. I could hear the waves undulating behind us, hear the rustle of the wind, almost taste the briny air. All my memories of her were precious because they were the only thing I had left of the person I'd loved most in life. I liked to imagine her as still close by, watching over us. It might have been a childish notion, but I clung to it for dear life. And now my dad had decided the time had come to move on.

How *could* he? Mom hadn't been gone six months and he was going on *date nights* at the Santa Monica pier like some kind of lovestruck teenager. What kind of man would do that? Didn't he care about keeping our family together? Didn't he know we were already hanging by a thread? I missed my mother more than anything. I felt her loss every single day, like wounds in my body that refused to heal over. Sometimes I felt like I was merely going through the motions of life. Most of the time I felt nothing at all. I would have given anything to have Mom back.

All my faith in my dad evaporated. If he thought we could play happy families with his new girlfriend, he was sorely mistaken. I would have no part in it. That was the least I could do to protect my mother's memory. In hindsight, it wasn't exactly the most mature reaction. But in that moment I was blinded by emotion; there was no room for reasoning.

I got to my feet, flung open the closet and dragged out the duffel bag that had been gathering dust since my return from England. I didn't bother to fold anything; I just hurled items in — some T-shirts, a few pairs of jeans. I made sure to dump my computer and schoolbooks in as well so I wouldn't have to come back for them. I zipped up the bag, then, as an afterthought, snatched up the brooch from my bedside table and tucked it deep in my pocket.

Rory stumbled out onto the landing. "Chloe?" he asked groggily. "What's going on?"

"Nothing. Go back to bed."

"Where are you going?"

My father appeared at the foot of the stairs. He looked up at me and his brow crumpled like an old napkin. "Oh, for Christ's sake, Chloe, what are you doing?"

"*Leaving*," I said as I marched past him. I wanted to seem dignified, but it was hard when the bag I was lugging kept crashing into my knees.

"Don't be so childish. Where are you going?"

It was clear from his tone that he didn't believe I'd actually go through with it. To him, this was just a teenage temper tantrum. I'd get in the car, drive around for a few blocks until I cooled down, and then come home.

"Anywhere but here!" I yelled at him.

"Wait!" Rory ran down the stairs, wide awake now, and sprang hopefully by my side as I reached for the door. "Can I come with you?"

"No, you can't go with her," Dad snapped.

"Why not?"

"Because nobody is going anywhere!"

"There's nothing you can do about it," I told him. "I'm eighteen. *Legally* you can't stop me."

"Chloe …" he began, but I pushed past him out the front door, letting the screen slam shut behind me.

They both followed me into the balmy California night, where, as per usual, starlight failed to pierce the smog.

"Chloe," my father said sternly. "Come back inside right now and stop making such a scene. We can talk about everything in the morning, okay?"

"*No!*" Anger overtook me again and I spun around to face him. I couldn't hold back the hot tears; they came thick and fast and I could barely see through them. "No, it's not okay! None of this is *okay*. How can you even think that? You can't just erase Mom from the picture and replace her with the first person you meet with boobs and hair. It doesn't work that way!"

"I'm not trying to replace your mother," my father said quietly.

"You have a *girlfriend*?" Rory asked incredulously. Eyes wide, he took a step back.

"I haven't … She's not … Would everyone just calm down!"

For the first time in my life I witnessed my father lost for words.

"You don't know how hard all this has been on me," he said eventually.

I felt that acrid taste creeping up my throat again. Didn't he know how hard it had been on Rory and me too? I couldn't look at his face any more, so I flipped open the trunk of my car and tossed the duffel bag inside.

"I hate you for this," I said, before getting behind the wheel. "I'll never forgive you."

I slammed the door and reversed aggressively out of the driveway, tyres crunching over gravel. My father watched dejectedly, but didn't try to stop me. My heart broke for Rory, who was standing there like a bedraggled puppy who didn't know where he belonged any more.

I drove aimlessly for a while before pulling over to think. I had no clue where I was going. I could have texted Sam or Natalie and crashed at one of their houses, but I couldn't do that without lengthy explanations and I just wasn't up for it.

I couldn't call on Alex either. He was off dealing with a crisis of his own, and besides there was no way of reaching him. It wasn't like at Grange Hall when he'd always sensed when I needed him and just appeared.

As I scrolled through the contacts in my phone, I realised there was only one person who wouldn't judge me or give me a hard time. Zac Green. The last time I'd seen him was in the cafeteria when I'd reacted so badly to hearing Alex's name. Zac had asked if I was alright, and told me he was there for me if I needed him. I remembered too how he'd shared something personal with me before I left for England: he'd told me that his baby sister had died. He didn't say how it happened, only that he understood what I was going through.

Zac Green. Just last year I would never have dreamed of asking him for anything. It would have gone against the protocol that governed our teenage world. But things like that didn't matter any more. I needed help and, unlike the old Chloe, I wasn't too embarrassed to ask for it. So I called.

"Hello, Zac?"

"Hi …" He trailed off uncertainly. Why had I expected him to recognise my voice?

"It's Chloe Kennedy."

I'd been crying so hard it was impossible to hide it, and Zac clued in right away. "Hey, Chloe, is everything alright?" He sounded genuinely concerned.

"Sort of," I began, then realised that lying would defeat the whole purpose of the call. "Actually, not really. Not at all. I just had a huge fight with my dad so I packed my stuff and left. Only now I don't know where to go or what to do. I realise it's kind of weird for me to be calling you —"

He cut me off. "It's not weird at all. Why don't you come over? I'll text you my address."

"Are you sure? It's pretty late. What about your parents?"

"Don't worry about it."

"Okay. Thanks."

Suddenly there was a solid plan in place and it took me by surprise. I'd expected him to suggest a late-night coffee and a heart-to-heart. I'd never spent time with Zac one on one before, yet here I was about to land on his doorstep and bring all my troubles with me.

His house was in Malibu; a little further than I'd anticipated, but the midnight drive down the Pacific Coast Highway helped me clear my head. The ocean stretched as far as the eye could see, curling along the shore that hugged the rugged cliffs. The waves rushed at the rocks, rearing like an angry wall only to shatter like glass seconds later, exploding through the air and landing quietly back in the sea.

When I reached the address Zac had given me, I had to double-check that I'd come to the right place. The house, hidden by foliage, stood behind vast mirrored metal gates. I noticed Zac had included an access code in his message so I leaned out the window and entered it on the keypad. An automated voice thanked me and the gate slid noiselessly open.

As I drove past the trees, the house came into view: a lavish contemporary construction made mostly of glass and steel. It was perched high above the Pacific Ocean, an expanse of blue unfurling as far as the eye could see until it blurred with the horizon. In either direction I could see the muted lights of other houses nestled higher into the cliffs. It was the sort of house you'd find in *Architectural Digest*. It looked so cutting edge I felt sure cyborgs rather than humans lived there.

"Hey!" Zac appeared on the driveway. He was wearing sweats and a polo shirt. "You made good time."

"There was no one on the road … and I was definitely driving over the limit."

He laughed. "Well, I'm glad you made it in one piece."

"This place is amazing," I said.

"It's alright." He shrugged. "A little sterile for my taste."

"How did you end up at Sycamore High? It's not exactly close."

"Yeah, that's why I chose it. There were too many memories at my old school; too many people who looked at me and saw my sister."

"I'm sorry," I mumbled. "I should have guessed."

"It's fine. I wanted a fresh start. Why don't we go round the back?"

"Good idea. I'd hate to wake your parents."

"Actually I live out the back," Zac said. "I needed my own space, so last year I moved into the pool house."

He pointed it out as it came into view. It was a sleek, flat building with glass walls overlooking the pool on one side and the ocean on another. The pool was built to look as if it was pouring off the edge of the cliff. It gave me the feeling of being caught in a strangely modern fairytale.

Inside, Zac's bed was hidden behind a long Japanese screen. There were electric guitars hanging on the wall, a huge flatscreen TV and a fully stocked bar. It made me think his parents must be very open-minded. Soft rock music played from speakers I assumed were hidden in the walls.

"Can I offer you a nightcap?" Zac asked. "You look like you could use one."

"Why not? Thanks."

"How about an Old-Fashioned?"

I only smiled rather than admitting I didn't know what an Old-Fashioned was. "I didn't know you were a student by day and James Bond by night," I said as he fixed the drink.

"Oh God, no." He shook his head. "I hate all this ostentatious crap."

"You do?"

"Yeah. Actually, my dad's super pissed at me right now because I won't let him buy me a flash car. He said I could choose between a BMW or a Porsche so I got a Prius just to spite him … a *used* Prius." He chuckled. "I thought he might have a heart attack when I showed up to dinner driving it. He's also pushing for me to do commerce at college, but I think I want to be a musician — not a very secure career in my dad's view."

I laughed. "Well, I'm all about hating on fathers right now. I get making your own career choices, but I'm not sure I'd knock back the offer of the car."

"What kind of idiot turns down a BMW, right?" Zac smiled. "I was just trying to prove that something doesn't have to be fancy for it to have value."

He pulled a jar from the mini fridge and garnished my drink with a cocktail cherry.

I raised an eyebrow. "Speaking of fancy ..."

"Hey, if I'm gonna make it, I'm gonna make it right!" he said, pushing the drink across the bar toward me. "Also, I'm a little OCD, so making it without the cherry would be a real problem for me. Do you like it?"

I took a sip. It tasted classy, like I should be sitting in a library puffing on a cigar.

"I do," I told Zac. "More than I expected."

"Why don't we sit outside?" He motioned for me to follow him through the glass doors to the edge of the glittering pool.

I could smell the ocean and almost feel its salty dust on my skin. He sat on a pool lounge, watching as I crouched by the water. Even though the night was balmy, I shivered as I leaned down to trail my fingers through it.

"It's so warm." Zac looked at me with a twinkle in his eye. "Are you up for a midnight swim?"

Floating on my back in the warm water, I could almost feel the anxiety being leached from my body. I felt weightless for the first time in a long time. I knew my troubles weren't gone, only abated, and was sure they'd descend again the moment I emerged from the water. But I'd have plenty of time for worrying later. Right now I felt spacey in a good way, like after an amazing massage.

Even though I hadn't planned to, I ended up telling Zac everything that had happened at home. Maybe it was because he didn't push that I felt comfortable opening up to him. He just waited patiently until I was ready to talk. I told him about my dad as well as Alex showing up out of the blue, although naturally I neglected to mention the part about him being dead. I told him Sam and Natalie were driving me crazy, and how scared I was that Rory would flunk out of school and end up flipping burgers for a living. In fact, I told him every minute detail and the load seemed to lessen with every word.

"So I guess that's how I ended up here," I said finally. "I felt bad calling you, but I didn't know who else to talk to."

"I'm glad you called." He was quiet for a moment as he bobbed in the water. "You've got a lot going on right now, Chloe. That boyfriend of yours really shouldn't be screwing with your head."

"He's not doing it on purpose," I said. "And for the record, he's not my boyfriend."

"Sorry, I shouldn't have said anything. It's not my place."

"No, I want your opinion. It's just that Alex isn't exactly …" I trailed off. "He's just different."

"Different how?"

"He's got a lot of baggage," I said carefully. "More than most."

"Well, I don't know his deal so I shouldn't comment. But can I say one thing?"

"Sure."

"It's about your dad. Look, I know it must really suck to imagine him with someone else. And I'm not defending him — don't get me wrong — but I wouldn't automatically assume it means he's moved on."

"What else could it mean?"

"Well …" He shrugged. "It could mean he misses your mom so much that he's willing to do anything he can to fill the void. He did spend twenty-three years of his life with her. I bet everything in your house reminds him of her. Maybe that's why he's never home. Not because he doesn't want to be with you and Rory. You guys probably remind him of her too."

"I didn't think of it that way," I murmured. "I know this is hard for him too and I wish I didn't feel so angry with him, but I do. Instead of stepping up, he's running away. It's just so selfish."

"You're right, it is, but pain can make people that way. Maybe he's just not as strong as you."

"I thought *he* was supposed to look after *us*. Isn't that what adults do?"

Zac laughed humourlessly. "First rule of life: there's no such thing as adults, Chloe. They're just children who've gotten bigger and less cute."

I smiled. "You're a wise one, aren't you?"

"Yep. I'm like an owl." He kicked back in the water. "Look, you're welcome to hang out here for a couple of days until things settle down."

"Oh, no, I appreciate you listening and all, but I couldn't do that."

"Why not? My dad isn't even in town right now, and Mom's usually half-drunk by mid-afternoon." He grinned, making it impossible to tell if he was joking or not. "I'll drive us to school every day, and then we can chill here. No one has to know if you don't want them to."

"Why would you do that for me? You barely know me."

"Because I'd like to get to know you better. After all these years don't you think it's about time?"

He smiled and lifted himself easily out of the pool, his torso rippling from the movement. I noticed the moonlight reflected in the droplets of water that clung to his skin.

"Come on," he said, offering me his hand. "It's past our bedtime."

CHAPTER EIGHT

Back inside, Zac directed me to the bathroom so I could take a shower. "There are fresh towels on the rack."

As expected, the bathroom was ultra modern, all chrome and slate. I showered quickly, then changed into the Nike shorts and Pink Floyd T-shirt I always slept in. I was starting to wish I'd packed nicer clothes.

As I folded my jeans, the antique brooch slipped out and fell onto the polished concrete floor. I snatched it up quickly, examining it for any damage. It seemed intact. I pinned it to the inside of my T-shirt for safekeeping; something told me I should keep it close.

I was yawning again by the time I returned to the living room, where Zac had transformed the leather sofa into a pull-out bed.

"Here you go — all ready," he said, plumping some pillows.

"Thank you. Where did you learn to be such a perfect host?"

"Don't tell anyone but Martha Stewart is my real mom." Zac winked at me as he turned out the lights. "Get some rest, Chloe. See you in a few hours."

"Night, Zac."

I climbed into the bed and immediately fell into a deep but not dreamless sleep.

Today I have been entrusted with the daunting task of cleaning the library. It is so vast, and I am terribly anxious about damaging Mr Reade's books, which sit in their glass cases like ancient seers. As I dust, I scan the spines, trying to memorise all the exotic titles. I am humbled by the treasure trove of knowledge contained in this room. There are books on every subject imaginable, so many it is hard to believe anyone could have the time to read them all. Our scant and well-thumbed collection at home cannot compare with these. They look wonderfully mysterious, each one a portal into a different world; so many places waiting to be visited, adventures waiting to be had. For someone like me, who has not a hope of real adventure, they are my only chance.

To my surprise the bookcases are not locked, I look around to make sure nobody is watching, even though I am the only person here, then I slide open a glass door and carefully remove one of the books. I marvel at how heavy it is as I trace my fingers over the gilt lettering on the cover. It is about bird species in Great Britain and contains beautiful watercolour illustrations. They are so mesmerising that I abandon my chores for a moment to take a closer look. I sink down on the floor, cradling the book and reverently turning its pages.

I am not sure how much time passes, but whatever spell has come over me is broken when I become aware of someone else in the library. A young gentleman watches me from the doorway. I leap to my feet, clutching the book to my chest, and feel an overwhelming urge to explain myself, to apologise, to ask for another chance. But I know I must not speak unless spoken to. Mortified, I bow my head.

The young man walks into the room. "Are you interested in ornithology?"

He speaks softly as if not to alarm me, but I am already alarmed — mostly at my own impertinence. I wonder if he will call Mrs Baxter, or simply send me to pack my bags at once. I hope he doesn't shout or make an example of me in front of the other staff.

He is still waiting patiently for an answer. Whatever ornithology is, I am sure it is nothing a housemaid has any business meddling in. So I shake my head vehemently.

"I beg your pardon, sir, I don't know what came over me. I forgot my place. But it won't happen again. I didn't mean to —"

He shakes his head. "Please, do not trouble yourself to explain anything to me." He looks around and shrugs. "As far as I can see, you have done no harm."

Surely there must be graver consequences for such unprofessional conduct? I flinch when he comes over to me, but he only kneels to retrieve a book from the bottom shelf. When he glances up, I see that despite the sharp angles of his face there is no censure in his expression. His eyes are the palest shade of blue and they seem to be smiling at me.

"Think no more about it," he says, and I can see he truly means it.

I feel the panic subside, replaced first by confusion and then recognition. He is the master's younger brother! I have only seen him from a distance, but it is unmistakably him. I recognise his hair — long and dark gold in colour, bound loosely at the nape of his neck with a black velvet ribbon.

"You are new to the household," he says, straightening up. "What is your name?"

"Rebecca," I mumble. "I mean Becky, and yes, sir, I've been here a little over a month."

"Becky, I am Alexander. I am pleased to make your acquaintance."

I decide the world must have gone mad in the time I have spent browsing the library. Since when do gentlemen take the time to make small talk with servants? I curtsey, feeling as clumsy as a donkey.

"Is it true you have come from Paris?" I hear myself ask. What am I doing? I know full well it is impudent to question him.

He smiles. "It is. I enjoyed it very much."

I do not know what to say next so I drop my gaze to the floor.

"Please do not let me interrupt you any further," he says. As if what I am doing here is of the highest importance.

"Yes, sir," I say. "Thank you, sir."

I allow our eyes to meet briefly and find myself startled. Not by the beauty of his eyes, although they are startling to be sure, but by the sadness in them, as if Mr Alexander (as I now refer to him) carries the woes of the world on his back. His eyes drift past me to the window and the storm clouds gathering in the sky. He looks wistful, nostalgic even. Does he miss Paris perhaps? I imagine returning to the English countryside would be a rude shock after living in such a cultured city. He looks the way I imagine a Parisian artist might look: tortured and ever so slightly dishevelled.

He tears his gaze away from the darkening sky and looks back at me. I scurry out of his way and begin dusting the gleaming desk in the corner. Writing implements are laid out neatly on it, and the paper looks so buttery I feel it might melt in my hands.

A moment later I hear Mr Alexander's footsteps receding. Instead of breathing a sigh of relief, I find myself turning to face him. To my surprise, I say, "Excuse me, sir."

I must feel emboldened by his kindness; there can be no other explanation for detaining him further.

He stops and tilts his head. "Yes, Becky?"

"If you don't mind my asking, sir," I say meekly, feeling my neck burn with embarrassment, "what is ornithology?"

Mr Alexander's mouth curls into a smile, but when he answers me he could not sound more earnest. "Ornithology is a branch of science that relates to the study of birds."

"Thank you, sir, and I'm sorry to trouble you."

I nod gratefully and return to my work, but he is not quite finished.

"Do not be sorry. Asking questions is the best way to learn. When all else fails, knowledge is the only thing we can rely on, Becky. Seek it out at all costs and never be ashamed to do so. You have my permission to avail yourself of the knowledge contained in these books whenever an opportunity presents itself."

Then he disappears out the door while I stand speechless. I cannot imagine why a gentleman would bother showing kindness to someone like me. But I know that whatever happens during my time at Grange Hall, Mr Alexander shall have my undying loyalty.

I was woken by the sun peeking over the palm trees and streaming through the glass walls of Zac's pool house. I was disoriented for a second before my mind cleared and the events of last night came rushing back to me. I rolled over and felt something sharp dig into my chest. It was Grandma Fee's brooch.

Even though I'd slept, I didn't feel rested at all. Poor Becky. I felt for her, all alone in her new world with few opportunities for social interaction. Alex had possibly spoken the only kind words she was likely to hear there. Would he play a role in shaping her life, I wondered. It was unlikely; the gaping difference in their social standing would limit his influence.

The dream had left me exhausted, confused and caught between different worlds. Alex's face was still fresh in my memory after seeing him through Becky's eyes. I half-expected to find him here, but it was Zac I saw when I finally sat up. To my surprise, he was already dressed and in the kitchen fixing us a cooked breakfast.

"Morning," he said. "This will be ready in exactly seven minutes. Feel free to take a dip in the pool while you're waiting. It always wakes me up."

Jumping into an outdoor pool before 7 am wasn't an invitation I would normally take up, but in this new place I was a new Chloe. So I grabbed a towel and took his advice. Outside, the morning air gently caressed my cheeks. It felt so peaceful and private at this hour that I stripped to my underwear without even thinking about it and dove into the water. It was cooler now, but it only took a moment for my body to adjust and then I felt wonderfully refreshed. The water felt like a safe haven and I wished I could stay there all day. But I didn't want to keep Zac waiting after all the trouble he'd gone to.

Back inside and wrapped in a towel, I saw he'd gone all out with breakfast. He'd made an asparagus, goat cheese and egg-white omelette, which sat on the granite countertop along with breakfast sausages, bacon, coffee and orange juice.

"You really shouldn't have gone to all this trouble," I said.

It always made me uncomfortable when people did nice things for me. I felt like I needed to repay them somehow.

"No big deal," Zac said. "I do this every morning."

"Seriously?"

"Yep, healthy body, healthy mind."

"So you're like a fully functioning adult," I said playfully. "Like the ones you see in the movies?"

He laughed. "Well, if you act like a child, you get treated like a child. And there's nothing I hate more than that."

Zac did seem to have his life together, which was more than I could say for myself. He appeared in control of everything, from his emotions to the decisions he made. He didn't react to things, he simply responded to them. Maybe I should try taking a leaf out of his book. I wanted to become a one-woman island, completely self-sufficient and not dependent on anyone. I didn't want to be the girl who was constantly in need of rescuing. Even though my troubles seemed to be piling up like an avalanche, I wanted to be strong enough to carry the load.

I only wished I could turn to my mother for advice. She was the person I always used to confide in. I'd go to her knowing that soon everything would be okay because she could always fix things. Even in the rare instance where the problem wasn't fixable she could always make me feel better.

Who could I confide in now? My friends wouldn't believe me if I told them about Alexander, my father was otherwise occupied, and Rory was too young to be of any help. Mom had been my lifeline. Now I had to make life-changing decisions alone, and no matter how many pep talks I gave myself, I was terrified of screwing up.

"Are you alright?" Zac asked on the drive to school. "You seem distracted."

"I'm just thinking about everything … I wish I could switch off my thoughts."

"Okay," he said. "Let's try something for a moment. Picture your problem, and I mean really focus on it …"

"Don't you mean *problems*?" I replied light-heartedly and Zac smiled.

"Let's aim for one at a time."

"Okay …" I closed my eyes and thought about Alex and how he was grieving alone right now. He may show up again tomorrow or he may not return at all. Neither of us knew what was going to happen from one day to the next. "Got one."

"Think carefully," Zac said. "Is there anything that *you* could do *right now* to fix this problem?"

I was quiet for a moment. "No."

"Then let it go."

"That's a very Zen outlook."

He shrugged. "You're just torturing yourself otherwise."

We didn't speak for the rest of the trip, but I knew Zac was right. I was torturing myself and for what? It didn't actually change anything. But there was no off-switch in my brain. Or if there was, I didn't know where to find it.

We pulled into the parking lot and I looked out the window at the school, seeing it in a whole new light. Alex's arrival had changed everything. The familiar routines and predictability were gone, replaced by tension and anticipation. It was even reflected in the weather, which had turned suddenly overcast, the sun struggling to break through the dense cloud cover.

I steeled myself for the trouble I knew was coming, even though I had no idea what shape it would take.

Zac and I had lockers in the same block so we walked into school together. I noticed a few raised eyebrows and searching glances, but I was past caring. In fact, I was ready to snap at anyone who dared ask any questions.

It was nice having Zac by my side. He felt like a buffer; a wall between me and the world I didn't want to deal with. Today, I decided, would be a turning point. I would keep my head down, work hard and not be consumed by problems I had no answers to.

But that plan went out the window the moment I reached my locker.

I opened the door and immediately reeled back. The rancid smell emanating from inside was so foul it almost bowled me over. Zac was at my shoulder, but I couldn't tell whether he could smell it or not because his eyes were glued to the inside of my locker door. Scrawled on the metal was a message in bold red ink: *I AM NOT GONE.*

My first thought was of Alex. Perhaps he was letting me know that he'd soon be back. But seconds later, I knew the message wasn't from him. The lettering was manic and shaky, as if the person who wrote it had trouble containing their emotions. Just looking at it gave me an uneasy feeling in the pit of my stomach. I wanted to scrub the words off with my hands, but at the same time I didn't want to touch them.

"This isn't funny," Zac said. "Your friends have a sick sense of humour."

"My friends didn't do this."

"Who else knows your locker code?"

"I have no idea," I replied softly.

"Made any enemies lately?" Zac was glancing around as though the culprit might be lurking nearby to watch my reaction to his handiwork. But the hallway was thronging with students and none of them looked even remotely suspicious. "I think we should report this."

"No," I said, "it's just a stupid prank."

"You don't know that."

"Come on, Zac, what else could it be?"

"I don't know. But I don't like it. If anything else weird happens today, you'll tell me, right?" He'd gone into strangely protective mode.

"Of course. Right now I just need to find whatever's making that disgusting smell."

We both peered into my locker, but there were only folders, protein bars and piles of books, all stacked neatly. The only other item was my gym bag, tucked in the top right-hand corner.

Zac motioned to it. "May I?"

I nodded and he tugged it down. The moment he opened the zipper, the cause of the putrid smell was revealed. Dark brown slime bubbled from the bag, seeping over Zac's fingers. He yanked his hand away and stared in horror. Everything I kept in there — my hairbrush, toiletries, tampons, a towel — was coated in this oozing substance, which was viscous like honey and filled the corridor with the stench of rotting meat.

Zac instinctively covered his mouth and stepped back as if someone had punched him in the face. "Okay, this we *have* to report."

"No! I mean … I'd rather not."

He stared at me, dumbfounded. "Chloe, this is destruction of personal property accompanied by what we can only assume is some kind of threat. Are you really gonna let it slide?"

"It's not the right time to stir things up. Trust me."

"What does that mean? You can't just ignore this."

"I can," I said, shoving the bag back into my locker. "I'll deal with it later. Please don't say anything, okay?"

Zac hesitated. "Well, I don't get it, but okay, if that's what you want."

"Thank you. I appreciate it."

"If you're in some kind of trouble, I want to help …"

"I can't explain right now, but I can handle this."

My tone was so emphatic that Zac had no choice but to accept my decision. Even if he was uncomfortable with it, I knew he didn't want to jeopardise our newfound friendship.

"Can I at least help you clean this up later?" he asked.

"Sure," I said, even though I had no intention of dragging him into my complex life. "That's nice of you."

We parted ways and headed off to our respective classes. First up for me was a double period of Biology. Shaken though I was, I went anyway and sat there writing reams of notes but absorbing nothing. What we'd found in my gym bag had brought back a disturbing memory. I'd seen that foul-smelling mud before, oozing from my wardrobe at Grange Hall, dripping from Isobel's decaying corpse. Only then I hadn't realised its significance: Isobel and her infant son both lay in a muddy grave and her spirit was forever hostile. If Alex was back, did that mean Isobel was too? The thought made me shudder.

As soon as class ended, I ran back to my locker, determined to dispose of the soiled gym bag. But when I opened it, already holding my breath, the smell was gone and the bag was clean. In fact, everything was just as I'd packed it yesterday with no sign of any interference.

I slammed the door shut, breathing hard. I didn't like this one bit.

★ ★ ★ ★ ★

I spent morning recess trying to find Alex, checking the theatre first and then wandering around the rest of the school. I wanted to tell him what had happened. I wanted to warn him that we were both in danger. He knew now about the tragic events of his short life, but not about the aftermath that was still raging over one hundred and fifty years later. He had to know the whole story.

But he was nowhere to be found and I was beginning to have second thoughts about the things I'd already told him. Perhaps I'd been wrong to think that the truth would bridge the gap between us. It seemed to have done the exact opposite, and Alex had withdrawn even further into himself. Being dead didn't make him superhuman. Obviously he needed as much time as anyone else to process the news I'd so tactlessly dumped on him. I just hoped he'd come around soon. Whatever was happening at my school, he was an integral part of it. I had to believe he would put aside his grief long enough to address the current situation. There was no way I could do it alone. I just had to be patient (not one of my virtues) and wait. Alex was desperately trying to put together the puzzle and had yet to realise that I was the missing piece.

I spotted Zac standing with a group of friends by the football field, playing some game on his phone. I waited for him to notice me, but he was too engrossed, so I pulled my own phone out and sent him a text: *Look up.*

As soon as he did, I waved and watched his face break into a smile. I could have navigated my way through the crowd to talk to him, but sending another text seemed faster: *Meet me for lunch?*

He glanced down, then gave me a thumbs-up.

The last thing I wanted to do was lead him on, so to clarify I sent a final message: *There are things I need to talk to you about.*

He nodded gravely this time, as if we had reached a secret understanding.

I was about to turn away to head off to my next class when a movement near Zac caught my eye. I saw a shadow like a dark aura, indistinct at first as it flitted around him, almost playful. Then the shadow grew, stretching and looming over him until I could clearly see the silhouette of a woman with long wild hair and a tattered nightdress. The shadow was faceless yet I got the prickly feeling it was looking for someone. *Me.* Memories rushed at me with the speed of an express train.

As if it could read my thoughts, the shadow extended spindly fingers that crawled spider-like over Zac's shoulders. Darkness fell across his face, blocking out the light, but he was on his phone again and didn't register a thing.

Instinctively I called out to him: "Zac!" He didn't hear me, but the shadow seemed to. The tendril fingers retreated, creeping backward over his face, to merge again with the black shadow, which faded to grey and dissolved into the air.

I knew we hadn't seen the last of it. The message had reached me loud and clear.

I AM NOT GONE.

CHAPTER NINE

I had to get through one more class before lunch: a double period of Social Studies. Luckily for me, Mr Nolan was short-sighted, arthritic and looked like he should have retired about a decade ago, which meant he didn't pay half as much attention to us as some of the other teachers. You could pretty much do what you wanted in his class as long as you didn't knock over furniture or swing from the rafters. He never said much either, just wrote reams of notes on the whiteboard, and if you didn't copy them down that was your own damn problem.

I took my seat feeling like all the wind had been knocked out of me. There seemed to be a shock waiting for me around every corner and it wasn't even midday yet. Who could live that way — always on the lookout, always bracing for the next attack? Right now, the routine of Social Studies was a welcome reprieve.

Mr Nolan began the lesson, but despite my efforts I couldn't concentrate. *Comparative Economic Systems* was the heading on the board, but I had no idea what that meant and, to be honest, couldn't care less about finding out. My brain was in overload, drowning in thoughts and worries and questions. It was enough to drive anyone mad.

As my tension grew, I found my hand slipping into my pocket to trace the ridges of Grandma Fee's brooch. I thought touching it might help stop my brain from exploding, and it worked. The more I rubbed my thumb over the smooth stones, the more I relaxed, until the pen I was holding in my other hand dropped to the floor. This was becoming a familiar routine now, but it had never happened in public before. Should I risk falling into a dream-like state surrounded by others?

I could have let go of the brooch and returned to Mr Nolan's monotone voice summarising the latest chapter in our textbook, but I liked the drowsiness overtaking me. It pushed all the troubling thoughts away. I wondered if anyone would even notice if I just lay my head down for a moment. Mr Nolan probably wouldn't.

My breathing was already slowing and my eyelids closing. A catnap. Two minutes tops. What harm could there be in that?

There is a different mood in the house today. With the master away, everybody seems to go about their business with a lighter step. It is as if someone has opened a window in an overheated room to let in a burst of fresh air. The strained look on Mrs Reade's face is gone and I even catch her smiling to herself for no apparent reason. When she and Mr Alexander are together they are like two carefree children contemplating their next adventure. There is a genuine affection between them that is infectious, lifting the spirits of everyone who comes into contact with them. Only old Isaac, Mr Reade's valet, shakes his head in disapproval, but no one takes much heed of him and his talk of hellfire. He thinks everyone should always be pious and even smiling is a misdemeanour to him.

Even though it makes no sense given he is my superior in both years and social standing, I cannot help feeling a protective instinct toward Mr Alexander, as if he needs to be shielded from the harshness of the world. I have not stopped thinking about him since our last encounter. I am not so naive as to think we could ever be friends, but even that brief exchange with him has reignited my confidence. I am not yet certain how our paths will cross again, but I feel certain they must.

Mr Alexander has none of the arrogance often demonstrated by those with privilege. In fact, apart from my own darling mother, he may be the kindest soul I have ever encountered. He is always courteous and civil to everyone, and takes a personal interest in the staff, asking after them and their loved ones. I do not know how he remembers these tiny details about people. Perhaps he listens intently when they talk, which is a rare quality. He treats everyone as his equal, which I suppose we are in God's eyes. I heard talk only yesterday that Mr Alexander is destined for the church, and if it is true I can think of no employment more fitting for someone with his gentle temperament.

Since our encounter in the library, his words have continued to ring in my ears: "You have my permission to avail yourself of the knowledge contained in these books whenever an opportunity presents itself." It was like receiving an unexpected gift; I feel honoured that someone as educated as Mr Alexander sees potential in me. However, I am yet to take him up on his offer. The pursuit of knowledge is a wonderful thing but it requires free time, and when is a servant ever free?

To my delight, an opportunity presents itself right when I least expect it. I have just finished sweeping the kitchen and find that nobody is about. Cook and Mrs Baxter have gone to the market to fetch supplies for tonight's supper and will be away at least an hour.

This allows me to slip into the library unseen. Admittedly I take a few shortcuts with my chores to enable this, but I doubt anyone will notice.

Inside the library I feel I am floating on a cloud, surrounded by so many possibilities I barely know where to begin. I realise how odd I must look, browsing the titles in my maid's outfit rather than dusting them. But my hunger for knowledge overrides all other emotions and makes me brave. I do not plan to stay long; I only wish to steal a few luxurious moments to cast my eyes over some illustrations so I may call them to mind this evening when I am trying to fall asleep.

Feeling as if I am liberating it, I carefully lift a volume from behind its glass panel in one of the bookcases, choosing it for its shiny cover. I ensconce myself in a window seat, shielded behind velvet drapery in case anyone should walk in, and sit there cross-legged, the pages of the open book fluttering on my lap. From my position I have a full view of the driveway and can see all comings and goings. I relax now; it is a rain-spattered day with no sign of life outside other than the old gardener planting bulbs before the first frost sets in.

To my delight, the book I have selected is about art from a period known as the Renaissance. Aware that my time is limited I flip to the illustrations first, stopping at a glossy image of the Madonna and Child surrounded by angels. The artist has an Italian name I cannot pronounce. One of his angels instantly catches my attention. The serene countenance, long burnished locks and chiselled nose remind me so much of Mr Alexander that I find myself peering closer, examining the features in detail. Unlike the master of the house, who is often distant and vexed over business matters, his brother has a face full of light, as if the sun has claimed him as its own. I cannot help but wonder if this is a result of Mr Alexander's choice to occupy himself with loftier matters such as art and philosophy. What a charmed life that must be to spend one's days in happy contemplation.

I do not know how much time passes as I turn the pages, enthralled and unable to tear my eyes away from the paintings. But eventually I become aware of whispered voices. There are other people in here! They must have entered stealthily or surely I would have heard them. The voices are muffled, making it difficult to catch what is being said. I hear gentle laughter and the unmistakable tones of intimacy. I wonder fleetingly if two of the servants have found a quiet place to have a secret tryst. But I know very well that none of them would dare.

I am well and truly trapped! I cannot announce myself without admitting I am shirking my duties in favour of self-advancement. Who will believe that my visit here is sanctioned by the master's brother? More likely I will be accused of lying as well as being lazy. Besides, the moment to reveal myself has come and gone. At this point it will look as if I am listening in on a private conversation — a grievous sin for a servant.

I part the curtains a fraction and catch sight of two figures, a man and a woman, talking closely beside a plaster column. He stands behind her, whispering something in her ear that makes her burst into a fresh peal of laughter and lean her body affectionately against him. Even from a distance there is no mistaking them: Mr Alexander and Mrs Reade.

I am thoroughly frightened now and I tuck my feet further under my body, wishing I could sink right through the floor and disappear. I hunch against the window, praying they will leave soon, before Mrs Baxter returns and wonders where I have got to. I am so busy attempting to shrink into the corner that I do something careless. As I adjust my position, the heavy book slips from my grasp and falls onto the wooden boards with a resonant thud.

I hear a sharp intake of breath, then an imperious voice demands, "Who is there? Show yourself!"

The voice belongs to the mistress of the house. There is nothing to be done now but to slip out from behind the curtains and try to explain myself as best I can.

Upon seeing me, Mr Alexander's face creases with concern while Mrs Reade goes pale with rage.

"What is the meaning of this?" she cries, eyes flashing. "How dare you hide in here and startle us half to death, you stupid girl!"

"I do beg your pardon, madam," I blurt, feeling my face burn with humiliation and my knees about to buckle. "I did not mean to interrupt you. I expected the library would be empty at this time."

"As this is my house, I believe I may enter the library any time I please," she says coldly. "And you have not answered my question. Kindly explain yourself before I send you to the attic to pack."

To my surprise, Mr Alexander comes to my defence. "I am afraid this is all my fault," he says.

Mrs Reade looks at him, perplexed.

"You must not blame the child. You see, I gave her permission to look at these volumes whenever she had a moment to spare. She is merely acting on my instructions."

The mistress's face is a mixture of surprise and irritation. I sense she would have enjoyed asserting her authority by sending me packing; and that she cannot fathom what need someone like me might have for books. She clearly does not approve of people rising above their station; however, with Mr Alexander watching she has to keep her anger in check.

"I see." She flashes Mr Alexander a tight smile before returning her attention to me. "And what is your name, girl?"

I open my mouth to answer, but am so nervous I seem to have forgotten my own name. Mr Alexander is once again forced to come to my rescue.

"This is Becky," he answers, and I see vexation blaze in Mrs Reade's eyes.

"Tell me, Becky," she says coldly, "have you completed your morning duties?"

"Yes, madam," I mumble, remembering to curtsey.

"Then I must conclude they have been shoddily done," she snaps. "I must say, I am shocked at your impertinence. Alexander, what is to be done with this ungrateful child?"

"Perhaps, my dear, you should leave this to me," he says. "I do hate to see you so upset."

Mrs Reade seems placated by his concern for her and allows him to steer her to the door. "I shall see you at dinner," she says, and throws me a glance as she exits that says she would like to see me obliterated from the earth.

"I beg your forgiveness, sir," I say when Mr Alexander turns back to me. "You gave me a privilege and I abused it. I am undeserving of your kindness. You must know I meant no harm."

"Please, I am not angry with you, Becky. You have abused nothing. Rather, I am glad you took my advice. I hope you will not take Mrs Reade's words to heart. She has much on her mind of late. Please don't think too harshly of us."

I am overwhelmed by his words and feel tears pricking behind my eyes. I feel terrible for putting Mr Alexander in such a position.

"Thank you, sir," I manage. "There is nothing to forgive."

I expect him to leave, but instead he lingers. I watch a range of emotions cross his face as he deliberates over what to say next.

"It is my brother's birthday," he begins, then winces as if aware of the flimsiness of the explanation. "My brother shall be thirty-three in the spring, and Mrs Reade and I are planning a small gathering. We sought refuge in here to discuss the details." His eyes search my face for a reaction. *"Perhaps it would be best if you forgot this ever happened."*

I nod, even though I am unsure what he is asking me to forget.

"What I am saying, Becky, is please keep the events of this morning to yourself. It is easy for innocent matters to be blown out of proportion, if you understand my meaning."

Outside, voices and boots crunching over gravel announce Mrs Baxter's and Cook's return. Eager to bring the conversation to a close and get back to work, I look earnestly at Mr Alexander. "Consider it forgotten, sir."

"Thank you." He gives me an encouraging smile. *"I am much obliged. And do not fret about Mrs Reade. I shall clear things up with her."*

As I watch his retreating back, I cannot shake a niggling concern at the back of my mind. Why should Mr Alexander feel the need to explain himself to a servant?

I cannot guess the real reason why he and Mrs Reade were alone together today, but I resolve to keep their secret safe no matter what. Even though I have a sinking feeling that whatever they are up to might have serious consequences.

The tinny sound of the lunch bell woke me and I sat up quickly, feeling sure all eyes must be on me. But as I looked around at the others hastily gathering their books I realised that everyone was too focused on themselves to really care about what I'd been doing.

While making my way across the campus to the cafeteria, I got the eerie feeling I was being watched. I stopped in the middle of the quad and allowed the student traffic to part around me as my eyes examined the space, making sure to sweep every dark corner. I could see no sign of anything suspicious and yet the feeling remained. Clouds passed over the sun, plunging the quad into temporary shade. It caused me to look up and that's when I saw her.

On the uppermost floor of the science wing, a child stood by an open window. I recognised her face. It was the same ghost child I'd found locked in my car. Everything seemed to grow slower as she looked down at me, hair streaming even though there was no wind. Her face was blackened with soot, and behind her huge sheets of fire were quickly devouring the room. When the child climbed onto the windowsill, I wanted to look away but something kept my eyes glued to her. I zeroed in on her scuffed lace-up brogues as they lifted from the sill and she leapt from the inferno to a fate no better.

"No!" I couldn't help the cry escaping even though I knew the child couldn't be harmed.

The scene of her death continued to play out as if it was really happening. Halfway to the ground she disintegrated to ash, then faded completely away.

Up in the window I could see another figure framed by a blazing backdrop of fire. She stared at the sky with a strangely resigned look on her face. I wondered if she would follow the child and plummet to her death, but she didn't. She turned and walked straight into the fire, which hungrily swallowed her up. Her agonised screams echoed through the quad, heard by no one but me.

It was then I realised that people were staring at me. I couldn't say I was surprised. After the incident in the cafeteria I was bound to publicly embarrass myself again sooner or later. But I was so disturbed by the vision of death, I didn't have the energy to care what people thought of me. I held my head high and went on my way acting as if nothing had happened.

Zac was waiting for me in the cafeteria as planned. We chose the most secluded table we could, tucked in a corner at the far end of the room. I looked up to see Sam and Natalie interrogating me with their eyes from the salad bar, but when I met their gaze they tossed their heads and turned away. They were giving me the silent treatment. I knew they felt confused and abandoned, but I couldn't help that. I knew they'd eventually come around just as I knew that for now keeping a distance between us might be in everyone's best interest.

"So," Zac said as he took a bite of his ham and cheese on rye, "there's plenty you're not telling me, isn't there?"

"Yes," I admitted. "But only because I don't want to drag you into it."

"What if I want to be dragged into it?"

"You wouldn't say that if you knew what was involved."

Zac gave a nervous laugh. "You make it sound like you've got hit men after you. You don't, do you?"

"Of course not."

"Then why not let me be your friend? Sounds like you could use one."

"Well," I said slowly, "there might be one thing you could help me with. I need to know more about the history of this school."

"That's it?" He looked surprised. "Piece of cake. There are archives in the library — you just need permission to access them. What do you want to know?"

"I'm not sure, but I've picked up enough signs now. I have to find out what they mean."

119

"What signs?" Zac asked, lowering his voice.

Despite what he might have been thinking, I wasn't being deliberately cryptic. "I can't really explain."

"Why not?"

"Because if I do, I'm pretty sure you'll think I'm completely nuts."

"It's a little late for that."

I rolled my eyes at him.

"Oh, come on," he urged. "You don't know me very well yet, but I'm the least judgmental person you'll ever meet."

My reluctance wavered. Deep down I desperately wanted to tell someone, even if just to temporarily alleviate the burden.

I sighed. "Fine. But don't say I didn't warn you."

Zac stopped eating and leaned in closer, waiting for me to continue.

I chose my words carefully. "Recent events have led me to believe there are some people at our school who don't belong here."

"Like the weirdos in drama club?"

I shook my head. This was proving harder than I'd thought. "No. Like people that *really* don't belong. I'm not sure I can even call them people."

"Yeah, I'm not following."

I needed to be blunter. "I guess they were people ... once."

Zac was starting to squirm a little. "Chloe, what are you on about?"

"This isn't their world," I said emphatically.

He gave a short nervous laugh. "I think the world belongs to everyone, doesn't it?"

"Not to those who've already left it."

Spoken out loud the words sounded absurd, like lines from a B-grade horror movie. Zac looked at me oddly, clearly wondering if this was my idea of humour.

He cleared his throat. "I'm sorry … are you talking about people who are …"

He trailed off so I finished the sentence for him. "Dead? Yeah."

"Okay," he said slowly. He sounded surprisingly rational. "But you know the dead can't hurt us, right?"

"That's what everyone thinks, but they're wrong."

"Chloe, listen to yourself —"

"Hey, what happened to no judgment?"

"You're right." He held up his hands. "I apologise. Go on."

"Look, I didn't believe it till I saw it either. But I know what I'm talking about here. There was a kid in my car a couple of days ago. She was badly burned and screaming for help."

"*What?* What kid?" Zac frowned.

"It doesn't matter. I couldn't help her. She was already dead."

Zac opened his mouth, then closed it again. It was painfully clear that this was no joke and he hadn't the faintest idea what to say next. That was fair enough. It wasn't something you heard every day.

"I can get you access to the archives," he said finally. I was grateful he'd decided to change the subject rather than press me further.

"You can?"

"Yeah, I'm on the magazine committee. It counts toward your SATs." He frowned again and bit his lip. "Chloe, are you sure you don't need any … y'know … help?"

I laughed drily. "Oh, I need help alright, but not the kind you're thinking of. And you're already helping me."

"Of course. I'll do whatever I can."

"Does that make us partners in crime?"

"It's not exactly criminal activity." He took another bite of his sandwich. "Although I guess that depends on what we find."

I turned at the sound of someone clearing their throat behind me. Sam and Natalie were standing there, arms folded, lips pursed. They clearly had something to get off their chests.

"Chloe," Natalie said, "we've just come to let you know we're not speaking to you."

"Kinda breaking the golden rule right now, ladies," Zac said with a smirk.

"Shut up," Sam retorted. "This doesn't concern you."

"Look, guys," I said, adopting my most diplomatic tone, "I have a lot on my mind right now. I didn't mean to upset you."

"Then why aren't you talking to *us*?" Natalie asked, shooting Zac a resentful look. "Instead of a stranger. We always tell each other everything."

"No, we don't," I said. "I stopped doing that a long time ago."

Natalie looked taken aback, as if she was registering something for the first time. "Why?"

"Because I knew you wouldn't understand, and no one likes to be judged."

Sam let out an indignant gasp. "We never judge! We're only trying to help you be normal again."

"Okay. Well, here's something you haven't considered," I said, standing up. "Maybe I'm just not normal."

When I walked away, leaving my unfinished lunch behind, they didn't try to follow me.

CHAPTER TEN

I decided to go home that afternoon before my dad finished work to get some clean clothes and check on things. My car was still parked at Zac's place so I had to take an Uber, but luckily it wasn't that far. When I got to the house, I checked the kitchen to find the fridge full of take-out boxes. I found a sticky note, wrote *BUY GROCERIES* on it and stuck it to the door of the microwave. I could see things were already starting to fall apart and I'd only been gone twenty-four hours. I wished Dad would take more responsibility. I thought I might as well do a load of laundry for them while I was there so Rory didn't have to show up at school in dirty clothes.

I was in his room picking up gym shorts and socks when a sudden weight pulled me down. The brooch in my pocket felt as heavy as a rock. Leaving Rory's clothes on the floor, I walked quickly into my own room and closed the door. I took out the brooch to examine it. It hadn't changed much other than its weight, but as I held it it emanated a bright glow, as if trying to tell me something. I placed it on my desk behind some books to create some distance between us. The last thing I needed right now was a trip through time.

But it happened anyway, even though the brooch wasn't in my hand. I felt a wave of dizziness strong enough to make me sink to the floor with my head between my knees, and when I looked up the walls of my room had melted away. In fact, I wasn't in my house at all.

With the master away, Mrs Reade and Mr Alexander choose to dine in the parlour rather than the imposing dining room. Mrs Baxter has assigned me the task of waiting on them. As I ladle soup into their bowls, I keep my eyes downcast, feeling conscious of every movement. I was worried there would be repercussions for the incident in the library, but it seems to be forgotten. They are immersed in their own world, planning activities for the morrow. I have become invisible again for which I can only feel grateful.

As I take my place against the wall to wait statue-like for them to finish before serving the next course, my eye falls on something under the table. Mrs Reade's dainty foot, clad in a grey satin slipper, inches forward until it is positioned snugly between Mr Alexander's black riding boots. The seemingly small gesture is so intimate and so improper that the truth hits me like a bolt out of the blue. Suddenly everything makes sense: Mr Alexander and Mrs Reade are lovers. There can be no other explanation.

I feel as if I have been trampled by a carriage drawn by four horses. I am finding it hard to draw breath and wish I could erase this newfound knowledge from my mind. There are not many secrets in our village and folk delight in discussing matters that are not their own. But being privy to such private, not to mention scandalous, information only makes me uncomfortable. I have but one desire now and that is to be anywhere but in this room. How can they be so careless? Do they think a housemaid is too slow-witted to notice their intimacy? Or are they indifferent because I am young and my opinion matters so little?

"That will be all, Becky," Mrs Reade says, as if she can hear my thoughts.

I know I am being dismissed so they can be alone and I scamper quickly out of the parlour. Instead of returning to the kitchen in search of Mrs Baxter, I retire to my room to gather my thoughts. There are no fireplaces in the attic and I immediately begin to shiver, though I cannot say whether it is from cold or shock. I reach for my mother's shawl hanging from my bed rail and wrap it around me. I wish my mother were here to advise me now as there is no one whose counsel I value more. But it will be a while before I see her next. We servants are released one afternoon every month to visit our families, except for Mrs Baxter who, so the other servants say, has never taken a day off in her life.

I have always prided myself on my common sense so how did I miss this happening under my very nose? Perhaps that is what happens when one is silly enough to elevate people to a level above that of mere mortals; one sees only their virtues, shining like stars and obliterating all their flaws. I must come to terms with the fact that Mr Alexander is not as superior as I once thought. He is as weak as any man, only his addiction is not to drink like my father's, but to lust and beauty. I cannot decide which is worse.

Little signs that I missed, or chose to ignore, come rushing back to me: Mr Alexander's hand accidentally brushing the nape of Mrs Reade's neck, a lingering look, a secret smile shared over the rim of a teacup, an eagerness to hear one another's next utterance as if it might hold the very meaning of life. In fact, every time I have seen them together there has been some sign that could have been picked up by a more discerning observer.

As the shock subsides, my mind strays into darker territory. How long can this go on before they are discovered? There is no telling what the master might do if he ever found out. Mr Reade could very well disown them both and leave them destitute; and the Reade family name would be sullied for generations to come. A single moment of foolishness may result in a lifetime of regret. For what else other than foolishness can have led them down this dangerous path? I may be young and, at fourteen, ignorant of some of the ways of the world, but I know enough to see that no good can come of this.

Yesterday, the world I lived in was black and white. Now I find it full of shadow. I so admired Mr Alexander; and although Mrs Reade treated me with contempt, I still thought her a noble and virtuous woman. Now I wonder if passion can be stronger than morality? Do the sacred vows of marriage mean nothing in the end? Mr Alexander and Mrs Reade are guilty of the kind of wickedness the rector warns against from the pulpit on Sundays. What has come over them to make them so reckless? Do the wealthy believe themselves immune to the laws of God and man?

They must put a stop to this before things get out of hand. But who will keep them in check? The only person in the house with the power to do so lives in ignorance and is absent a good deal of the time. If I could catch Mr Alexander alone, perhaps I could make him see sense. But that would be overstepping the mark. Who am I to lecture anyone, let alone someone of his standing?

When I finally go to bed that night I toss and turn, unable to settle until dawn breaks and I have to get up to begin my chores. I barely have enough energy to beat the rugs outside. All the while I find myself worried I may stumble upon Mr Alexander and Mrs Reade in some passionate embrace.

Feeling irked with myself, I vow to put the knowledge out of my mind. There is nothing to be done, and even if there were, I am hardly the one to do it. Interfering now would be a sure way to get myself thrown out of Grange Hall. I must remember what *brought me here in the first place. My wages may be meagre, but my family will not manage without them. Whatever my misgivings, my family's survival must come first.*

I decide I will tell no one what I have seen. This secret shall be my burden to carry.

When my room came into focus again I was curled on my rug. The clock on my bedside table told me it was 5 am. I'd been out for hours. No wonder my neck felt stiff and my muscles ached as if I'd run a marathon. I groaned and shook myself back to the present. It wasn't easy getting back into my own head; it seemed harder each time to leave Becky and her troubles behind. The brooch was still sitting where I'd left it on my desk.

I checked my phone to find several voice and text messages from Zac asking if I was alright as he hadn't heard from me all night. I could tell he was worried, especially after our last conversation that must have left him with a million questions. I quickly sent back a message, letting him know I was fine and that we'd talk soon.

Not wanting to run into Rory or Dad, I got changed as quietly as possible and headed downstairs. I walked to the Starbucks at the end of our street and tucked myself into a seat by the window where I could watch the early commuters come and go. Most of them were half-asleep and responded half-heartedly to the cheerful server. I nursed my latte and nibbled a bagel as I watched the world outside come to life. Early morning was the most peaceful time of the day. Now I understood why some people woke up at crazy hours to go jogging. There was nothing quite like watching the sunlight slowly creep over all the cracks of the city, chasing the shadows away. I only wished the world wouldn't wake up so fast. Soon the cafe was teeming with people, signalling it was time for me to call another Uber and head to school.

My first period was French, which I'd been dreading since my heated exchange with Doctor Ritter. I hadn't been called into the principal's office yet though, so perhaps he was willing to let the incident go. I would find out soon enough.

When I walked into the classroom I tried to make myself as inconspicuous as possible, taking a seat in the very back row. When Doctor Ritter arrived I felt his gaze lock onto me for a second. I was ready to apologise and blame hormones if he made any reference to our last encounter, but to my surprise he didn't say a word. He just subtly raised an eyebrow, then turned his back to us to scrawl something on the whiteboard.

"Please open your books to page forty-seven," he said.

Keeping my head down, I followed his instructions until I heard the door open again and someone enter. "My apologies for my lateness," said a soft-spoken voice with a British accent.

My head shot up to see Alex standing at the front of the room perusing the students. Adrenaline bolted through me, nearly causing me to leap from my seat.

Alex had no textbooks, no notepad and no writing implements whatsoever, and his face was set in a calm mask. Something about him had changed: he no longer seemed overwhelmed by the modern world. In fact, he looked as if nothing could faze him. What had happened to cause this transformation?

"Who might you be?" Doctor Ritter asked. "I don't remember seeing any additions to my class list."

"My name is Alexander Reade," he said, without offering any further information.

"Are you certain you're in this class?"

"It has taken me a while to get my bearings, but yes, I am in the right place."

"Why don't you take a seat then, Mr Reade? We're glad to have you."

Alex slid into an empty seat beside a girl named Michelle Kramer, who snuck a long and unsubtle glance at him. He was wearing all black again, with his dark gold hair tied away from his face. So far he seemed oblivious to my presence. He hadn't so much as glanced in my direction.

"If you could open your textbook to page forty-seven," Doctor Ritter said.

"I am afraid I do not have a book," Alex said unapologetically.

A strange energy shot through the room and, one by one, heads lifted until everyone was paying attention.

"I'm going to assume that's a joke." It was clear Doctor Ritter was pissed now. He was running the tip of his tongue along his upper teeth and his eyes had narrowed to slits. He must think there was a serious discipline problem at this school.

"I rarely jest," Alex replied. "But when I do, it is apparent."

I couldn't tell if this performance was deliberate or not. Was he trying to push Doctor Ritter's buttons, or did he simply have no idea about student–teacher decorum? A line like that might fly at a nineteenth-century ball, but here it just sounded sarcastic, like he was asking for trouble.

"Tell me," Doctor Ritter's voice had gone stone cold, "how do you expect to learn the syllabus and pass your exams without a textbook? It's rather an essential tool, don't you think?"

The whole class was now riveted by the exchange. They looked at Alex, expecting him to be intimidated, but he only smiled.

"I am not concerned about that," he said. "I doubt I will learn much from this class."

Doctor Ritter was growing more flustered by the second, speaking now through clenched teeth. "What do you mean by that? Are you questioning my pedagogy?"

Alex shrugged. "I am not here to judge your competence. But I am already proficient in French."

"Is that so?"

"Yes. I lived in Paris for several years."

"Where?"

"Saint-Germain-des-Prés."

"I see." Doctor Ritter gave a smile so forced his skin seemed to stretch like plastic. "If you really can speak French, then by all means go ahead. Amaze me."

"Very well," Alex said. *"Je ne voudrais pas vous offenser, mais parler français est facile pour moi. Si vous avez besoin, je serais ravi de vous aider."*

Doctor Ritter's annoyance seemed to morph into suspicion. He watched Alex curiously, drumming a finger against his chin. Had he figured out Alex didn't belong in this world? No, he couldn't have.

"If you don't need to learn, what, may I ask, are you doing in my class?"

"I am here because Miss Kennedy is here," Alex said, as if it should be obvious, and he turned in his seat to look at me.

As he did, every other head in the room swivelled in my direction. Whispers broke out all around me. What the hell was he doing?

When our eyes met, I held his gaze and gave a tiny shake of my head as if to say, *Please don't do this here.* That kind of display would get the whole school talking and it was the last thing I needed.

"Enough of this nonsense!" Doctor Ritter cut in. "I don't know what game you two are playing, but any further disruptions and I will ban you both from ever attending this class again. Have I made myself clear?"

Alex was having difficulty containing his amusement. It was obvious he was untroubled by the threat. In the grand scheme of things, I supposed our whole world must have seemed trivial to him.

"Yes, sir," I said quickly. "Crystal clear."

Doctor Ritter gave me a withering look before turning his attention to Alex. "And you, Marie Antoinette." The class sniggered. "Will I have any more trouble from you?"

I could tell by the way he stiffened his shoulders that Alex wasn't accustomed to being insulted. In his lifetime he'd been a gentleman and had probably never had to take orders from anyone. There was a flicker in his eyes that told me he wanted to offer a reply worthy of his class and education, and I bet he would have known exactly what to say to put Doctor Ritter in his place. Something witty and acerbic. But something stopped him. *Me.* He didn't want to do the wrong thing by me, so with great restraint he swallowed whatever was on the tip of his tongue and said, "Definitely not."

★ ★ ★ ★ ★

As soon as the lesson was over, I grabbed Alex and hurried him out into the corridor so we could talk. I was about to launch into a speech about the importance of flying under the radar when I realised that almost every student from our class was now lingering in the hall. They watched us intently, straining to catch snippets of our conversation. We had suddenly become noteworthy and what schoolkid doesn't love a drama to break up the monotony of the day?

I glared at Michelle Kramer, who was dawdling near us under the pretence of checking her phone, and took Alex by the arm. "Come on. Let's go somewhere a little more private."

I made sure to say it loud enough for everyone to hear, but I still felt their curious eyes burning into the back of my head as I led Alex away.

We walked until we came across an empty science lab. I checked the timetable on the door and it looked like the room was free for the next two periods so nobody was likely to disturb us.

"Okay, what the hell was that?" I exploded as soon as the door clicked shut behind us.

"I am back," he said simply.

"Yeah, I got that. In fact, I think the whole school probably knows you're here by now."

"You are angry with me?"

He looked so confused that I let out a long breath and decided to change my tune.

"I'm not angry. I'm glad you're back, I really am. But do you really think extra attention is what we need right now?"

"You are right. I apologise." He shook his head. "I have been attempting to work out this whole operation, but I simply cannot understand it."

"What operation?" I asked.

Alex waved a hand around the lab. "This place. You keep your books in strange metal boxes on the wall, there appears to be no set dress code, and when I went to the dining hall people were drinking a strange effervescent brown liquid and eating what I can only assume was yellow gruel."

"I think that was probably mac and cheese."

"What is mac?" he asked. "And why was the liquid bubbling?"

"It's called soda. It's carbonated."

"I do not care what it is called," he replied with a slight shudder. "It cannot be good for you."

"Things that are popular aren't always good for you. I'm sure it was the same back in your day. What about those opium dens?"

"Is that where you picture me spending my time?"

"No, of course not."

This was going to be harder than I'd thought. How much had changed since the nineteenth century? *Everything.* Half the things we used on a daily basis hadn't even been invented during Alex's lifetime. So I couldn't blame him; it was a natural human instinct to mistrust things we didn't understand.

"Just forget the soda, okay? I didn't think you'd be back so soon."

"I have been longing to return," Alex said and I noticed a twinkle in his eye. "There is something I must tell you."

"Okay."

"Chloe, I remember."

I waited for him to elaborate. When he didn't I said, "You remember what?"

He watched me with a small smile on his face and I realised he was looking at me differently somehow. My heart started pounding against my ribcage. Something in his eyes had changed. Before they had been shutting me out. Now they seemed to be inviting me in.

"Are you saying …" I broke off, too timid to finish the question.

Alex drew a little closer and the new playfulness in his manner reminded me of our time together at Grange Hall.

"Yes," he said. "I am saying I remember you."

CHAPTER ELEVEN

I heard Alex's words, but my brain refused to believe them. It was a way of protecting myself in case they turned out not to be true.

"Don't say that unless you really mean it," I said in a trembling voice.

"Chloe, I am so sorry for my recent distance."

"It wasn't your fault," I said, but the sting of it hadn't left me yet.

He moved closer so his face was only an inch from my own. "I remember meeting you in the woods and wondering if the dusk was playing tricks on my eyes because you seemed to be looking right at me, and you were so beautiful. I remember nursing your foot the night Isobel attacked you and promising myself I would never let her harm you again. I remember every word we ever exchanged, but most of all I remember wondering how, after everything that happened, you could still bring yourself to love me."

I was so moved by his words, my eyes welled with tears. "You do remember me," I whispered and a strangled laugh of relief followed. "I thought everything that happened between us was lost. I thought the Alex I knew was gone for good."

I gave up fighting the tears and let them fall freely. Alex reached out and brushed them from my cheeks with his finger. It had been so long that his touch was startling at first. Then everything blurred into the background as I buried my face in his shoulder. My lips brushed the skin of his neck as I breathed in his familiar scent, something I never thought I'd do again.

"I don't just remember you, Chloe." Alex's voice was thick with emotion as his fingers combed softly through my hair. "I remember *us*."

As his lips found mine, I descended into a dazzling dreamlike state where I was aware of nothing but his touch and the sound of his breathing. I drank him in like some rare nectar, savouring every last drop. His arms enveloped me and his body gave off a warmth that was almost tangible. It seemed to wrap our entwined bodies, bathing us in a golden light. Even if only for a moment, we were back in our world where no one and nothing could touch us. I could no longer feel my feet on the floor. The walls of the classroom had fallen away. We were somewhere else entirely, moving through space and time.

"You came back for me," I whispered.

"Where else would I go?" Alex said into my hair. "I always knew I would find you again."

I wanted to answer him but found myself slipping away. Darkness closed in around me. I could see Alex's mouth moving but could no longer hear his words. I saw his face fill with alarm when he realised what was happening and his mouth formed my name. I felt myself go limp in his arms.

Chloe? Chloe? Chloe?

But I couldn't answer. I was being dragged under, and all I was aware of were my eyelids closing.

The disaster I expect to befall Grange Hall does not eventuate. To my surprise, in its place come weeks of calm. Mr Alexander is his usual friendly self whenever I encounter him in the halls or grounds, while the mistress maintains her cool aloofness. I keep an eye out for any signs of misconduct, but other than the mistress looking paler than usual, there is nothing out of the ordinary. I conclude that the pair have come to their senses and put an end to their dalliance. But my relief is short-lived.

This morning Mrs Baxter informs me that the mistress is out of sorts and will not come down to breakfast. Instead I am to carry a tray up to her room and serve her there. As I am rarely called to attend to the mistress in her chamber, I make doubly sure that my hair is neatly tucked under my cap and my apron is spotless.

When I reach the gleaming mahogany door that leads to her bedroom, I tap gingerly on the wood. The last thing I want to do is startle Mrs Reade when she is unwell.

"Come," her floaty voice answers.

I turn the handle and enter as quietly as a mouse to find a blazing fire in the hearth and the curtains drawn, allowing only a feeble light to penetrate. It is a gloomy November morning, already threatening rain.

The mistress is lying in bed propped against lacy pillows. Her eyes are closed, and because she does not open them when I approach I am able to study her briefly. Even with the roses gone from her cheeks and her usually lustrous locks hanging limply around her porcelain face, she still looks regal. I wonder that she does not have the power to command all who enter her orbit.

The tray rattles a little when I set it down, but the noise elicits no response.

"Shall I pour your tea, madam?" I venture.

She opens her eyes then and I see that even feeling poorly is not enough to drive the sparkle out of them.

"Yes," she murmurs. "I shall take it black today." A heavy sigh follows, then suddenly she comes to life, tossing off the bedclothes and sitting up. She fans her face with her hand and her eyes wear a feverish brightness. "It is stifling in here. When you have finished there, Becky, you must open a window and let in some air!"

"Are you sure, madam? The wind is bitter today."

I set down the teapot and hand her the steaming cup. Before I can stop her, she raises it to her lips and takes a large sip. I wait for a reaction, but there is none. How peculiar. The tea must be scalding hot and yet she does not seem to notice.

"I welcome the cold," she declares. "All the better to shake off this lethargy!"

I make no move to open the window.

Mrs Reade is astute and guesses the cause of my hesitation. "Oh, Becky, I see you are worried I shall catch my death and they will hold you accountable. Well, you need not worry. I shall survive. Now, unless you are too deficient to follow instructions, kindly do as you are told. I will not ask a third time."

I only open the window a crack, but immediately a gust of cold air invades the room, like a wolf about to pounce. I shrink away, shivering, but Mrs Reade sinks back against her pillows with a satisfied look.

"Ahhh," she sighs. "Much better."

Now that the mistress is more comfortable, she turns her face toward me and I am surprised to see that she looks pained. I wonder if she is sorry for her earlier harshness, but if I am expecting kinder words I am disappointed. Mrs Reade does not waste her breath making apologies to people like me. But what she does say makes me squirm with discomfort.

"I am so unhappy, Becky." She gives a heartfelt sigh.

I can hardly believe my ears. If it were anyone else making this disclosure, I might feel some pity, but having witnessed her self-absorption firsthand I am more wary than moved. All I can think is that she wants something of me that I will not be able to deliver. Why else would she choose a housemaid as a confidante?

"What is to be done?" she continues in a plaintive tone.

"I'm not sure what you mean, madam. If I'm not needed, I think Mrs Baxter is waiting for me downstairs."

"Let her wait. Can you not stay a while?"

I stand in the room, waiting for further instruction, but her face has taken on a faraway look. When she speaks I am not even sure it is me she is addressing.

"There must be a way out. Why does he not find one? Must I take charge of everything?"

She seems to expect me to know what she is talking about, and I wonder whether the fever has caused a mild delirium.

"You are not well, madam. You should eat something. Shall I ask Mrs Baxter to send for the doctor?"

"What troubles me is not physical," she replies.

"Shall I call for Mrs Baxter?" I say again.

"No, leave that silly old dragon where she is! Just stay a moment. I need to unburden myself and you are the only person in this house who can be trusted."

I stand stock-still, wishing I could decline the honour of this unexpected confidence.

"The funny thing is, I have brought it all on myself," she says. "I have no one else to blame."

"You are mistress of this fine house," I blurt without thinking. "You can do or have anything you want."

"Status and freedom are not the same thing, Becky. I shall never be as free as you. Why do you look so surprised? Has it never occurred to you that you may take your labour wherever you please? As for me, I must remain mistress of Grange Hall and fulfil all that position entails until the end of my days."

I hardly think being mistress of Grange Hall is a hardship, but Mrs Reade makes it sound as though it is a burden heavier than she can bear. Has it not occurred to her that it is the middle of the morning and she is still lying idle in bed? But of course I do not voice that thought aloud.

"I am sorry you are feeling poorly, madam."

She leans forward. "I must ask a favour of you, Becky. I need a friend in this big lonely house. Will you be that for me?"

"Of course, madam," I say, eager to bring this awkward conversation to a close.

"I can see you are a loyal person," she says, sinking back against the pillows. "And loyalty should always be rewarded. Bring me that jewellery box on the dressing table."

She points to a black lacquered box with gilt paw feet and decorated with scrolling vines and flowers. I carry it reverently by its handles and place it beside her on the bed. When she opens it, I see its interior is a soft velvet the colour of a robin's egg.

"Come closer."

She beckons me forward until I am standing right in front of her. Only then does she open her hand to reveal a glittering brooch in her palm. I have never laid eyes on an object of such delicate beauty. She holds it out to me, but I spring back as if it is tainted.

"Take it," she says. "It is yours."

I shake my head. Something about this exchange does not feel right. I cannot accept a gift intended to buy my silence.

"I cannot," I mumble helplessly. "There is no need."

But Mrs Reade is not someone to be argued with. "I will not take no for an answer!" She grabs my hand, places the brooch on my palm and closes my fingers firmly over it. The sharp edges press into my skin as if in warning. "Consider it a token of our gratitude."

It is not possible to refuse now without causing myself further embarrassment. But what does she mean by "our"?

When Mrs Reade releases me, I stumble from the room without waiting to be dismissed. In the hallway I open my hand to examine her gift. It is shaped like a flower and the stones have a soft sheen as though coated in starlight. I wish I knew the name of the polished milky centrepiece and almost wished I had asked.

I have never owned anything so valuable before and it looks out of place in my work-roughened hands. I certainly will never have occasion to wear it, so I decide to keep it in the trunk under my bed, which now feels like a secret treasure trove.

Despite Mrs Reade's protest that she does not need an old quack to tell her that she is well, in the afternoon a grim-faced Doctor Webb pays a visit. I do not hear the diagnosis, but his prescription is clear broth, a baked potato and a sliced apple if the patient can keep it down.

Mrs Baxter scribbles importantly in the little notebook she carries on her person lest her memory prove unreliable.

Refusing the offer of tea, the doctor takes his leave. I see him out and return to help Mrs Baxter make up a tray in the kitchen.

"Is the mistress going to get better?" I ask.

"Oh, yes!" She seems in unusually high spirits given the situation. "She'll be just fine."

"Well, that is good news."

"Indeed, though I think we can expect to receive even better news very soon."

"Really? What sort of news?"

Normally my questions try Mrs Baxter's patience, but today she is in an indulgent mood.

"Have you not guessed, child? You really do live in your own little world, don't you?" Her voice drops an octave or two. "Mrs Reade is in the family way."

"You mean she is to have a baby?" My hands fly to my mouth as I wonder if this has been the cause of the mistress's peevish mood.

"Some six months from now by the doctor's calculations. But mind you don't speak a word of it to anyone. We must wait until the formal announcement is made. What a boon if it is a boy! Then Grange Hall will have an heir. Just think of that!"

Mr Alexander's face flashes through my mind and a mixture of dread and excitement overtakes me. But I refuse to allow myself to give in to such thoughts. They are too terrible to contemplate. The birth of a babe is meant to be the happiest of occasions. I can only hope it will prove so for Grange Hall and all its occupants.

I woke on the floor of the science lab with Alex kneeling over me and gently shaking my shoulders. When I opened my eyes, he dropped his head and exhaled with relief.

"Are you alright? You frightened me. I see you are still having those troubling turns."

I realised he was remembering the visions he'd witnessed me experiencing at Grange Hall. "Something like that," I said, trying to shake off the remnants of the dream. "But I'm fine now. How long was I out?"

"Only a few minutes."

"Is that all?"

"It felt like a lifetime," he said as I tried to sit up. "Be careful, you are still shaky. We need to get you some water and then to the infirmary."

"No, that's not necessary. I didn't pass out. I think I just fell asleep."

"Asleep? Just like that? It does not seem natural."

"It's been happening a bit lately, and every time it's followed by a vivid dream. It's strange because it usually doesn't happen without —" I broke off.

Alex looked at me encouragingly. "Without what?"

I went quiet for a minute. I didn't want to turn the conversation to Isobel and the past life they'd had together. This was our time and she had no place here. That was probably exactly what she wanted — to come between us, to remain the centre of attention. Even as a ghost Isobel couldn't bear to be forgotten, but I was tired of her monopolising Alex.

"You know what? Never mind," I said. "Can we just forget this happened and go back to five minutes ago when you said you remembered me and we were having a special romantic moment? I don't know about you, but I'm not ready to move past that just yet."

"But, Chloe —"

"Please?"

He looked into my eyes and didn't argue; he just nodded.

I saw the tension ebbing from his face and hugged him. I couldn't describe the feeling of being back in Alex's arms. It wasn't until he was holding me again that I realised how terribly cold I'd been. Not in a physical sense, but inside, as if a bitter winter had settled on my soul. But now the snow was melting and I was filled with warmth. The feeling came from the knowledge that I had everything I could possibly need right in front of me. It was so strong it obliterated the outside world entirely.

I didn't know how long we stayed locked in our embrace, like a sculpture of two lovers entwined for eternity. I held onto Alex so tightly even a tornado couldn't have ripped us apart. What we had was timeless. Nothing could ever change that.

"I admire you, Chloe," he said eventually, and I lifted my head from his chest.

"You do?"

"Of course." He was running his hands comfortingly up and down my back. "Look at the way you have coped with this whole bizarre situation. There must have been so much you wanted to say and yet you restrained yourself. I don't know if I could have done that. It shows great strength."

"It wasn't easy," I admitted. "But I was afraid if I said too much, you might think I was crazy."

"Perhaps you are." He laughed. "But so am I."

A thought occurred to me then and I loosened my grip to look at him. "Alex, what happened to make you remember everything?"

"I wish I had a clear answer." He released me and I settled at a desk to listen to his story. "It happened a few hours after I left you at the theatre. What you said must have triggered something because I could not clear my head. My mind was full of voices, strange conversations I did not remember taking part in. Then came the images — the faces of every occupant of Grange Hall. I saw them all as if I were tumbling through time, the memories colliding until I thought my head would explode. But then I saw your face … and a wall came down. Suddenly I was myself again. I remembered dying, I remembered grieving, and I remembered the hundred and fifty years of solitude that followed. I remembered the day you arrived at Grange Hall, and the immense joy of knowing I was no longer alone in a bleak and endless afterlife. I remembered your face, the light that emanates from your eyes, the soft curve of your lips, the way your nose crinkles when you laugh …"

Before he could say another word, I took his face in my hands and kissed him so fervently that when we eventually broke apart, it took a moment for my surroundings to take shape around me. If we hadn't been in a place where we might be discovered, I'm not sure I would have been able to let go.

"Just so you know," I said, "telling you the truth wasn't easy. I think that's what actual heartbreak feels like."

"I could see it was painful for you, although at the time I did not understand why. But I am glad of your bravery, Chloe. Without it, I might still be lost."

"Speaking of lost … do you remember anything about how you got here?"

"Not much. I do know one thing for certain: I had passed on. I was no longer a shadow lingering at the edge of a world that had long forgotten me. I was truly on the other side of the veil … and then something pulled me back."

"Something?" I echoed intently. "Like what?"

"I do not know. It felt as if I were being gripped by an invisible hand and dragged back through the darkness until I saw light. I thought perhaps it might have been you, or at least my desire not to leave you."

"Can I ask you something?" I said quietly. "What was it like there … beyond the veil?"

I waited with bated breath for his answer. This was the question humankind had been asking for centuries. What awaited us on the other side in that great unknown: was it God? Was it infinity? Was it only emptiness?

"My memory of it has faded since my return," Alex said. "But I remember feeling weightless, stripped of all earthly grievances. Every regret, every painful memory, everything I had held myself responsible for, simply melted away. I was pure energy."

"That doesn't sound too bad. Do you remember anything about what it looked like?" I whispered. I think Alex knew I was thinking about my mom.

Alex gave a wistful smile. "How I wish I could recall. I have tried. All I know is that I was not alone. I was a light connected to thousands of other lights in the darkness."

"Were you happy?"

"I do not recall feeling any emotion at all." He paused to reflect. "I suppose that makes sense. Emotion comes from the brain, and my brain felt as if it had been switched off."

"I bet that was peaceful," I said. "I wish I could switch my emotions off."

"Indeed, they cloud everything. But they are not all bad, I hope?"

Our eyes met and a smile crept onto my face. "Definitely not."

I wanted to kiss him again, but something occurred to me that made my breath catch in my throat. I couldn't believe it wasn't the first question I'd asked.

"Wait a minute," I said slowly. "If you've come back from the dead, does that mean that you're now …" I could barely get the word out. "*Alive?*"

"No," Alex said bluntly, and the balloon of hope in my chest popped and disappeared as quickly as it had swelled up. "At least I do not think so."

"How do you know for sure?"

"Well, I keep disappearing. That seems a clear sign."

"I'm sorry, you what?"

"It is beyond my control." He frowned and sat down opposite me. He looked weary now and I realised these disappearances must be taking their toll on him. "It happened that day at your house after we first met. I never know when to expect it, but I know it is happening because I feel my strength wane. Then I fade into a strange shadow world where everything is made of ash, like a charcoal drawing. I wander in the semi-darkness until I am transported back here, where I look and feel human again. Each time I return to the theatre, although I cannot say why."

"Maybe because you feel safe there?"

"It is possible."

I'd listened to everything he'd said yet I wasn't ready to accept it. "Disappearing like that doesn't necessarily mean you aren't —"

"No, Chloe," Alex said firmly, sensing where I was going. "I have tested my theory."

"Tested it how?"

"The only way I could think of." He pulled a pocketknife from the back of his jeans.

"Just what do you think you're doing?" I asked nervously.

"Watch," he replied, flicking the blade from its handle.

I read his intention in his face. "No! Don't you dare!"

But he did dare and my hands flew up to cover my eyes a second too late. I couldn't miss seeing him stab the knife into his wrist, slicing through what should have been muscle and tendon so the blade protruded like a spear on the other side. I let out a gasp, expecting blood to gush forth, but that didn't happen. Alex held out his wrist, twisting and flexing it to show how his skin seemed to meld like dough around the shifting metal. When he pulled the blade out, the gash it had made closed up before I could blink.

"See?" he said.

"Alright," I managed. "I guess you're not exactly flesh and blood."

"Definitely not." He gave a resigned shrug, but it was going to take more to satisfy me.

"You have to admit, things are different this time," I said. "I mean, why are you warm when I touch you? And why can other people see you too? At Grange Hall it was only me, but this time you're *really* here. There must be a reason you've come back. What do you think it is?"

"I have thought about that." Alex's voice was sombre. "There is only one explanation I can think of." He went quiet and waited, as if expecting me to guess.

"Which is …?" I asked rather impatiently.

"Witchcraft."

I was about to let out a shriek of laughter, then realised he was serious.

"Witchcraft?" I repeated dubiously. "You mean like an old woman with warts flying around on a broomstick?"

"No, I mean dark arts, Chloe. Powerful black magic that should never be meddled with."

"You can't be serious," I said apprehensively. "I mean ... *magic*?"

Alex folded his arms and examined me closely. "Interesting," he mused. "You are conversing with someone you know is dead and yet the idea of magic shocks you."

"It isn't shocking," I explained. "It's just that when I think of the word *magic*, I think of fairy dust and cauldrons and, y'know, Harry Potter. And the fact that you're a ghost doesn't prove magic is real. It just proves there's life after death; that other dimensions exist alongside our own. A lot of people believe that. But the kind of thing you're talking about — witchcraft and spells and all that stuff — it just doesn't seem real."

"I believe it *is* real," Alex said, casting a glance around the science lab as if suspicious of every test tube and beaker. "How else can you explain why I have a body yet I do not bleed? I am not a magician."

He had me there. Back at Grange Hall, Alex had been intangible, without physical form. Now he had a real body and could hold me in his arms. So what had changed?

"There is something else," he began.

"Tell me," I encouraged.

"I know black magic is real because Isobel used it." His jaw tightened the moment the words were out, like he'd just betrayed a confidence. "I would have told you sooner, but this memory was the last to surface."

"Really?" I could hardly believe my ears. "What did she need it for?"

"My brother was bewitched by her, enough to marry her. Carter was never the romantic type."

"Are you saying Carter didn't want to marry her?" I couldn't keep the astonishment out of my voice.

"No, I think he wanted her very much. But in the way one covets a rare treasure in order to display it in a cabinet. Isobel was enchanting, a goddess of unrivalled beauty. But apart from her physical attributes, she had nothing else to recommend her — no fortune, no name and no prospects."

"You mean like in *Pride and Prejudice* when Mr Darcy thinks Lizzie is beneath him?"

He sighed. "I am afraid Isobel's situation was worse than that. Isobel wasn't simply from a lower class than our own; her parentage was questionable. Beautiful though she was, it was an unthinkable match for my brother. He might have wanted to bed her, but he would never have considered making her his wife."

"When did you find all this out? You never mentioned it before."

"I was too busy trying to protect you. And I didn't learn the truth until long after we were both dead. When you are facing eternity, there is little point in keeping secrets."

"So how did Isobel change Carter's mind?"

I was teeming with curiosity now, although I would have preferred fewer references to Isobel's great beauty. I knew it was ridiculous to be jealous of a dead girl, but I got the picture: she was hot. There was no need to remind me every two seconds, especially when I was wearing a faded Hotel California T-shirt and hadn't bothered to cover the circles under my eyes with concealer.

"She was not powerful enough to perform magic herself," Alex explained. "But she paid a visit to a sorcerer who used some kind of binding spell on my brother. Isobel never disclosed exactly what the ritual involved, but she did say the sorcerer broke the neck of a turtle dove right before her eyes."

"That's disgusting." The image made my stomach turn. "How could you still love Isobel after she told you that? Didn't you think she might be a bit … how do I put this nicely? *Disturbed?*"

Alex's voice grew heavy, like he was dredging up memories he'd sooner forget. "Isobel took that secret to her grave. As I said, the truth did not surface until long after we were both dead. If I had known in life, I would have rejected her. She knew this."

"She sounds evil," I said softly.

"If evil is defined by putting one's own needs ahead of all others', then yes, she was."

"Well, we dealt with her once and we'll do it again if we have to. But it still doesn't help us figure out who brought you back."

"Bringing a person back from the dead is no small feat. He or she must be very powerful."

"I just assumed it would be a she," I said.

He nodded. "Indeed, witches are female as a rule. But I have a feeling we are dealing with someone more formidable than an ordinary witch."

"I don't like the sound of that," I said nervously. "What could be more formidable than a witch?"

Alex took my hand and squeezed it gently. "I hope I am wrong, Chloe, but I am almost certain that we are facing a necromancer."

CHAPTER TWELVE

Alex disappeared again sometime after sixth period. It happened without me even noticing and I wondered whether he'd been able to conceal it from others. When by the end of the day he hadn't resurfaced I wasn't so concerned as we'd already discussed what to do in such a situation. I agreed to check the theatre every morning until I found him waiting there for me. Neither of us wanted to address the bigger question hanging in the air: what if he didn't come back at all? I didn't want to think about that.

After school, I met up with Zac in the parking lot. I needed to collect my car from his house so I could go home. I couldn't stay away forever and I'd realised that if things were happening in my family before I was ready for them, there wasn't much I could do about it. I just had to accept it.

Except by the time we pulled into Zac's driveway, the last thing I felt like was braving the peak-hour traffic back to the valley.

"I'm *so* sore from track practice," Zac groaned as we walked into the pool house. "I gotta get in the hot tub pronto." He tossed his backpack aside and went to grab some towels. "How about you?"

"I'm not in the mood, but thanks anyway."

"Are you sure? It's a great way to unwind and, no offence, you look a little tense."

"I'm always tense." I gave a faint smile. "Alright, what's half an hour?"

Half an hour quickly turned into two. Before I knew it, I was looking up at an outline of the moon growing steadily bolder against the canvas of sky. Zac was so easy to talk to I'd lost track of time.

"Believe it or not, I can see why you like that new guy," he said out of the blue.

"You're talking about Alex, right?"

"Yeah. He's mysterious, just like you."

"Don't be silly, I'm not mysterious," I replied dismissively.

"Are you kidding?" Zac made a face. "Girl, you're a closed book!"

"Did you just call me girl?"

He nodded. "I did, and I enjoyed it a little too much."

We talked some more, ordered take-out, and laughed until it was too late for me to think about driving home. But the moment I climbed into the sofa bed, I knew I wouldn't be getting a wink of sleep. I'd been distracting myself all afternoon but now, without Zac to keep me occupied, my last conversation with Alex kept replaying in my head. It was like someone had mixed up the pieces of different puzzles and none of them seemed to connect. Thinking about it was making me crazy. Sleep was what I needed most, but when I glanced at the clock I saw it was almost two in the morning. Dammit! How long had I been lying here obsessing? There was nothing I could do right now anyway, so why couldn't my mind just settle and leave me in peace? Instead, I was stuck in an endless loop of thoughts with no exit sign in sight.

An idea hit me and I reached to grab Grandma Fee's brooch from the coffee table where I'd left it. I lay down again, clutching the cool silver to my chest, for the first time inviting it to work its magic. I had spent so much time thinking about Alex and his world that I thought I may as well travel back there. Besides, there had to be a reason Becky was so determined to share her story with me.

In what seemed less than a minute my mood changed. My mind actually emptied without any effort on my part. It was like someone had just thrown a blanket over all the spinning wheels in there. When the heaviness descended I embraced it willingly.

My mother could not afford the luxury of retreating from the world just because she was expecting. She worked until the very day both I and my younger sisters were born. But things are very different for the upper classes. The moment Mrs Reade's condition is announced, she gives up all activity and keeps to the confines of her room. It seems out of character for a woman who was always hankering to be out of doors. On occasion the warm weather draws her out to sit in the garden for a short time or to take a brief walk about the grounds, but she soon hurries inside again, as if worried too much fresh air might have some adverse effect.

Mr Reade, when he is home, is more attentive to his wife, as if she is a priceless ornament that requires special handling.

"It troubles me to be away at such a time," I overhear him say to Mr Alexander one morning before climbing into his carriage for yet another trip to London. "Isobel has such a delicate constitution and you know how she misses me when I am absent."

The mistress might look as delicate as a dandelion, but I am sure she has the constitution of an ox.

"I know, dear brother," Mr Alexander replies. "But she has a surprising strength. Do not weigh yourself down with troubles at such a joyous time."

"I am sure you are right," the master declares. "I fret over nothing. Just promise me she will be given the utmost care in my absence. I entrust her wellbeing to you."

"And I shall endeavour to ensure her every need is met."

The master looks relieved and, in a rare display of affection, gives his brother a hearty embrace before bidding him farewell.

I note that throughout the exchange Mr Alexander looks composed, but the minute the carriage is out of sight his face darkens and he seems to sag a little.

He stays true to his word and, like a devoted brother, does not leave Mrs Reade's side. Attending to her every whim and fancy becomes his primary focus. She often complains of being bored and bedridden and he will attempt to lift her spirits with card games or by reading to her from her favourite books. I am relieved to see no return of their former intimacy, which would be most inappropriate in the mistress's condition, and feel confident that this new life on the way has put an end to their folly.

On 22 April I am woken well before dawn by the sound of running feet and people shouting orders in the hallway below and I know the birthing has begun. I dress quickly and descend the stairs. Other housemaids come flying past me carrying armfuls of linen and pitchers of steaming water to Mrs Reade's chamber.

I reach the foyer to find Mrs Baxter with her cap askew. She is wringing her hands as she shouts directives to nobody in particular. "Becky!" she exclaims upon seeing me. "Cook needs you in the kitchen. Make haste!"

For what seems like hours muffled moans and cries drift down to us from upstairs. Everyone in the household is anxious for the wellbeing of the mistress, except for me. Having been present at the birthing of both my sisters I recognise the sound of pain that has a purpose. Mrs Reade is not as breakable as others seem to think.

Cook sends me to wait on the master, who is pacing in the drawing room and sipping whisky to steady his nerves. Every so often he throws a helpless look at the staircase but does not ascend. I look around for Mr Alexander, but he is nowhere to be found.

The doctor finally emerges, his brow glistening and his sleeves rolled up past his elbows. He comes jovially into the drawing room and Mr Reade jumps to attention. Even the servants cluster at the door, anxious to hear the news. I can tell from their faces that they are as anticipatory of the announcement as if awaiting a new addition to their own families.

"Congratulations, Reade," the doctor says and touches him on the shoulder. "You have a son. Eight pounds and bouncing with life."

"A son?" the master repeats before breaking into a beaming smile. "I have a son!"

After she has rested and her husband has been allowed up to visit, the mistress asks after Mr Alexander. I am delegated the task of finding him, which proves difficult until I eventually catch sight of him in the garden. He is leaning against the old willow tree, his features plagued with worry, the locks of his hair damp with the early morning dew. (Still morning, just hours after dawn?)

He looks up when he hears me approach. "How is she?" are the first words out of his mouth.

"All is well with Mrs Reade," I assure him. "The doctor said there were no complications and he will have trouble keeping her abed."

"And the child?"

I am excited to be the bearer of such good tidings. "Grange Hall has an heir and you have a nephew, sir. The bonniest babe by all accounts, although I have yet to lay eyes on him. Will you come inside, sir? The mistress is asking for you."

Strangely, my joyous news seems to cause Mr Alexander consternation rather than delight.

"I will come in presently," he murmurs.

His lack of enthusiasm surprises me, but it cannot deflate my own spirits. I hurry back to the house to let my mistress know he will come soon.

You would never guess there is a newborn in the house. Baby James is a quiet and well-behaved infant who sleeps and eats at designated times without complaint. Mostly he is kept isolated in the nursery for fear of infection. This manner of bringing up a child seems rather unnatural to me, raised as I was in such close proximity to my family and sharing everything with them.

A prune-faced nanny named Mrs Everest has been brought on staff and guards the baby with the fierceness of a dragon. We are lucky to catch a brief glimpse of him. Mrs Everest may possess years of experience in child-rearing, but I cannot help thinking how discomfiting it must be to wake each day to that dour face.

I seek out opportunities to lay eyes on the child, and on Sunday I am rewarded when Mrs Everest unexpectedly takes to her bed to nurse a slight cold. This means I am excused from attending church to watch over James for a few hours.

When I reach the nursery, I am immediately entranced. No expense has been spared here. There is a frieze of dancing bears around the walls, several newly upholstered chairs for nursing, and a mahogany rocking horse with a saddle and bridle of real leather. On a table are the gifts that keep arriving from well-wishers. The *villagers send whatever they can afford — a basket of oranges, a seed cake or a homespun blanket — but the gifts that arrive daily by post are lavish: silk pantalettes and embroidered smocks, engraved silver mugs and rattles, and wind-up toys in velvet-lined boxes.*

I approach the sleeping babe, who casts a spell on me the moment I set eyes on him. He looks so peaceful in his frothy crib and I wish he could stay that way forever, unaware of the cares of the world. Careful not to wake him, I reach down to stroke his hair, dark like his mother's but as soft as duck down. He responds by making a gentle snuffling sound in his sleep. His hands lie open like tiny flowers, but when I trace across one wrinkled palm his fist closes tightly around my finger. He is the prettiest child I have ever seen and I wonder how the mistress can bear to be away from him for even a moment. I know that if he were mine I should not entrust his care to anyone.

Suddenly the infant opens his eyes and the world is awash with blue. They are a crystal-clear blue, like sapphires.

I start, not because the child is awake and looking right at me, but because I know those eyes. I have seen them at close quarters in the face of another.

Zac offered to drive us both to school and, as I wasn't up to a long drive, I accepted. I planned to drive myself home later in the afternoon when I was hopefully feeling more alert. From the moment we pulled into the school's parking lot I had a feeling Alex was around. Luckily I had a free period first thing, so I parted ways with Zac and went straight to the theatre. Nothing in my life felt stable these days so I liked the way the theatre remained a fixed point, unchanged each time I visited. The light never seemed to change in here and the air always smelled the same.

My intuition turned out to be right. Alex was in his customary seat on the balcony, staring attentively at the dimly lit stage as if it were swarming with actors in lavish costumes. I wondered if a performance was unfolding in his head.

"We have a lot to talk about," I said when I reached him.

"I know." He stood to stretch his legs. "I have been sitting here since daybreak. I am beginning to miss the sun."

"Come on then," I said. "Let's get you some vitamin D."

"I'm afraid I do not follow your meaning." I had to stop doing that — putting him on the spot by making references to things outside his realm of experience. It was easy to forget how many scientific advancements had occurred since 1853.

"It means let's go enjoy the sunshine."

We headed to my locker so I could put my stuff away, then went into the quad and tucked ourselves away on a stone bench, hidden from prying eyes.

"I feel like things are about to get weird around here," I told him. "Like something's building. Something bad."

"What makes you say that?"

"There's something I haven't told you yet." I paused briefly; there was a part of me that wanted to shield Alex from more bad news. I thought he'd had more than his fair share over the last few days. But there was no point hiding anything from him now, not if we were really a team. "The other day I opened my locker and found my gym bag full of this foul-smelling muck. When I went back to clean it up at the end of the day it was gone."

Alex's face reflected his horror. "Why haven't you told me this?"

"I was waiting for an opportunity."

"It can only mean one thing."

"I know. Isobel must be back too. We just haven't seen her yet." Alex looked defeated for a moment, then his eyes found mine.

"There is not much we can do while we lack a vital piece of information. If there is a necromancer at large, and there seems little doubt of that now, we need to find him."

"If that's really what brought you back. We can't be sure."

"You do not believe me?"

"It's not that," I said. "Deep down I know you must be right, but that doesn't make it any easier to accept. It's a terrifying thought. I mean, this person could literally have this whole place overrun by the walking dead at any time."

"That will not happen." Alex adjusted his stance like a warrior steeling himself for battle. But his confidence didn't convince me.

"How do you know that? I don't imagine necromancers are the most stable people in the world."

"Whoever is doing this has a clear plan," Alex replied. "And time is his or her ally."

"It would help if we knew what that plan was."

"Of course, but we know that nothing has happened without reason. Everything is being carefully calculated. The last thing this sorcerer will want is to draw unnecessary attention that may hamper them."

I groaned. "That makes me even more nervous. Are we any closer to knowing who this person might be?"

Alex thought for a minute. "Perhaps it could be the school headmistress? She looks rather witch-like."

"Mrs Kaplan?" I said dubiously. "She might not have the best fashion sense and she needs a new hairstylist, but why would she want to let a bunch of ghosts loose in her own school?"

"You raise a valid point."

"And wouldn't this necromancer have to have a connection to you?"

"We can make no assumptions. Besides, the only person at this school with any connection to me is you —"

"Are you suggesting *I'm* the necromancer?"

Alex rolled his eyes. "*No.* I am saying that none of this makes sense yet. The necromancer must know about me and Isobel, our history. Have you ever spoken to anyone here about us?"

"Not that I can remember," I said, racking my brains in case there was an instance I'd forgotten about. "I mean, Sam and Natalie bugged me for information when I got back from England, but I never told them much. How could I? They would have had me committed."

Alex's brows knitted together as he thought. "Is it possible your friends could be craftier than they look?"

"I highly doubt that. And we'd better head inside — my next class starts soon."

We were almost at the library when a reedy voice cut through our conversation. "Excuse me, might I have a word?"

We looked across to see Doctor Ritter standing in the doorway of his empty classroom. He invited us in with a wave of his hand. Alex and I flashed each other a look before following him inside.

Doctor Ritter shut the door and settled against his desk, hands folded in his lap. "I think we can all agree that there has been some tension between us lately, correct?"

"That's fair to say," I replied, wondering where he was going with this.

"You can relax, Miss Kennedy, you're not in any trouble."

"I'm not?"

He shook his head. "I actually wanted to say that I understand senior year is a stressful time for students and teachers alike, and animosity in the classroom will not benefit anyone. So I would like for us to put aside our differences and start afresh. What do you say?"

"That's a very generous offer, sir."

Truthfully, I thought his proposal a little strange after our last interaction. Why the change of tune?

"Very good." He rubbed his hands together. "Before you go, Mr Reade, I was wondering if we have met before? There's something very familiar about your face."

Alex frowned. "I do not think so."

"Ah, my mistake." Doctor Ritter smiled, picked up his briefcase and strolled out of the room whistling.

"What was that about?" I asked as soon as he was out of earshot.

"I have no idea," Alex replied. "Let us find somewhere more private to talk."

"If I cut any more classes, I'll be in big trouble."

He gave me a funny look and I immediately got the irony. If we didn't get to the bottom of what was happening, cutting class would be the least of my worries.

"Sorry, priorities," I said.

We were scouring the library for an empty aisle when Alex started to lag behind me. I was so busy looking for a spot to ensconce ourselves that I didn't pay attention at first.

"Chloe," he said, but I wasn't really listening. I was too busy thinking about the fact that there might be a necromancer on the loose at Sycamore High. Not just teenagers messing around with stuff they didn't understand, but a person with a lot of experience and power. The idea was hard to process, but I knew Alex was right. This situation we found ourselves in was no accident, which meant someone had deliberately brought him back from the afterlife for a reason currently unknown. Sure, there was a slight, maybe two per cent chance this was a friendly necromancer who just wanted to give Alex a new lease of life, but somehow I doubted that. There weren't many altruistic reasons for raising the dead that I could think of.

"Chloe, wait!"

I turned to see Alex's face twisted in a strange expression. He wasn't standing up tall the way he usually did. In fact, he seemed to be wilting in front of me.

"Hey, are you alright?"

"No." He was breathing heavily. "It is happening again, right now. I cannot stop it."

"Stop what? What's happening?" I was confused for a moment until I remembered what he'd told me earlier and my eyes went as wide as saucers. "Wait, are you saying you're about to *disappear*?"

"That is exactly what I am saying. But do not be alarmed; it is only temporary." As he spoke, his eyelids drooped and he leaned forward as if falling into a trance.

This was not good. The main study area was teeming with people. How would they react to somebody keeling over and evaporating like smoke?

"Holy crap!" I said. "We have to get out of here. How long until it happens — five minutes, ten?"

"More likely sixty seconds." Alex threw out an arm to support himself against a shelf.

I needed to get him out of sight and pronto. But where could we go with so little time?

I grabbed his hand. It was buzzing with static and he was starting to look completely disoriented. I moved in front of him to shield him from view, but it was useless. We were bound to be seen!

That was when I spotted it … The janitor's closet, just across from the library's entrance a few feet away. We could make it if we moved fast.

"Can you hold on for just a few more seconds?" I asked.

But Alex was fading at the edges. His hand had already disappeared and I found myself holding an empty sleeve. I slipped what remained of his arm over my shoulder, trying to look casual and not like I was helping a wounded soldier to safety. By now we were attracting curious looks, and the librarian on duty seemed to have singled us out as potential troublemakers.

By the time we reached the janitor's closet, Alex was the consistency of jelly — jelly that was crackling with electrical currents. I pulled open the door and hauled us both inside, knocking over mops and buckets that clattered to the ground. I released Alex for a second to shut the door behind us. The only light now came from the cracks around it, and the sounds from the hallway were muffled. It took my eyes a while to adjust to the gloom.

"Can you hear me?" I asked, extending my hands to locate Alex's face in the dark.

There was no answer.

"Alex?"

A weak flash lit up the interior of the closet. It was pale green and lasted only a second before vanishing into the air. As it faded, I realised I could no longer feel Alex by my side. He was gone.

I hated to be apart from him with so many still-unanswered questions looming. But at least this time I believed he'd be back. And I knew where to find him.

I decided to wait until the crowd in the hallway had thinned. Dashing into the janitor's closet with a member of the opposite sex would have looked suspicious enough. Emerging alone would just fan the flames of gossip. So I sat on an upturned bucket, with the smell of cleaning agents giving me a headache behind one eye, until the voices faded. When I thought everyone was gone, I opened the door a crack only to see a face staring back at me.

"Ugh!" I jumped back, tripping over the bucket and landing painfully on the tiles.

When the door opened fully I instinctively shielded myself, but it was only Miguel's startled face staring down at me.

"I am sorry, Miss Chloe," he said. "Are you okay?"

My alarm quickly dissolved into plain and simple embarrassment. I pushed aside the broom that had fallen on top of me and quickly got up, tucking my hair behind my ears.

"Yes, I'm fine, thank you. I know this probably seems pretty strange, but it's just a silly misunderstanding."

"Of course," he said tentatively. "So what happened?"

"What?"

"How did you end up in here?"

"Oh, I was playing a silly game and hiding from someone. I thought this was a classroom — oops!" I let out a terrible fake laugh. "Anyway, sorry to get in your way. I'd better go."

I ducked past him, my ears burning. He must have thought I was a total freak lurking in the closet like that.

"Wait," he called after me and his tone was kind not angry. I turned to see him holding out a small card. "Please, take this, Miss Chloe."

It was a holy card, the colour of parchment and carefully laminated. On one side was an image of the Archangel Michael, his mighty sword poised over his head ready to slay the dragon in one swift motion. His expression was completely unmoved. When I flipped the card over, I saw that the other side held a prayer for protection against evil.

"It's very sweet, but you can't give me this, Miguel," I said, trying to hand it back to him. "It looks special."

He refused, shaking his head and stepping away. "I want you to take it," he insisted. "You need it more than I do."

Before I could ask why, he gave me a sympathetic smile that seemed to say *I don't envy you* and walked away with his cart.

I stared down at the card. Things just kept getting weirder. Why did Miguel think I needed help? Did he know something that Alex and I had missed? As I turned the card over in my hand, the last line of the prayer seemed to float in front of me: *And all the evil spirits who roam throughout the world seeking the ruin of souls.*

The ruin of souls … That hit just a little too close to home.

CHAPTER THIRTEEN

Slipping the card into my back pocket, I headed for the bathrooms. I was feeling a little light-headed and hoped splashing some cold water on my face might help. It was surprisingly cool in there and I was grateful for the silence while I deliberated what my next move should be. Something had to be done, but what? I wasn't good at sitting around being idle. Alex had sure chosen a bad moment to pull a disappearing act. I sighed, knowing it was beyond his control. It probably frustrated him as much as it did me. But now he might not appear again for hours … even days.

I thought about heading home, but my car was still at Zac's. That made things tricky. Perhaps taking refuge there hadn't been the smartest idea after all. Should I spend another night at his house? And if I did, how would Alex feel about that? Maybe he wouldn't care given the bigger problems we had to face.

The constant stream of questions made me want to scream. The cold water wasn't helping much so I turned off the tap and that's when I heard something creak. In the bathroom mirror I saw that one of the stall doors had swung open. It was the last one, tucked into a corner, a little narrower than all the others.

I froze. I could have sworn I was in there alone. Until now there had been no indication of company; not a single sound. I waited for the mystery occupant to emerge, but nobody did. Were they embarrassed or deliberately trying to frighten me?

"Hello?" I called out hesitantly. "Anyone in here?"

The silence stretched for another long minute before I heard someone crying with jerky, gasping little spasms, as if they were too upset to answer.

I edged closer, wishing they would say something. "Do you need help?" I asked.

A reedy wail filtered from the cubicle.

I decided to bite the bullet and look inside. What I saw disturbed and confused me. A child with a shaved head and scuffed shoes sat huddled on the grubby tiled floor clutching a dirty handkerchief. It was sobbing, knees drawn to its face, so I couldn't tell if it was male or female. But I knew it was dead and that was all that mattered. All the signs were there: the air had dropped several degrees in temperature, the child's outline was ever so slightly blurred, and the hairs on the back of my neck were standing on end. I was about to beat a hasty retreat when it occurred to me that ghosts might be the only ones able to shed some light on what was happening around here.

"Why are you crying?" I asked softly.

The child looked up, a sob catching in its throat. I saw then that she was a little girl, with blue eyes as deep as the ocean and wearing a tattered coarse dress that barely covered her matchstick limbs.

"They cut off my hair," she hiccuped. "They said I had to be punished and they took it all away!"

"Who did?" I asked. I felt overcome with pity for the poor kid even though I knew she wasn't really there.

"That wicked Mrs Marsh! Don't let her catch me again!" She broke into a fresh wave of tears and looked up at me imploringly. "I want to go home. Won't you help me?"

"I … I want to," I stammered. "But I'm not sure I can. What's your name?"

"Amelia," she answered, getting to her feet but still hugging the cubicle wall. "Amelia Alcott."

Only once she was standing did I see the little flames licking almost innocently at the hem of her dress. "Oh my God!" I cried as they climbed higher, fanning out and snaking around her knees, eating away at her skin.

Amelia seemed oblivious to her scorched limbs, now crackling like spindly tree branches. "Take me home!" she demanded as the fire reached her hands. It looked as if she was holding great fistfuls of flame.

I stood rooted to the spot, unable to look away. "I'm sorry," I choked out.

"Take me home!" she continued to shriek as the blaze consumed her.

Her little body rushed at me then and I reeled back, hands flying up to shield my face. But just before she reached me she evaporated with a hiss, leaving nothing but a tiny scorch mark on the floor.

Her screams still echoing in my head, I bolted for the door. You'd think I'd be accustomed to seeing spirits by now, but every time I did my heart felt like it was beating right out of my chest.

In the empty corridor, I yanked my phone from my

pocket. Involuntarily my fingers flew over the keypad and I realised I was calling Zac.

"Hey, Chloe," he answered. "What's up?"

"Where are you?" I panted. There was no time for formalities.

"At the gym. You don't sound so good. Is something wrong?"

"You have to meet me at the library. I need access to those archives right now. It can't wait."

"Okay, I'm coming," he assured me. "Just take a breath, alright?"

"I would if I could. I'll see you there in five minutes."

It was rude to hang up on him, but I didn't even think about it. My nerves were shot from jumping from one drama to another. When would they end? Or would they just intensify until I reached breaking point?

Something sinister was happening — that much I could feel. But too many pieces of the puzzle were missing, which meant I was in the dark. It was the worst feeling to know danger was just around the corner, especially when any new information I received only served to confuse me further.

Zac arrived at the library in his sports gear and we got straight down to business. I hovered anxiously behind him as he used his magazine committee keycard to unlock the filing cabinets in the restricted room behind the checkout desk. On the back of the door hung a black and white photograph of Sycamore High on the day it was founded in 1941.

I was expecting to be questioned, but the librarian didn't bat an eye when Zac sailed past her.

"Hi, Mrs Willis," he said breezily.

"Hello, Zachary dear. Are you having a nice day?"

"It's always nicer when I see you."

"Oh, aren't you sweet. There are some brownies on my desk if you're hungry."

Wow, I guessed being on boring committees really did have some perks.

Zac collected an armful of files — just enough not to raise suspicion — and carried them to a secluded corner of the library. We tucked ourselves in at a table with our backs to the communal couches. The place was pretty empty on a good day, but this afternoon we had almost total privacy. There was only one other student there, plugged into headphones and hunched over his computer.

"So are you going to tell me what happened?" Zac asked as I began leafing through the documents. Some of them were quite old and had to be handled with care.

"I saw another one," I replied.

"Another what? Oh, man, you're not talking about ghosts again, are you?"

"I'm sorry to bore you, but it's true. There was a little girl in the bathroom. She was on fire and asking for my help. Don't you see? There's a pattern emerging. Something terrible happened here once and we have to find out what."

He looked at me searchingly, conflict scrawled all over his face. Unlike Alex, Zac wasn't able to hide what he was feeling. Or maybe he didn't try. I could tell he genuinely wanted to help me but was also wondering what he was getting himself into. For some reason Zac's opinion of me mattered and I didn't want him thinking of me as a nutcase.

"Let's get started then," Zac said finally.

I blinked. "Does that mean you believe me?"

"Let me put it like this: I know crazy and you're not crazy, Chloe. So if you tell me something happened, I'm going to take your word for it. And we're going to get to the bottom of it."

He picked up a folder and began searching in silence.

"Thank you," I said. "Most people in your position wouldn't be this cool."

"Well, I'm not most people." He smiled. "And we both know I can't resist a challenge. Now what exactly are we looking for?"

"Anything related to the history of the school."

He leafed carefully through a bunch of documents for several minutes, then pulled a sheet of paper from one of the folders. "You mean like this?" He read the contents aloud. *"Sycamore High School was founded in 1941 by Mr Robert G Sycamore of San Diego, California, who bought the property after it was neglected by its previous owners. At the time of sale the property had been badly damaged by a fire only six months prior that killed a number of victims."*

"I knew it." My whole body was trembling. "That's why they're always burning."

Zac glanced up from the page; he looked pale. "So people did die here."

"Does it say anything about who they were?"

His eyes flew over the remainder of the page. He sighed when he reached the end. "Nope. Nothing."

"The information must be in there somewhere," I said.

"True. And I can think of a faster way to find it."

He tucked the document back into the folder and motioned me toward a row of computers. We huddled together at the end one even though the only people nearby were two exchange students absorbed in study.

"It's times like these that make me thankful for the digital age," Zac said. He typed *SYCAMORE HIGH SCHOOL FIRE 1941* into the search engine. "Bingo," he said as the very first item to pop up contained the information we were looking for.

"Thank God for technology," I agreed, my eyes already flying over the article.

April, 1941. On Tuesday night, tragedy struck the Alameda Orphanage in Southern California when it was destroyed by a devastating blaze that claimed the lives of several children and their devoted caretakers. The cause of the fire remains unknown, although authorities suspect it began in a room on the second floor of the building. There were thirty-seven children in the care of the orphanage, ranging in ages from five to twelve. Twelve of the children were unable to escape the inferno in time and perished alongside their nurse, Miss Sarah Boyle, and the headmistress of the orphanage, Mrs Agatha Marsh ...

I stopped reading. Agatha Marsh. As in the Mrs Marsh the girl in the bathroom was so scared of? The woman who'd cut off her hair? I scrolled down, combing the article for clues, only stopping when I came across the photographs. The dead children stared at me, solemn as tombstones in black and white. It was unnerving to look at people who had probably died not a stone's throw away from where Zac and I were now sitting.

There she was, in the bottom right-hand corner of a photo: Amelia Alcott. I recognised her even though she looked completely different with a smile on her face and a gentle curl in her golden hair. She looked nothing like the terrified and shivering entity I'd seen in the bathroom.

My gaze lifted to the photograph above hers. It was a stern face, with eyes that held little emotion. I didn't have to read the caption to know this was Agatha Marsh. But where had I seen her before? It took a moment for the penny to drop, for everything to click into place. When it did, I stifled a gasp.

"What is it?" Zac asked eagerly. "Chloe? Tell me."

But I couldn't articulate my thoughts. I couldn't explain what was happening because I didn't understand it myself. I had first seen Agatha Marsh in the vision of the burning building before she melted into the fire. Like Amelia, her face would be forever emblazoned on my memory. But why was she appearing to me? Why had some kids and a woman who had died more than seventy years ago suddenly returned to haunt Sycamore High?

Zac followed me and kept watch while I made copies of the relevant documents. They weren't supposed to be removed from their protective plastic covers. We were probably the first people to look at them in years.

I wanted to go someplace more private to study them without fear of being interrupted. I wanted to make sure there was nothing we'd missed. My plan was to compile all the information I could get my hands on, even though I suspected it probably wouldn't be enough to answer my and Alex's questions.

"Well?" Zac asked.

"Well, what?" I replied.

"Seriously, Chloe, you have *got* to stop doing that."

"Doing what?"

"Making discoveries and not telling me what they are."

"Okay," I said, realising he was right. Zac had gone out of his way to help me and that entitled him to some explanation. "But you're not going to like it."

"I haven't liked a lot of the things you've told me, but I'm still here, aren't I?"

"That you are," I said with a smile. "Okay, well, it's pretty simple. I have it on good authority that the people who died in that fire are now back ... or at least their spirits are."

"What kind of authority?"

"Okay, I'm the authority. I already told you — I keep seeing them everywhere." Zac started to say something, but I cut him off. "And I *know* I'm right because the people I've seen are the same people in this photograph."

I waved the sheet of paper at him, but he didn't take it. He'd gone rigid.

"Look," I continued more gently, "I know you don't want to hear this, but something or someone is raising the dead at this school, and I'd bet my life that whoever's doing it is the same person who brought Alex back —"

I realised my mistake too late. The words had slipped out in a moment of carelessness.

I watched as incredulity settled over Zac's face. "What did you just say?"

"Never mind."

"It's a bit late for that. You mean Alex as in your old boyfriend, don't you?"

"Yes."

His eyes went wide. "Please tell me you're not suggesting what I think you are."

"I told you it was a complicated relationship," I muttered, unable to meet his gaze.

"That's the understatement of the year! Chloe, how can you be in a relationship with someone who's ... who's dead? I mean it's impossible! It's unnatural —"

"It's very possible actually," I jumped in. "Honestly, it's no different from having a relationship with a living person only they're harder to hold onto."

Zac rubbed his temple, unable to believe he was having this conversation. "Okay, for argument's sake let's say you could have a relationship with a ghost. Why the hell would you *want* to?"

"It's not like they're monsters, Zac."

He shook his head. "Yeah, what am I thinking? People love ghosts. That's why they're such a dominant theme in romantic comedies. Wait, no, I'm thinking of *horror* movies."

"I'm telling you, they can be just as loving and loyal as you and me. Besides, you've never met one so how do you know how you feel about them?"

"I've never met a werewolf either, but I'm pretty sure we wouldn't get along."

"You're just thinking of all the negative stuff you've ever heard about ghosts," I told him. "People are afraid of the dead because they remind them of their own mortality. But the truth is, sooner or later we're all going to join them so why bother being afraid? They're not that different from you and me."

"Right, except for one huge whopping difference."

"Don't be so narrow-minded. Can't you at least meet Alex before deciding to hate him?"

"I don't hate him," Zac clarified. "But I am scared of him, like any normal person would be. Like you should be."

"That's ridiculous. Alex is one of the gentlest people you'll ever meet."

"He's not a person!"

"And you're not being very politically correct right now."

"Oh my God!" Zac threw up his hands. "This has got to be the most bizarre conversation I've ever had."

"Hey, you wanted to know."

He let out a low whistling breath. "You're right about that — I did ask for it. And we're going to finish this talk later. But right now I have a swim meet to get to."

I checked my watch to find the day had slipped away from us. I guess time flies when you're freaking out.

Zac promised the swim meet wouldn't last more than an hour so I agreed to walk over with him and wait. I wasn't sure I wanted to go home anyway — I still wasn't ready to give my father that satisfaction — and besides, I had plenty to mull over. There had to be a connection between the new visions, Alex's return and the necromancer he was certain had brought him back. But what was it?

I couldn't help thinking about the strange timing of it all. For me, high school had always been an uphill battle, like some grim initiation ritual into the real world. For years I'd had to navigate my way blindly through this obstacle course, hoping for an end in sight. Now that end was almost upon me; the finish line was within reach. I just had to keep my head down for the next few months, get through graduation and I'd be home free. It should have been smooth sailing. Instead, it felt like the whole school was on the brink of catastrophe. One hurdle after another just kept popping up and slapping me in the face.

I suppose I was so busy worrying about senior year and lamenting the bad timing that I didn't stop to consider something vital. Looking back on it now, I should have read the signs better. I of all people should have seen the little things for what they really were — precursors of real danger to come.

A strong wind had picked up. It rattled the windows and made the tree branches creak, and seemed to be alive with a melancholy personality of its own, screaming one minute and moaning the next. It caused an ominous atmosphere — a sense of rampaging manic energy. My skin prickled all over and I knew something bad was about to happen. I just didn't know what or where. I felt like I had a responsibility to inform someone. But what would I say? I could produce no tangible evidence. It wasn't like the principal would thank me for alerting her to a "paranormal attack" and close down the school until further notice.

As I glanced around the bustling parking lot, a feeling of helplessness crept over me. I didn't know every student by name, but I knew all their faces. They were average Californian kids, rooted in the here and now. For the most part, their days were sun-filled, their nights balmy and their minds free of trouble. They were completely oblivious to the dark worlds that existed alongside the bright one they occupied and their complacency made them vulnerable. Whatever storm was brewing, it would catch them completely off guard.

CHAPTER FOURTEEN

When Zac and I reached the pool, the rest of the team was already outside, waiting for Coach Curtis to unlock the door. As we made our way up the gravel path lined with succulents, I realised I hadn't set foot in this place since the ninth grade when swimming was a compulsory component of PE.

"Hey, guys," Zac said. "What's with the windows?"

I saw that the building's floor-to-ceiling windows were covered with a heavy fog. Usually you could see straight through and watch the swimmers at practice, but today it was like a white wall had appeared.

One of the boys shrugged. "Dunno. I think the A/C is down."

"I hate it when that happens," Zac said. "It's like swimming in a sauna."

"Yeah, it's gross," the boy agreed, then turned his attention to me. "Hey, Kennedy, are you here to cheer Zac on?"

"That's right," I said sarcastically. "I'm his number one fan."

"Where are your pompoms?"

"Shut up, Daniel," Zac said, saving me the trouble of telling him myself.

Coach Curtis appeared jangling a set of keys in his hand. "Okay, boys," he said. "I hope you're ready to train hard today. Oh, dammit, don't tell me the A/C is out again. I've been at admin about that for months, but does anybody listen?"

He unlocked the door and the team traipsed inside, groaning in complaint. The steam was almost impossible to see through and made the air stiflingly hot. The tension in my body grew.

"Chloe, you'd better take my hand," Zac said. "These tiles can get pretty slippery."

"Oh, Chloe, please take my hand!" someone nearby mimicked in a high-pitched voice.

"Shut up, Daniel!" Zac and I chorused.

I gripped Zac's hand. He was right about the floor and I didn't trust myself not to lose my footing. My hair was damp now and clinging to my forehead. I felt the unpleasant sensation of my heart thumping against my ribs.

"Where the hell is Anderson?" Coach Curtis asked. "He's usually the first one here."

He was talking about Hart Anderson, captain of the swim team. Everybody knew Hart, if not personally then by reputation.

"Uh, Coach," a boy said. "There's something in the water."

From where I stood it looked like a black shapeless mass.

"There's nothing in the water," came the gruff reply. "You're dreaming again." There was silence for several drawn-out seconds, then Coach Curtis yelled, "Jesus Christ!"

Zac released my hand and sprinted to the edge of the pool. The other guys followed. I couldn't see through the mist or past the throng of bodies in front of me, but I could hear the swimmers talking over one another in confusion.

Then the fog lifted and I saw that the mass at the bottom of the pool was a body curled in foetal position.

"Is that ...?" someone began.

"Oh my God!"

I heard a splash as two of the boys leapt fully dressed into the water.

"Get him out!" urged the coach. "Hurry! Hurry!"

"Is he breathing?"

"Jesus! How did this happen?"

The crowd parted to make room and I saw that the two boys who had dived into the pool were now struggling to haul out Hart Anderson's body.

Coach Curtis grabbed him, lay him on his back and pressed his ear against Hart's lips. He started CPR, pushing against his chest and breathing into his mouth. But we all knew it was too late. Hart's normally athletic body was already looking bloated, his lips tinged with blue. It was hard to know how long he'd been at the bottom of the pool, but his skin had puckered in places.

You could tell there was no reviving him. But Coach didn't give up though, he kept at it until it was clear Hart was never going to respond.

The swimmers clustered together in shock. They stared at their lifeless captain, horror plastered over their faces. I'd never seen Coach look so white. Things like this just didn't happen. Hart Anderson was a hero, invincible and destined for glory. If he could be cut down so randomly, what hope was there for the rest of us?

Finally, Coach snapped to his senses and asked if anyone had dialled 911. There was no urgency in his voice though and I knew he was simply going through the motions.

I couldn't look at Hart's face. It was too awful. I'd always thought of drowning as a peaceful death. I didn't think so now. A shudder went through me, like an animal sensing the proximity of danger. And that's when I saw her. It's not like I hadn't expected it; I just hadn't expected it to happen so soon.

The mist vanished altogether to reveal a figure on the other side of the pool. A woman in a white nightdress, her black hair streaming behind her like tentacles even though there wasn't a hint of wind. Her lips were twisted in a cruel smile and her eyes were two black chasms in her death mask of a face. Still I recognised her; I'd know that face anywhere. Even if I was eighty years old and suffering from dementia, it would never lose its clarity.

My worst fears were realised as Isobel Reade stared back at me. Her expression was mocking as if to say, *Surely you didn't think you could escape me that easily?* My mind flashed back to the message in my locker: *I AM NOT GONE.*

Isobel had followed me across the world … followed me through time. I had never seen her outside the grounds of Grange Hall. Strangely, the modern setting, where she was distinctly out of place, made her more terrifying. With trembling limbs, I stared at her; this time she had gone too far. Taunting me with cryptic messages and foul apparitions was one thing. Randomly taking an innocent life was quite another. Hart Anderson was a strong and healthy eighteen-year-old with so much life ahead of him. He would have graduated, gone on to college and eventually become a husband and a father. Now that future had been snatched away from him. It was hard to fathom. And why Hart? If Isobel's motivation was revenge, what had he ever done to her?

Someone would have to break the news to his mother and father. What would they tell them? That their only son had suffered an unexpected stroke or seizure and happened to be in the water when it occurred? No matter what cause of death the coroner came up with, I knew the truth: Hart's drowning was no accident; it was a violent murder. What made Isobel think she could get away with this? This was my school, I knew these kids. Isobel couldn't just show up here and start tearing lives apart. I wouldn't stand by and let that happen. I wouldn't leave my friends and fellow students at the mercy of an invisible enemy who could strike at any time.

Whether I felt capable or not, it was up to me to do something.

An ashen-faced Coach Curtis hung up the phone and turned to his team. "Go home, boys. The paramedics are on their way. I'm going to wait here with Hart."

He took off his windbreaker and used it to tenderly cover the dead boy's face. Before that moment I don't think the others really believed Hart was gone.

"But, Coach," one of the swimmers protested weakly.

"*Please.*" Coach Curtis's voice cracked. "Please … just go. I'm sorry you had to see this."

Zac gently touched his teammate on the shoulder. "Come on. There's nothing more we can do here."

One by one they followed his lead, turning their backs on their friend's body with difficulty. I'd never seen so many grief-stricken faces.

Outside, I took Zac by the arm and steered him away from the crowd. "We have to get to the theatre."

"Chloe, for God's sake, a guy just died!" He was barely managing to blink back tears. I knew he'd been close friends with Hart Anderson.

"I'm sorry," I said. "I know how awful this is, but Hart's death was no accident."

"What are you talking about?"

"Hart was murdered."

Zac looked around frantically in case anyone had heard. "Chloe, you can't say crazy stuff like that!"

"I'm saying it because it's true. Isobel did this. I saw her on the other side of the pool."

"Who the hell is Isobel?"

"A vengeful spirit," I explained. "I've encountered her before and she's not someone you want to mess with."

"Okay!" Zac held up his hands and backed away from me. "I can't do this right now. I just need a moment."

I stepped forward and grabbed his hand. "We don't have a choice! There'll be time to grieve for Hart, but that time isn't now. We need to stop Isobel before there's another tragic accident. And trust me, there will be one."

Zac didn't argue any further. He swallowed down his emotions, nodded and followed me to the theatre in silence.

I walked as fast as I could against the wind, hoping that Alex would be there. If he wasn't, we were royally screwed. He was the only person who could help us now.

But when I flung open the theatre door and ran inside, his customary seat in the balcony was empty.

"Damn!" I yelled, tears spilling. I couldn't shake the image of Hart's blue-tinged face from my head. "How

could this happen? How could we have let this happen?"
I kicked the wall hard and stubbed my toe.

"Hey, it's okay." Zac put his arms around me.

"Nothing about this is okay. And now Alex isn't here
when we need him most."

"We'll figure it out."

"You don't get it. We can't do this without him!"

"So we'll wait for him."

I knew Zac was trying to comfort me, but he didn't fully
understand the danger we were all in.

"He might not show up for hours, days even," I said.
"Honestly, sometimes I think we're cursed."

I sank down into a chair and buried my face in my hands.
Cursed. The word echoed in my head, triggering a new
wave of hopelessness.

"We have to hold it together," Zac said. "Especially if
there is something weird going on. Look, I'm going to go
call my parents. Can you wait here for me?"

"Sure."

"I won't be long."

As I watched his retreating back, I felt that physical
tug, that sensation of falling that always came just before
a vision. What could Becky possibly want to show me
now?

*It is a crisp, bright morning and as I round the corner of the house,
my arms laden with freshly chopped firewood, I see Mr Alexander
sitting on the back steps as if waiting for someone.*

He rises when he sees me and I curtsey as required.

"Good morning, Becky. I trust you are well?"

"Very well, thank you, sir."

"Good." He lingers, seeming to want to say more. "Do you need help with that?" he asks eventually. "It looks heavy."

"Oh, no, sir!" I am aghast at the very idea of accepting his assistance. "I can manage quite well, thank you."

Nevertheless, the bundle is heavy and I am keen to get inside and unload it into the grates, which I cleaned earlier.

"I think you must have a very low opinion of me," Mr Alexander says suddenly.

My face must reflect my surprise at the personal tone of his conversation. "Why do you say that, sir? You have shown only kindness to me," I reply honestly.

"That may be, Becky, but I have also done things of which I am deeply ashamed."

It occurs to me that this unburdening of guilt should be taking place in the presence of a cleric rather than a servant, but his sweet face is so pained that it melts my heart. There must be something I can say that might prove comforting to him.

Suddenly it is my mother's voice I hear in my head and I find myself speaking her words aloud. "All sins may be pardoned, sir. We need only to ask God's forgiveness, then make our amends."

He becomes thoughtful, and when his eyes meet mine I see a new brightness in them, as if a secret has been unlocked.

"Out of the mouth of babes," he whispers. "Yes, I believe I know what needs to be done now. Thank you! You have been most helpful."

"I did nothing, sir," I reply, before shyly adding, "Although I should like to see you cheerful again."

"What a good heart you have, Becky. I hope you receive only blessings in your lifetime."

I am gazing into those crystalline blue eyes when an admonishing voice calls from within. "Becky! What's taking you so long?" It is Mrs Baxter. "You'd better not be dawdling."

Mr Alexander holds a finger to his lips and winks as if we are partners in crime. "Mrs Baxter is on the warpath," he whispers. "I will let you get on with your work." And he walks off purposefully.

The encounter leaves me unsettled and that night I toss and turn, my inability to sleep compounded by Martha's soft snoring in the adjoining cot. I stare at the ceiling until I can lie here no longer. Aided by the light from a tallow stump, I find my way to the kitchen in search of that bitter brown tincture Mrs Baxter keeps hidden in a scullery cupboard. I am unconcerned about my bare feet and nightgown as I do not expect to encounter anyone at this late hour.

As I creep down the back stairs, I become aware of a strip of light coming from under the drawing room door. From within I hear heightened voices and realise an argument is in progress. I know the master is not currently at home so it must be Mr Alexander and the mistress. I have not heard them speak to each other like this before.

The mistress's voice is petulant, rising in volume, while Mr Alexander's remains calm and measured. I have no inkling of what they might be talking about, but the topic is clearly not to Mrs Reade's liking. Mr Alexander sounds resolute, which makes me admire him, until I hear the unmistakable sound of weeping followed by hushed and soothing tones. It seems the mistress has won this argument. I shake my head. If she is able to bend him to her will so easily, he is done for. There can be no saving him.

In the library, I have been secretly reading about the travels of Ulysses. When his ship came upon the sirens he ordered his men to stop up their ears with wax so they would not be seduced by the sirens' song. He himself remained tied to the mast, his cries to be released unheard. That is how I think of Mrs Reade, as an alluring and cruel siren who has robbed poor Mr Alexander of his senses.

In the scullery it does not take me long to find the blue bottle. I remove its cork stopper and count half a dozen drops into a glass of water. I have seen Mrs Baxter do this countless times before when one of the servants has a toothache or aching joints.

I barely have time to raise the glass to my lips when I am startled by the sound of hooves on the gravel outside. With a pounding heart, I peer through the window and see the master. His arrival must be unexpected because he leads his horse to the stables himself. I notice that he is unsteady on his feet, and have seen my father in a similar state enough times to recognise inebriation.

Terror makes my mind go blank. It is possible that the occupants of the drawing room have not noted his return. What should I do? Return to my bed and act as if I never came down? Where does my allegiance lie? Not with the master surely, that stern and exacting man. I am beholden to Mr Alexander, and he is not strong enough to extricate himself from the spell that has been cast over him. If truth be told, he didn't stand a chance from the minute he arrived here from his sojourn in Paris and Mrs Reade set her sights on him. The intrigue has been going on for months and I wonder how she can live so comfortably in her web of deceit.

I listen intently as the master enters the house. I imagine him stopping to throw off his cloak. Unless he is too intoxicated to notice, it will not be long before he hears voices and stumbles upon his wife and brother in the drawing room. The truth has a way of coming out, and perhaps this is for the best. Perhaps this is the only way the lunacy will come to an end.

I am too small and insignificant to get involved in such a drama. Instead I quickly down the contents of my glass before retreating to *my room. As I climb into bed, I consider how I have changed from that wide-eyed girl who first arrived at Grange Hall. I shall never look in the mirror and see her again. That gloss of innocence has been erased, never to return.*

This house is cursed, I think, and so are all who dwell within it. I lie in my bed under the flimsy cover and wait for the axe to fall.

I was glad to be released from Becky's memories before Carter found Alex and Isobel in the drawing room. I knew what horrors would follow and didn't need to witness them firsthand. That would be too heart-wrenching.

As I woke from the vision, I became aware of two voices arguing.

"Why weren't you watching her?"

"I was watching her. She's fine, aren't you, Chloe?"

"She is unconscious!"

"Word to the wise: when people are unconscious they're generally not standing up."

I opened my eyes to see Alex peering into my face and snapping his fingers under my nose.

"Chloe, can you hear me?"

"I'm fine," I said. "I was just someplace else for a few minutes."

"So it is still happening," Alex said. "Are you going to elaborate?"

There was no point telling him what he already knew when there was something much bigger at hand. Hart's death took precedence over Becky's scattered memories.

"I'm just so glad to see you!" I said, walking straight into his arms.

"You have been crying. Why?"

The words choked in my throat the first time I tried to get them out. I had to take a deep breath before whispering, "She's back. Isobel is *here*."

Alex released me instantly and a shadow fell across his face. "Are you certain?"

"I saw her with my own eyes. And she's done something awful."

Alex waited for me to say more, but I was too overcome to speak. I just shook my head and left the explanations to Zac.

"Hart Anderson, a student, was killed in a freak drowning accident. He was captain of the swim team." Zac's voice gave out and he turned away to compose himself.

Alex stared at me, realisation dawning. "I am very sorry," he said to both of us.

I could see from the look on his face that he felt responsible for the tragedy. He was probably thinking that if he hadn't come back from the afterlife, this wouldn't have happened. But there was more to it this time, I was sure. And somehow we had to work together to figure it out.

CHAPTER FIFTEEN

No one spoke for a while. We each needed some time to process what had just happened. I knew that Zac especially was torn apart by losing his friend. I was surprised to see him holding up as well as he was.

"I do not understand," Alex finally murmured. "How can this be happening again? What does Isobel want? To hurt me? Or you? She cannot still harbour so much vengeance."

"Vengeance is her middle name, remember?" I said. "And you know what the worst part is? I think she's just warming up."

"This isn't like she's vandalised your car," Zac said angrily. "Somebody died! Somebody I cared about. So what are we going to do about it?"

Alex shifted his gaze to Zac, who was standing in the aisle with his arms folded, his face dark with emotion. "I do not believe we have been introduced."

"I'm sorry," I said quickly, before Zac could reply. "Alex, this is Zac Green. Zac, meet Alex Reade."

"I'm a friend of Chloe's," Zac added.

"Indeed?"

I thought it best to set the record straight before any more testosterone went flying.

"Zac's been helping me try and piece everything together. Do you remember the girl we saw in my car on your first day here?"

That got Alex's attention. "How could I forget her?"

"Well, it turns out she used to live here once when Sycamore was an orphanage run by a woman called Agatha Marsh. She died here in 1941, in a fire along with twelve little kids and their nurse. I keep seeing flashes of the victims; and now I've seen Isobel. What does that mean? How are they connected?"

"It means whoever this necromancer is, he's running circles around us," Alex said, as calmly as if he were announcing the day's weather forecast.

Zac did a double-take. "Back up! Necromancer?" he asked sharply. "You've got to be yanking my chain."

"I wish he was," I said.

I knew Zac must be getting used to me dropping these paranormal bombshells, because instead of debating further he just looked directly at Alex. "Well, at least that explains how you got here."

"I thought so too," Alex said, sounding mildly offended. "Then I realised that a necromancer does not raise the dead out of generosity, to let them walk free. Rather, he uses black magic to bind spirits to his control, like dogs on a leash. Rest assured, I am not on a leash."

"How else do you explain your being here?" Zac asked.

Alex offered a small smile. "I cannot pretend to explain it. Perhaps the afterlife returned me so Chloe and I could be together again."

Was he deliberately taunting Zac by mentioning our shared history?

When I saw Zac's glare, I jumped in as conciliator again. "There's only one way to get to the bottom of this and that's if the three of us work together," I said firmly. "We're the only ones who know what's really going on."

"What do you suggest we do?" Zac asked.

"We have to find the necromancer."

"That could be anyone."

"Not exactly," Alex said. "We are talking about a dark and ancient art; it takes many decades to perfect it. This person is old, although they may not appear so. And if they have raised Isobel, there must be a reason."

"Any ideas?" Zac asked.

"I cannot say for sure."

"Well, that's helpful," Zac muttered.

Alex looked at him with raised eyebrows. "If you have a theory to offer, please be my guest."

"This is your territory, dude. You have more in common with *them* than us."

I didn't like what Zac was implying. Turning Alex into the enemy wasn't just ridiculous, it was a digression we couldn't afford.

"What are you suggesting?" Alex replied. He straightened his shoulders, lifted his chin and looked like he was about to challenge Zac to a duel.

"I'm not suggesting anything. I'm *saying* you're one of them so why should we trust you?"

"Stop it! Both of you," I said. "This isn't helping."

They both looked sheepish for a moment before returning to staring each other down. I decided I needed to come clean, get everything out in the open.

"There's one more thing you should know."

That got their attention. They both turned to me, waiting for me to go on.

I looked at Alex. "It's about Becky Burns."

A surprised look crossed his face. "How do you know that name?"

"She's been visiting my dreams," I answered. "Or I've been visiting hers — it's hard to tell. All I know is, I'm reliving her memories in visions or when I'm asleep."

"Are you sure it is not your imagination?"

"You tell me," I said, and repeated the advice he'd given Becky that day in the library: "*When all else fails, knowledge is the only thing we can rely on. Seek it out at all costs and never be ashamed to do so.*"

Alex stared at me, dumbfounded.

"Straight after she asked you what ornithology was," I said. "Isn't that how it happened?"

"Word for word," he said softly. "How very strange you should have seen that. How often do you have these episodes?"

"Whenever this is close by." I withdrew the moonstone brooch from my pocket and handed it to Alex.

His frown deepened as he held it up to the light. I could tell from his eyes that it wasn't the first time he'd seen it.

"Where did you get this?" he asked.

"Grandma Fee sent it to me. It used to belong to Becky."

"No," he said adamantly. "This belonged to Isobel."

"Hold up, I'm getting confused here," Zac said. "Becky ... Isobel ... who are these women?"

"Ghosts of the past," Alex murmured. He handed the brooch back to me, as if it held memories too painful to recall.

"Who, for whatever reason, refuse to stay in the past," I added.

"Becky was a sweet, devoted girl. I wonder how this item came into her possession."

"Oh, she's already shown me that," I said. "Isobel gave it to her."

"A bribe?" Alex murmured.

"No doubt." I really didn't want to go there.

"The brooch allows you to access her memories," he continued. "I have heard of objects imbued with such powers."

"But why is she sharing them with me?" I asked. "They're like random pieces of a puzzle."

"The staff at Grange Hall saw much and said little. Perhaps there is something Becky wants you to know. Or perhaps she wants to put her own mind at rest. Have you seen anything out of the ordinary yet?"

"Did anything happen at Grange Hall that wasn't out of the ordinary?"

Alex gave an enigmatic smile. "Tell me what you have learned so far."

"Well, I know her father was a drunk and that her mom had a tough time, but I don't think that's relevant to our situation." I mentally shuffled through the dreams. "Like everyone else, she steered clear of Carter, but she liked you a lot and appreciated the interest you took in her."

"That's not much to go on."

"Maybe there's more to come. Maybe she'll show me something important soon."

"I hope so," said Alex. "In the meantime we keep looking."

I groaned and sat down on the edge of the stage. "We can't just wait around for me to have more dreams. Isobel is here *now*. People are in danger *now*. If only there was some way I could talk to Becky directly."

Alex rubbed his chin and grew thoughtful for a moment, and then I saw his eyes light up and the corners of his mouth crinkle into a smile.

"Perhaps there is."

"Absolutely not," Zac said after Alex had outlined his proposal. "It's completely out of the question."

"It may be the only option we have," I countered.

"Have you gone insane? I am not helping you guys summon a dead girl!"

"She's really quite friendly," Alex said.

Zac rolled his eyes. "That's good to know."

I could see that he was struggling to keep it together. Not only had he just witnessed the death of his friend, he was now being asked to help us access the afterlife for answers.

"Don't you think we've got enough ghosts running amok here?" he said. "We should be trying to expel the ones we have, not adding to them!"

"A seance will not bring Becky's spirit into this world," Alex explained calmly. "It will simply allow us to communicate with her. She has already made contact, so perhaps there are other things she wants Chloe to know."

"It's okay," I told Zac. "If you want to go, I completely understand. This isn't your fight."

He shifted uncomfortably. I knew he wasn't weak or faint-hearted; he just wasn't sure how much more of this he could handle.

"But first, consider that you are already talking to the dead," Alex added.

Zac looked surprised for a second, as if he'd forgotten Alex was a ghost. I didn't blame him; Alex seemed so real these days.

"So where are we doing this?" Zac tried to sound stoic, but the little quaver in his voice gave him away. "Here might be a tad exposed."

"We can't go to my place," I said. "My dad and brother will be home by now."

Zac squeezed his eyes shut like he couldn't believe what he was about to suggest. "I suppose we could go to mine. But I don't have one of those ouija boards or anything."

"That will not be necessary," Alex said. "A black scrying mirror will suffice."

"I didn't see one of those lying around either last time I checked." Zac was using humour to stay calm, but the colour had drained from his face.

"That is easily rectified. They are simple enough to fashion."

"Great," I said. "But what exactly is a scrying mirror? How does it work?"

"Scrying is an ancient art by which one gazes into a reflective surface in the hope of communing with the dead. A scrying mirror is sometimes called a black mirror or magic mirror — all rely on the same concept. It is believed that when one clears one's mind, the surface of the mirror will become fluid, opening a door between the living and the dead."

"So how do we make one?" I asked.

"We must paint a small sheet of glass black."

"You mean like the glass in a picture frame?"

"Precisely."

"Okay," Zac said, resolved now to see this through. "What are we waiting for?"

We took a short detour to the art department's supply room and made off with a can of quick-drying black spraypaint. Zac assured us he had plenty of picture frames back at his place that we could use.

As we walked to his car, I noticed that he and Alex positioned themselves on either side of me. I knew it was partly because they were being protective, but also because they wanted to put some distance between each other. It was going to be one awkward drive to Malibu if they kept this up. Where was I supposed to sit? In the back with Alex or in front with Zac?

Don't be an idiot, I upbraided myself. *Seating arrangements are the least of your concerns.*

When we arrived at the Greens' residence, Alex seemed intrigued by the modern glass and metal structure.

"This is your home?" he asked.

"That's right." Zac tossed me the key to the pool house while he headed for the main building.

"Designs have changed over the years," I told Alex.

"Change is not always a good thing," he muttered under his breath.

"Anything else we need other than the frame?" Zac called back.

"Could you please bring a clean cloth, some vinegar, water and a newspaper?" Alex replied.

"Done."

Zac disappeared, and Alex and I went to wait in the pool house. I could tell he was uncomfortable in Zac's space. He regarded every high-tech appliance, from the coffee-maker to the air purifier to the flatscreen on the wall, with suspicion.

Maybe he and Zac would never be friends, but I just needed them to get along for the next few hours.

"I know you and Zac got off on the wrong foot," I said finally, "but he's a really good guy. If you give him a chance, I think you might actually like him."

"It is clear that you do," he replied.

"What do you mean by that? You must know there's nothing going on between Zac and me."

"That is reassuring. Do you often spend the night here?"

I followed his line of vision to the sofa bed, where my pyjamas were neatly folded on the pillow. I'd worn the same pair at Grange Hall and Alex had clearly recognised them. To me, the sight confirmed that Zac and I had slept in separate beds, but Alex obviously had different ideas rattling around in his head.

"I've spent a couple of nights here," I admitted. "I fought with my dad. He has this new girlfriend and I needed a friend to talk to." *And you were nowhere to be found*, I wanted to add, but bit my tongue.

"Friendship between men and women is not possible," Alex announced.

"Of course it is! This isn't the Middle Ages."

"One party will always entertain feelings of a more romantic nature."

"So you're saying no man and woman in the history of the world have ever been able to sustain a friendship?"

He sighed like I was a naive child. "I am sure there are exceptions."

"Like you and Becky," I pressed. "You were friends, right?"

"Becky was a servant and barely fifteen. I believe she may have harboured a girlish infatuation for me, but we were not friends. Such a relationship would have been impossible."

I scowled, but before we could continue what was fast turning into our first ever disagreement, Zac walked in with an armful of supplies.

"Let's get down to business," he said, dumping the lot on the coffee table.

Alex knelt and began sorting through the picture frames, discarding anything that looked too sleek or modern. "This will do nicely," he said, choosing a medium-sized round frame with embellished silver edges that looked a little tarnished. It contained a photograph of Zac's parents in their younger, happier days.

We followed him outside, where he laid several sheets of newspaper on the grass. Then he removed the pane of glass from the frame, careful not to tear the picture, which he handed to Zac for safekeeping. Using the cloth, he rubbed the glass down with vinegar, then water, making sure to erase every smudge and fingerprint.

When he was satisfied, he laid the glass on the newspaper and picked up the can of spraypaint. After puzzling over it for a moment, he passed it to me. "Chloe, would you mind?"

I took the can and, as instructed, sprayed three coats of paint over the glass until it was completely blacked out. While we waited for it to dry, my attention was drawn to the frame.

"Zac," I asked, "how likely is it that your parents will notice this missing?"

"Seeing as I found it in a closet, I'd say not very."

Without knowing why but feeling compelled in some way, I pulled off an earring and used the pin to etch a border of tiny stars and moons around the frame. I quickly discovered the silver wasn't solid, only paint that scratched away.

"What are you doing?" Zac asked curiously.

"I'm not sure yet."

When the paint had dried, Alex slid the glass back into the now-decorated frame. The black looked eerie, like the frame was empty and you could pass your hand right through it.

Zac led us back inside, where he shut the doors and rolled down his blackout blinds.

"How did you know we need darkness?" Alex asked.

"I didn't," Zac replied. "I just don't want my mom to see us and think I've joined some kind of cult."

"Do you have candles?"

"Yeah, in the bathroom. I'll grab them."

He returned with several scented candles in glass jars, which Alex lit and arranged in a half-circle on the coffee table. He then set the black mirror in the centre and we gathered on our knees around it. It was unnervingly quiet. On my left, I was aware of the rise and fall of Zac's breathing and the faint rush of waves in the distance.

On my right, Alex's attention was completely focused.

"Look into the mirror as if you are gazing into water," he instructed in a hypnotic voice. "Imagine what lies beneath the surface until it begins to ripple. But remember, it is vital that you do not look upon your own reflection. If tempted, you may look from a side angle."

"Why can't we look at our own reflections?" Zac asked in a nervous whisper.

"To do so may cause your soul to become trapped in the mirror. If that were to happen, I would not know how to free you."

"Well, that doesn't sound risky at all."

Alex ignored him and turned to me, candlelight dancing across his perfectly composed features.

"Chloe, are you ready to meet Rebecca Burns?"

CHAPTER SIXTEEN

Ready was the last thing I felt. All of a sudden what we were about to do seemed very dangerous. I'd attempted something similar once before, at Grange Hall, but then I'd been with Mavis and May, paranormal experts who'd guided me safely through it. I wasn't sure Alex knew what he was dealing with. On the other hand there didn't seem to be another choice.

I leaned closer to the mirror and it seemed to pull me in, as if it wanted to check me out before revealing its inky magic. It was hard to believe that putting a few everyday items together could have produced something with such power. The silence in the room filled with anticipation, but nothing appeared in the mirror. Something told me we needed to break through a final barrier to coax it to divulge its secrets.

Words spilled from my mouth without me realising what I was saying. To be honest, it didn't feel like it was even me speaking. I was a conduit, controlled by an unseen entity. I should have felt afraid, but I didn't. Somehow I knew this entity was a guide, taking the place of Mavis and May, so instead of trying to expel it, I welcomed it in.

"I consecrate this mirror in the name of the Sun and the Moon and the stars."

"Excuse me?" Zac's voice was surprised and very far away. All that existed now was the mirror and me.

"I banish all evil energies. I invoke the Ancient Ones to speak to us now. What secret knowledge you possess, I command you to divulge it now." My guide told me the words must be uttered three times and I complied, with extra emphasis on the last: "I command you to divulge it *now!*"

We all held our breath, waiting for a response. At first nothing happened. But then, as I gazed into the black, a swirl of grey appeared, like a tiny feather on the surface of a still pool.

My body began to loosen and relax and a strange sinking sensation came over me. Then, to my amazement, small explosions of colour burst across the glass before falling away like chalk dust. Faster and faster they came, until they were colliding with one another, streaking across the mirror like a private display of fireworks.

Could the others see them? I wanted to ask but didn't dare speak in case it interfered with the magic.

Then, as suddenly as they'd appeared, the colours vanished, leaving what looked like a yawning black space. Ever so slowly an image began to fill it. It appeared to be some sort of photograph or painting, but as it took shape I saw that it was neither. It was a face. The face of Rebecca Burns, staring at us.

I sensed Zac's body jolt as he drew in a sharp breath. That meant he could see her too. I didn't have to wonder if Alex could. We were making contact with his own kind.

"Do not avert your gaze," Alex warned me, before his voice turned gentle. "Becky, do you remember me?"

She blinked as she examined him. She seemed so young with her upturned nose, smattering of freckles and tumble of curls, yet there was unmistakable sadness in her eyes. As she stared at Alex, a look of recognition dawned on her face. She nodded and her colourless lips stretched into a wan smile.

"It is good to see you again," Alex said, then his expression clouded. "But you are so young. What happened to you, Becky? You should have lived a long life."

Becky didn't answer, but her eyes filled with tears.

"You cannot speak, can you?"

She looked around her temporary cage and shrugged unhappily.

Alex bowed his head. "I am sorry for you."

Upon seeing his grief, the ghost reached out a hand. To my shock, her pale fingers came right through the glass. As they stretched toward us, the blackness stretched with them like elastic.

"Ugh!" I gasped and the hand recoiled as if it had been stung. Becky looked offended.

"I'm sorry. You just startled me," I said, my heart still pounding. "Do you know who I am?"

She tilted her head. I could tell she recognised me from somewhere, but it was eluding her. She looked to Alex for guidance.

"Listen, Becky," he said, "we have summoned you here because we need your help. It is about Mrs Reade ... about Isobel. She has come back, you see."

Becky's eyes widened.

"Something or someone has brought her back," Alex continued, "and she is very dangerous. We need to know if you remember anything, even the smallest detail, that might help us."

Becky glanced over her shoulder with an alarmed look.

"She cannot hurt you, Becky," Alex said. "I promise you. Now tell me, do you know anything?"

Becky didn't look all that convinced, but she gave an almost imperceptible nod.

"If you cannot tell us, can you show us?" Alex asked.

Becky's gaze shifted to me and our eyes locked. She looked at me inquiringly and I gave her a small smile of permission. I knew what was going to happen, but there was no time to warn Alex and Zac. My body slumped and I felt Alex's arms catch me before the physical world ebbed away.

I wake to the sound of birdsong on this glowing September morning. Sunlight streams into the attic and I dress in a puddle of light, relishing its warmth on my skin. From the window I see a grand carriage waiting by the front entrance. Are we expecting visitors? Mrs Baxter did not mention any and she is usually so rigorous about informing us of changes to the daily routine.

I hurry downstairs to find a small party assembled in the foyer around Mrs Reade. Her glossy mahogany tresses are pinned back today and she wears a feathered hat and a sumptuous velvet riding cloak. As I approach, she throws a cursory glance in my direction, but I am not engaging enough to hold her attention. She looks away, bored, and I feel myself blush beet red. How plain she must think me. Plain as dry toast. I feel suddenly ashamed that I was born to be so ordinary.

"Ah, Becky, here you are!" Mrs Baxter declares. She steers me aside, speaking quickly under her breath. "Now listen carefully, I have an important task for you today. The mistress is making

a trip into town and she cannot go alone. Ordinarily I would accompany her, but we have just received word that the master will be returning and bringing guests so there are preparations to be made. So you are to go in my place."

My duties have never extended beyond the house till now and my face reflects my alarm. "Me?"

"It's an honour, girl, not a punishment! You only need follow the mistress and do as she asks. Now come here, you cannot go out into the world like that."

She whips off my apron, adjusts my cap and hastily wraps a cloak around my shoulders before bidding me to follow Mrs Reade to the carriage. I wipe my palms on my cloak feeling terribly anxious. I have never ridden in a carriage before and I do not know the proper etiquette. Do I sit next to or across from the lady of the house? Or was my place outside with the driver? There is no time to ask Mrs Baxter so I must hope not to make a fool of myself in front of my employer.

Once the mistress is comfortably ensconced, I am bundled into the carriage opposite her. Before I can so much as look out the window, I hear the crack of the driver's whip and we are away, rattling down the driveway. We travel in silence and I keep my gaze fixed on my lap. I dare not look directly at Mrs Reade lest I unintentionally offend her, which would be easily done in her current brittle mood.

"How old are you, child?"

The sound of her voice makes me jump and I look up to find her watching me with eyes the colour of woodland sunshine. I marvel at the way they seem to absorb everything yet reveal nothing. I have never been in such close quarters with her before and she hardly seems real. I feel as though I am gazing at a life-sized porcelain doll with immobile features except for her big searching eyes.

"I shall be fifteen come Candlemas," I answer.

"Will you really?" she exclaims with genuine curiosity. "I would have put your age much younger."

I am bothered by her implication that I look and behave like a child, but as I have no clever response to offer I fall silent. Mrs Reade rests her head against the window to watch the lush green fields roll by.

"I wonder sometimes about the life of a housemaid," she says. "It cannot have anything to recommend it."

"I don't know what you mean, madam," I say with some confusion.

"I simply cannot imagine it," she continues. "It is a wonder you can get out of bed in the morning."

"I am very grateful to have my position," I say quickly, in case she thinks otherwise.

"Well, I should never survive it."

"We accept the lot we are given," I say meekly.

Mrs Reade's glittering eyes regard me challengingly. "Not always," she murmurs, adding after a considered pause, "I believe we are masters of our own destiny."

The carriage takes us past the village, rattling along cobbled streets. It is still early so there are not many people about. Smoke curls from the chimney of the bakery and I know Mrs Mills and her three sons will have been up for hours. We pass the butcher and the haberdashery and the sweet shop but show no signs of slowing down. On the open road, we journey until the fortified walls of a large town come into view. The air has a briny tang and I wonder whether we are close to the sea.

I have never ventured beyond the confines of our village and I crane my neck, eager not to miss a thing. We drive along broad roads filled with other carriages and pass the smoking chimneys of

209

what must be factories. My eyes widen to see a horse-drawn bus full of common folk going about their daily business. Wistings has but a smattering of shops, but here the street is crammed with shopfronts advertising all manner of items from furnishings to ornaments. It would be easy to lose hours just perusing the windows.

There is so much to take in I feel dizzy. Even though I find it fascinating, I can also see this place is dirty and congested. Little wonder people die of epidemics in towns like this, all crammed in together.

We leave the main street behind and the carriage turns into a narrow alleyway. The shopfronts here are shadowy and marked by tarnished brass signs hanging over dusty doorways. The brick walls seem to close in on us, blocking out the light. I peer out the window with some trepidation while Mrs Reade reclines in her seat, calm as ever. Right at the end of the alleyway, set deep into a corner, is a small shop with a sign that reads Apothecary. This is where the carriage stops and the mistress alights.

Is she ill, I wonder. She seems to me the picture of health.

"Wait here," she instructs. "I shall not be long."

The shop's lintel is so low that Mrs Reade has to stoop a little to walk beneath it. The building looks as if it dates back to medieval times, and I see that the window is sagging on one side. Through it I spy a set of scales and various jars holding dried herbs. There is an old telescope and a globe and other implements I cannot identify. It is a place full of secrets for those who dare inquire.

Minutes pass and I begin to feel conspicuous sitting in this gleaming carriage. I sense eyes watching me from dark recesses, even though the alleyway is mostly deserted. A few harried-looking folk pass by, but they keep their heads down as if they wish not to be recognised. When the desperate eyes of a street urchin lock with mine I retreat out of sight. I hope the mistress does not keep us lingering here much longer. There is no telling what shady characters we might encounter.

I wait for what seems close to an hour, growing more and more concerned. It seems peculiar that the mistress has been gone so long. Could she be in need of assistance?

I wish I could ask Mrs Baxter the proper thing to do, but without her guidance I shall have to decide for myself. After some wavering, I step out of the carriage.

The driver frowns at me. "Where you off to, girly?" he growls, rubbing the whiskers on his chin.

"I am going to check on my mistress," I reply. "She has been gone a while now."

He brays like a donkey. "Nay, I wouldn't do that. She won't thank you for it."

"But it is growing late and I don't like this place."

"Mrs Reade's business is her own. Don't go sticking yer nose where it's not wanted."

Ignoring his advice, I approach the dingy doorway and turn the knob as quietly as I can. There doesn't seem to be anybody about so I grow bold enough to slip inside. The air is heavier here and smells of a combination of licorice and aromatic oils. Every wall is lined with hundreds of glass bottles, each seeming to contain a different potion or remedy. On the counter is a dusty ledger and bowls of strange, smoking herbs.

Upon hearing muted voices I instinctively shrink into a corner, only to realise they are coming from a small slanted room at the back of the shop. From my hiding place behind a shelf laden with assorted vials, I see Mrs Reade seated opposite a man, who is stooped in his chair with his back to me. All I can discern is his long silver hair tied with a black ribbon.

He chuckles affectionately. "Honestly, my dear, what would you do without me?"

"Luckily, I shall never have to find out," the mistress replies with a smile that would melt butter.

"We are in agreement then?"

"Undoubtedly."

"Excellent." He leans toward her and rubs his palms together. "I shall prepare the draught for you and you must take it three times daily. I must warn you, it is not very palatable."

"No matter," the mistress replies. "You must know by now that I am not such a delicate creature."

"I never underestimate you, my dear. You have the body of a woman but the spirit of a warrior. Now, did you bring what I asked for?"

"I did, although it was not easy." She reaches into her cloak and removes a drawstring pouch, which she dangles tantalisingly in front of him.

"Nothing worth having is easy," he scolds gently. "Besides, the ritual cannot be completed without it."

He takes the pouch from her hands and withdraws a glass vial partially filled with a ruby liquid. It is unmistakably blood and my stomach twists at the sight.

"It is all I could get without exposing myself," Mrs Reade says. "I told Carter I wanted to shave him and the fool was so drunk he didn't even flinch when my hand accidentally slipped. Will it do?"

The man removes the stopper and inhales deeply. "Oh, yes, it is more than ample. It only takes a single drop to complete the binding spell."

I know these words are not meant for my ears and yet I cannot tear myself away. I also know that if I am caught the punishment will be most severe.

Mrs Reade leans in close to the man, practically purring with satisfaction. "And how potent would the spell be if we were to use ten or even twenty drops?"

Her accomplice throws his head back gleefully and gives a throaty chuckle. "You are my girl! I would say it cannot fail. We make quite a team, do we not, Isobel?"

Mrs Reade's eyes light up and she leans forward and takes the man's gnarly hand between hers. Although I have yet to see his face, his hand seems disproportionately aged compared to his silken voice. "Indeed we do." She brings the hand to her lips and kisses it. "Father, how I have missed you."

While I'm still in the vision something changes. The images blur and shift and suddenly I'm not in the dusty shop any more. Becky's memories merge and I find myself suddenly back at Grange Hall, looking on the scene I most hoped to avoid. It's almost like Becky's in a hurry to show me everything now, whether I'm ready or not.

The gunshot wakes the entire household and I am sure I feel the floor shake. I race downstairs to find Cook and Mrs Baxter huddled outside the drawing room door. Mrs Baxter is still in her nightgown, silver hair braided down her back. All her bravado is gone and she looks vulnerable. She holds a candle in one hand, illuminating her face, which is paler than I have ever seen it. The door is ajar and through it I see servants huddled around a shape on the floor. A pair of hands wrings out a rag drenched in blood and I know who has been hurt before anyone tells me.

"There has been a horrible accident," Mrs Baxter cries. "Mr Alexander has been shot!"

Even though I am prepared, hearing it out aloud is like being impaled with a spear.

"Can you think of anything more awful?" she continues. "And it was the master himself who pulled the trigger, in a drunken fit! Now he has run off in a terrible state. Have you seen the mistress?"

I shake my head, barely registering her question.

"Find her," she instructs before dashing off to manage the chaos that has descended over the house.

I freeze when I see Mrs Reade at the top of the stairs, her hair unpinned and her eyes wide with terror. She is clutching a bundle in her arms and moving in circles, like someone without sight. She notices me and comes to life, flying down the stairs, muttering feverishly about fetching a doctor and her baby not breathing.

I am not accustomed to seeing the mistress of Grange Hall looking so panicked and I don't know how to react. Instinctively, I reach out to check the babe, but as soon as I do she jealously clutches him closer to her and pushes past me. Fearing for her safety, I grab a cloak and follow her through the kitchen into the night.

As I blunder through the moonlit grounds, I do not realise I am crying. I cannot believe what I have just heard. Why did I decide to go to bed when I heard the master return home? Why did I not warn Mr Alexander? The idea that I could have prevented this heinous act causes me to collapse to my knees and cover my face with my hands.

But it is too late to act now and I get up again and stumble on. As the lake comes into view, the first fat raindrops begin to fall, turning the ground to mud.

The lake has always been one of my favourite places at Grange Hall. But tonight its dark water looks like glass, reflecting distorted images of trees and sky, and there is something foul in the air. The nearby woods seem too dark, the lake's waters too deep.

I am gripped by memories of all the times I have seen Mr Alexander working at his easel on these grassy banks. I think of the portrait he painted of Mrs Reade, which now hangs in the upstairs gallery. It captures her spirit exactly, and when it was unveiled I thought it the highest form of flattery to be immortalised in such a way. Now its creator lies bleeding on the drawing room floor.

At the lakeside I come to an abrupt halt. Is there something in the water? What could it be? It seems too large for an animal. I draw closer to see the shape in more detail. That looks like lace. Has someone thrown a gown into the water, where it billows a little like the parachutes I've seen in books.

I am utterly perplexed for a moment, until I see the white hands and the hair streaming like seaweed, darker than the water. I swallow back a scream. The body of a woman in a waterlogged nightdress lies face down in the reeds, her head bumping gently against the shore. I can tell from the way her arms float limply in the water that she is already dead. It cannot be the mistress of the house, I refuse to believe it. Yet who else could it be?

Chilled to my very core and with a hammering heart, I edge closer, but stop short as a figure emerges from the trees. He is hooded and facing away from me, but in the moonlight I can see he is dressed in a dark frockcoat and wearing gloves.

Without hesitation, he wades into the water and gently turns the body to lie face up. My hand flies up to muffle my cry. It is the mistress! Poor Mrs Reade looks as cold as clay and I wonder how long she has been floating in her murky grave. And where is baby James?

I watch as the strange man bends over her, slipping an arm under her neck. With some effort, he manages to lift her into his arms. Water streams from her hair and nightdress, but the man seems not to notice. His posture does not suggest grief. Rather, it is commanding and full of concentration.

"Have no fear, my darling," he says tenderly. "You have not left us for long."

I freeze. It is the same unmistakable voice from the apothecary, where that strange transaction occurred. This man is Mrs Reade's father and her accomplice in something wicked.

He carries her body back toward the dense trees. Where is he taking her? Should I call out or attempt to stop him? But I am too paralysed by fear to act.

Before he disappears from view, I catch a glimpse of his face framed by that long silvery hair. He is handsome for his age, but there is something menacing in his features. Perhaps it is the pallor of his skin. Or the way I imagine his mouth curling between a smile and a sneer.

I opened my eyes to find myself lying under a duvet on Zac's sofa. Zac and Alex were leaning over me. On the coffee table behind them the candles were still burning, but I noticed the black scrying mirror we'd made had shattered.

"Thank God." Alex let out a sigh of relief. "You scared the life out of me."

"You sure you don't want to rephrase that?" Zac asked, although this time I could tell the barb was light-hearted. Despite that, he looked haggard. The strain of the past few hours was really starting to show.

When I tried to sit up, my head felt cottonwool cloudy. I was exhausted, like I'd just run a marathon.

"How long was I out?"

"Not that long, but it was pretty scary," Zac said.

"How do you feel?" Alex took my hand. "Are you able to tell us what you saw?"

"Well," I started and heard my voice come out shaky. "It turns out Becky knew exactly what to show me. Can I get some water, please?"

"Of course." Zac darted into the kitchen and returned with a bottle.

I downed half of it before going on. I was still trying to digest what I'd seen. It had stupefied me.

"I know who the necromancer is," I said, and felt Alex's hand tighten around mine. "Becky saw Isobel's body floating in the lake at Grange Hall, but someone got to her first. A man showed up and stole her away. I heard him speak to her, even though she was dead. He said she wouldn't be gone for long."

"Who was he?"

"You'll never believe it. I can hardly believe it myself. I mean, it doesn't seem possible."

Alex knelt beside me, his brilliant blue eyes shining. "Who was the man you saw with Isobel's body?"

I had the feeling he was anticipating my answer. Maybe he'd known all along and just needed confirmation. There was no way to soften the blow. I let out a long breath and gave a small shudder of disbelief.

"It was Doctor Ritter."

CHAPTER SEVENTEEN

I knew Alex well enough to read his face and right now it showed me his fears had just been confirmed. Zac, on the other hand, looked like he'd finally been given sufficient evidence to declare me officially crazy.

"Doctor Ritter?" he repeated, looking at me as though I might have concussion. "As in the French sub teacher?"

I knew how absurd it must sound to him because I was struggling to believe it myself. But I knew in my heart that Becky's memories were genuine. Everything had happened exactly the way I'd seen it. There was no reason for her to mislead us.

"I don't understand it either," I said. "But he was right there in Becky's memories and he looked exactly the way he does today. I'm just telling you what she showed me."

"Becky continues to be a loyal friend," Alex added. "She has tried to help us the only way she knows how: through sharing her memories with you."

"But how could a man who lived over a hundred and fifty years ago be walking around Sycamore High today?" Zac asked.

Alex threw him a look and Zac realised his mistake.

"No offence, Alex." Then he turned back to me. "Are you saying Doctor Ritter is a ghost?"

"No, I'm saying he's very much alive, and he's trying to bring Isobel back to life too."

I was a little embarrassed that I hadn't realised this earlier. I'd sensed something fishy about Doctor Ritter the moment I'd first laid eyes on him and my instincts had been right. You only had to look at his face to know something was wrong. His features were always composed, like a clay mask, and his skin was stretched tight. He didn't really look human because he wasn't; he was a walking, talking cadaver that should have been fertilising daffodils many decades ago. Now he'd found his way into our school under the guise of helping out, when in fact he'd probably orchestrated Madame Giles's accident in the first place to get himself hired. The thought made me furious.

"But how does someone manage to cheat death?" Zac asked.

I could see he wasn't dealing well with this new information. It was one thing to accept ghosts were real, but now we were talking about one of the teachers at our school having somehow made himself immortal.

"I don't know," I said. "But the first time Becky saw him, she overheard a conversation between him and Isobel in an apothecary shop. He was planning to make some kind of potion using human blood. He must have found a way to prolong life."

Zac shook his head. "That's one messed-up dude! This kind of stuff only happens in movies."

"Everything you have told us makes sense, Chloe," Alex said slowly — I could almost see the cogs turning in his head — "but it still leaves one significant question. What reason could Doctor Ritter have for bringing Isobel back? Did they have some kind of pact?"

"That's where it gets really weird. Before she left, she called him Father."

Alex looked surprised. "Are you sure? Isobel's father died shortly before she and my brother married."

"Maybe that's what she told everyone, but at this point I'd assume everything you knew about her was a lie."

"That does not surprise me," Alex said. I'd never seen him look so sad. "I have a very bad feeling about all this."

"Great," Zac muttered. "When even the ghosts are worried, you know something bad is about to go down. So what now?"

"What can we do?" I said. "It's not like we can barge into school and take out the French teacher."

"No, but we can't just sit around waiting for him to execute whatever twisted plan he has in store either," Zac argued. "He's not raising the dead for no reason."

"Indeed he is not," Alex replied. "Whatever his intent it will be up to us to intervene. You two should try and get some rest so we can deal with whatever tomorrow brings."

Alex's words struck a chord. We really had no idea what might happen next. Up until now I had taken comfort in the knowledge that the dead were confined by certain limitations that separated our two worlds. But now it seemed all restrictions had been lifted and the dead had free rein. They could show up at any time in any place with powers we couldn't even begin to understand. How could you fight an enemy like that? I sure hoped Alex was working on a plan because I felt totally unprepared.

It was this feeling that prompted me to finally go home. I didn't feel right leaving my father and brother unprotected with monsters like Isobel and Doctor Ritter on the loose. I didn't know what they had in store for us, but past experience told me Isobel would always strike for the heart, and in this case that would be my family.

I was glad of Alex's offer to accompany me home, especially in light of the disturbing new revelations. I drove as fast as I could along the winding Malibu coastline, cursing the traffic. Ahead the sun was melting into the horizon, creating a mirror effect on the surface of the ocean.

"It is strange how reality can prove so different from fantasy," Alex said. "This is not at all how I imagined our reunion."

"How did you imagine it?" I asked, feeling a rush of pleasure at the word *reunion*.

"I thought it would be full of happiness, not despair and chaos. And never did I imagine Isobel would have any further part to play."

"She's hard to shake," I agreed. "Deceased ex-lovers who refuse to move on do have a way of putting a damper on things."

Alex looked shocked for a moment and then he began to laugh. It was a crazy and contagious sound that quickly got me laughing too. It felt good, even if it was only a temporary distraction from whatever calamity lay around the next corner. At the very least it reminded me that I wasn't facing this battle alone. I had to believe we could come through it, that light would find its way through the darkness. We just had to stand firm and not lose heart.

It was about six thirty by the time we pulled into my driveway. It felt like I'd been away a lifetime instead of a couple of days. I was relieved to see my dad's car parked in the driveway, although my mind wouldn't rest until I saw him and Rory for myself.

"I shall wait here," Alex said. "I expect you will want to see your family alone. But fetch me at the first sign of anything amiss."

"Thanks," I said. "Just give me half an hour."

I felt nervous as I headed inside, worried I might find the place trashed or empty. But as I pushed open the front door, I heard the kettle whistling and the television chirping just like normal.

"Hello?" I called, not wanting to startle anyone by barging in. But there was no response.

I walked into the kitchen to find the kettle trilling away on the stove with no one there to answer its call. Feeling my throat grow a little tighter, I poked my head into the den. Cartoons played to an empty sofa.

"Rory?" My heart began to turn somersaults in my chest. I ran upstairs, feet thudding against the carpeted steps. "Rory? Are you home?"

I burst into his bedroom and immediately heaved a sigh of relief. My little brother looked up in surprise from his desk where he was plugged into headphones and engrossed in a computer game.

"Chloe!" He leapt up and flew at me, wrapping his skinny arms around my waist. "You're back!"

"Hey, kiddo. Is everything okay here?"

"Sure, but it's better when you're here. You are staying?"

"Yeah, I'm staying. Hey, what are you all dressed up for?" I asked, realising his hair was neatly combed and he'd put on a clean button-down shirt.

"Have you forgotten the school play opens tonight? Aren't you going?"

"Tonight?" I couldn't believe how time had flown. It seemed like only hours ago I'd found Alex hiding in the shadows of the theatre. "Wait, you're going to sit through *Macbeth*?"

Rory sighed. "Mrs Hudson says we have to be there to have a cultural experience. Even Dad and Marcie are going."

"Who's Marcie?"

"Dad's girlfriend. She's not so bad, Chloe. She helped me with my math homework last night."

"That's nice," I said. I didn't want to get into a discussion with Rory about our father's changed relationship status.

"Hey, are there any cool explosions in *Macbeth*?" he asked.

"Afraid not."

"How about sharks or crocodiles?"

"Sorry. But there are witches, murders, a scary ghost and a few bloody battles."

Rory perked up. "That doesn't sound too bad." He looked past me at the door. "Dad, look who's back!"

I turned to find my father standing there. He looked more haggard than I remembered and the lines around his eyes seemed deeper. Was the waistband of his pants a little looser too?

"Hey," I said, raising my hand in an awkward half-wave.

"Hey, Chloe," he said. "I've been worried about you. Are you alright? I phoned Sam and Natalie, but they said they hadn't heard anything. Maybe next time you could send a text letting me know where you are?"

"I'm fine. I've been staying with a friend in Malibu. I guess I just needed some time to cool down, y'know?"

"I figured," he said softly, staring at his shoes. "And I understand."

"Look, Dad," I began falteringly. "There's something I want to say to you."

He lifted his head and I caught a flash of hope in his eyes. Maybe Zac's analysis had been spot-on after all. Maybe I'd been too harsh on my father. Even though Mom had barely been gone six months, everybody grieved differently, right? Maybe he was just trying to comfort himself in his own strange way.

"I'm sorry I took off like that. I wasn't thinking clearly and I didn't mean to stress you out."

"That's okay," he said. "You were right — I should have been spending more time at home. You guys are my number one priority. I hope you know that."

I touched him lightly on the arm. "You deserve to be happy. And don't worry about me because ... I get it now."

I promised Rory and Dad I'd meet them at the theatre later, then hurried back to my car where Alex was still waiting.

"That was fast," he said.

"It looks like we're going back to school," I told him, jumping behind the wheel. "*Macbeth* opens tonight and the staff usually attend, so maybe Doctor Ritter will be there."

"And if he is?"

I turned the key in the ignition and paused. "Okay, I haven't thought that far ahead. But we have to check it out, maybe confront him. I'd better text Zac and tell him to get down there."

"If you think he will be of use."

"Don't be like that. We need all hands on deck here."

As I turned to fish my phone from the back seat where I'd tossed it, every muscle in my body stiffened. Isobel stood boldly in the middle of the road, illuminated by a streetlamp. She was barefoot, with black hair falling all the way down to her waist. Her nightgown was in tatters and her skin was as colourless as ice against the night.

There was something different about her. At first I struggled to put my finger on it, then it dawned on me. Isobel looked strangely solid standing there. Every other time I'd been unlucky enough to see her, she'd been a diaphanous form, faded at the edges or flickering unnaturally, a shadow or a phantom in the mirror. But tonight her every limb looked as sturdy as marble. Could this mean the necromancer had succeeded? Was Isobel now flesh and blood, like Alex?

Our eyes met and she smiled her demented smile. She seemed to be issuing me a challenge: *Which of us will get there first?* I knew then beyond a shadow of doubt that Sycamore High and its entire community were under direct threat. There was no need to puzzle over what had been brewing this last week because we were about to find out.

A sleek black limo with tinted windows purred up beside her and the passenger door flew open. Isobel disappeared inside and the vehicle sped off into the night.

Alex's expression was grim. "I do not like this."

"Me neither. They're up to something."

"Chloe, we need to follow them."

My shock transformed into action and I reversed wildly out of the driveway. By the time I reached the road, the car and its freakish passengers were no longer in sight, but I knew where they were headed. I slammed my foot on the gas and gave chase.

I didn't know exactly what Isobel's intentions were, but it didn't matter. I knew she was a collector of lives, tallying them up like notches on her belt. Whatever her plan, I would do everything in my power to thwart her. No one else was going to get hurt. Not if I could help it.

CHAPTER EIGHTEEN

When we reached the theatre, parents were milling around in the foyer, talking about local events and school news. I could tell whenever anyone mentioned Hart Anderson by the way their faces changed. His death had hit everyone hard.

Isobel's appearance had distracted me from calling Zac so I dialled his number now. There was no answer and I wondered if he might already be on his way. But how would he have known to come? I fired off a text: *Emergency. We need you. Come to school play.*

I quickly got some tickets and Alex and I walked inside the auditorium. There was nothing unusual going on in there, no impending threat of danger. Rather, there was an air of excitement as people chatted quietly, munched on boxed candy or studied the program, waiting for the lights to dim.

I didn't much like the idea of being trapped in the theatre should anything happen, so Alex and I didn't take our seats but hovered at the back, eyes peeled.

Silence descended as Principal Kaplan came onto the stage. I guessed by her expression what she was about to say before she even began. "The tragic loss of Hart Anderson has rocked our community to the core." A wave of disbelief went through the audience. I'd never known our principal to show even the slightest sign of emotion, but now her voice quavered. "Our hearts go out to his family and friends at this difficult time. Hart was one of Sycamore's best and he will live on in our hearts. When I think about Hart, there are two things that stand out in my mind: the first is how much he supported his fellow students, whatever their passion; and the second is that he was no quitter. It's for this reason that I've decided to allow tonight's show to go on. It's what Hart would have wanted. And so we dedicate this opening performance to him and the contribution he made to this school."

Mr Helton was next to walk onstage. By the look in his eyes I could see he lived for these moments. He began by giving an overview of the play, but went on so long about the elements of Elizabethan revenge tragedy that people started shifting restlessly. He then moved on to describe the drama club's talent and ongoing commitment since the start of the school year, and finally spoke the words everyone had been waiting for: "And now to Elsinore Castle …"

My heart rate increased as soon as the lights dimmed and the audience's voices died down. Alex and I sat in the aisle, which we figured gave us the best vantage point, and tried to look inconspicuous. I knew Isobel and her accomplice were here somewhere, but Alex and I had searched all the faces in the audience without success. That wasn't surprising; of course, they were too calculating to put themselves in full view.

The curtain lifted to reveal the three witches. The stage had been transformed to look like a barren heath, and a crack of lightning flashed across the theatre.

"When shall we three meet again?" the first witch cried out. "In thunder, lightning, or in rain?"

A shiver travelled up my spine and my hand sought Alex's. The words of the play were strangely foreboding. It felt as if we were walking a tightrope over a ravine, waiting for the shove that would send us plummeting to the rocks below. Every one of my muscles was wound to a coil and adrenaline pumped through me, swinging between a flight or fight response. But I refused to give up hope. *Just have a bit of courage, Chloe*, I told myself.

Alex squeezed my hand as if he could read my thoughts. The small gesture gave me all the courage I needed. I swore I could feel his energy flowing into me.

We didn't have to wait long for trouble to start. The second scene began and we heard soldiers fighting offstage. But before the kid playing Malcolm could finish his lines, a fog curled around his feet and moved upward like a snake. I wondered for a moment whether the stagehand was going overboard with the fog machine, until I saw it. It began as little blue and green flashes, almost too fast to detect, but quickly morphed into the figure of a child — a little boy wearing old-fashioned breeches with a button-up jacket and holding a cap in his hand. I knew immediately that he was one of the children from the orphanage.

His appearance was so unexpected that the audience gasped and whispers began to fly. "I didn't know this was a modern take on *Macbeth*," I heard one of the parents say.

But you only had to look at the actors to know this wasn't part of the play. They'd gone dead silent, faces drained of colour, and looked around nervously as if waiting for someone to jump out and say, *Gotcha!* But nobody did, and the silence was almost deafening.

"Come on." Alex tugged me gently by the hand. "We need to go backstage."

Once we reached the foyer, we broke into a run. I led the way around the building to the back entrance the stagehands used. In the wings we found Mr Helton reeling about like a spinning top, throwing commands to no one in particular. I could imagine his devastation. On opening night, his play had been brought to an abrupt halt before the end of the first act by the appearance of a ghost child with an unclear motive. The rest of the cast and crew watched open-mouthed, unwilling to intervene in what was happening onstage but unable to tear their eyes away.

Mr Helton flapped his hands, trying to get the attention of the actors onstage. "Do something! Improvise!" he called. Then his gaze fell on me. "I remember you! Do you know anything about this?"

"No, sir," I replied. "But you have to get those kids offstage."

"Why? What's going on?" he cried. "Where did that kid come from? Who's trying to sabotage my play?"

"There is no time to explain," Alex told him. "You must evacuate the theatre at once."

"Evacuate?" Mr Helton glared at him. "Are you joking?! The show must go on!"

"Sir, please," I began, but broke off when I saw what was happening onstage. Behind the actors, the walls of the set rippled then tilted dangerously forward.

"Good Lord," Mr Helton moaned and I saw his eyes

were glistening with tears. "This can't be happening. Get them offstage! Get them off!"

The stagehands responded, but not fast enough. The painted set fell onto the stage, breaking apart in a cloud of dust. The lights spluttered, then blew out with a shower of sparks. The actors ducked as props rained down around them, and the audience started jumping to their feet to leave.

As I peered closer, I realised the stage was now covered with figures, only they were hazy, masked by fog. Bit by bit the fog cleared to reveal Isobel surrounded by the twelve children who had perished in the fire. They were like a ghost army and it was unsettling to see such menacing expressions on their young faces.

At the sight of them, Mr Helton blanched and swayed dangerously as if he might pass out. The children weren't real; that much was obvious. At least, it was obvious to Alex and me. Their bodies were slightly translucent and the air around them looked like dimpled glass.

Before Alex could stop me I rushed onto the stage until I was only feet away from the circle of wraiths. "Isobel!" I hissed. "You have to leave."

Slowly her head cranked sideways like a mechanical doll until she was looking directly at me. I saw that her eyes were huge and black with murderous intent.

There was only one thing I could think to say. "I'll do whatever you want. I'll give Alex up ... for good this time."

I knew how much she hated me for taking Alex away, but the truth was Alex hadn't been hers for a long time now. She'd lost him decades ago but had never come to terms with it.

Isobel lifted an eyebrow almost playfully. "Keep him." Her voice sounded eerie and hollow.

"What do you want then?" I demanded, desperate to bargain with her and put an end to whatever disaster was about to unfold.

"Do you really think this is about you or him?" she said scornfully. "I want what you have — to live again!"

"That's not how it works! There are supposed to be rules. Please, Isobel, you have to let go."

But Isobel was a law unto herself, as she had always been. Her only response was a humourless laugh. "You of all people cannot talk about rules."

Before I could answer, Alex grabbed me and pulled me back into the wings. He didn't attempt to address Isobel. Perhaps he knew better than I did how futile it would be.

With me out of the way, Isobel was able to refocus her attention to the task at hand. She gave a slight hand signal to which the orphans responded immediately. To my horror, I saw weapons materialise in their hands — a spade, a hammer, a jagged shard of glass. Where had they come from? The little boy who had appeared first raised a pair of sharp scissors to his face, smiling as the metal glinted in the dim light. I could only assume those weapons had been conjured for them. How had Isobel managed to get all these ghosts under her command? What promise had she made them?

A tense beat of silence followed, then, with a sound like steel scraping across glass, the ghosts rushed forward and flew en masse into the audience. From where I stood they looked like a frenetic cloud. Alex and I moved just a second later, bolting onto the stage toward Isobel. She saw us coming and vanished into the wings on the opposite side.

Helpless, we looked out at the mayhem in the auditorium. The ghost children were slashing people with their weapons, slipping like vapour through the fingers of anyone who tried to grab hold of them. The weapons were real, as were the injuries they were inflicting, and people screamed as they tried to run or to shield their children. The dim light created the impression of a grotesque Halloween spectacle, but this was only too real.

Some of the ghosts had drifted toward the exits, barring anyone from leaving. I stared wildly around the theatre, but there was no sign of Dad or Rory. They should have arrived by now, so I had to hope they were somewhere safe, away from this madness.

I wondered why no one had called the police or an ambulance, but when I pulled out my phone there was no signal so the presence of ghosts must have blocked the reception.

"We have to do something!" I cried, although I hadn't the faintest idea what. I looked desperately at Alex, hoping he might have a plan.

"There are only two ways I know to repel ghosts," he answered. "Obsidian and salt. We have neither."

"Okay. Well, forget the first thing," I said, "seeing as I don't know what it is. But salt should be easy to get."

"From where?"

"The cafeteria will have a supply." I glanced around. "I don't want to leave you here alone though."

At that moment Mr Helton came rushing over, punching numbers uselessly into his phone with trembling hands. He was shaking so hard he dropped his phone when Alex took him by the shoulders.

"Your devices are not working," Alex said. "Would you like to do something that will help?"

"What? What can I do?" I'd never seen Mr Helton so panicked. "I don't understand what's happening!"

"There *is* something you can do. But I need you to pull yourself together first," Alex said. "Can you do that for your students?"

That struck a chord. Mr Helton swallowed and looked Alex square in the eyes. "Tell me what to do."

"Run to the cafeteria and bring all the salt you can find," I told him.

He looked at me blankly. "Salt?"

"I know it sounds ridiculous, but there's no time to explain."

He turned and stumbled toward the exit, calling for two of his older students to go with him. They peeled off their cumbersome costumes and raced after him, eager to help.

In the auditorium, the wraiths continued to attack and the shrieks from their victims grew more frantic as they scrambled for cover or tried to fend off their assailants.

I heard crazed laughter behind me and knew who it was before I turned to look. Isobel was larger than life now, her ivory nightgown flowing around her, the stiff lace of its collar circling her throat like barbed wire. She made me think of Bertha Mason, Mr Rochester's insane and violent wife locked in the attic of Thornfield Hall. Her arms were raised and her head was thrown back and her mad laughter bounced off the walls and ceiling. I couldn't tear my gaze away from her. There was nothing human left in her now and I wondered why she was clinging to the idea of being reborn. Hadn't she made a royal mess of her life the first time around?

Alex appeared at my side and, finally, spoke her name. "What has happened to you?" he asked.

She turned to him, her laughter fading, and I saw that whatever tenderness she had felt for him in the past was well and truly gone. I didn't think he had any influence left to wield over her.

She took a step forward, speaking in a strange, almost flirtatious way. "Alexander, my dear, do I repulse you? I remember a time when you could not get enough of me."

"I did not know you then."

"Hush, my sweet, I am as I have always been. Perhaps it was you who was blind."

"I was a fool." He looked around the auditorium at the devastation the ghost children were wreaking, then back at her. "Why are you doing this, Isobel? Have you no pity left? Has every last shred of humanity abandoned you?"

"Tell me, why should I relinquish life when you are still here?"

Alex's eyes narrowed. "You and I are not the same," he said in a steely voice. "I am no murderer."

"Perhaps not yet," she purred, and I felt Alex go rigid at my side. "But what if you were forced to choose between the life of an innocent and that of your precious adolescent admirer?"

It took me a second to realise she was referring to me.

"You shall not touch her," Alex spat. "If you try, I will —"

"You will *what?*" Isobel sniggered. "You cannot harm me and you cannot control me, Alexander. You are at my mercy now and I do not even have to get my hands dirty."

She looked past us and beckoned with a long, bloodless finger. Almost immediately a child manifested by her side. I recognised her as the little girl with the shaved head who had appeared to me in the bathroom — Amelia. In her tiny hand she clutched a shard of glass now smeared with blood. At first she looked disoriented, until Isobel placed a maternal hand on her shoulder and knelt to whisper something in her ear. I couldn't hear the words, but I saw the little girl's face change as if under a spell. Her eyes locked on me, blazing with malicious intent. She moved closer, close enough for me to hear her ragged breathing. Very deliberately she raised her arm.

Alex stepped in front of me, but the child was undeterred.

Looking into her eyes, I saw the flicker of flames and remembered. Her fear in the bathroom came back to me: *That wicked Mrs Marsh!* she'd said. *Don't let her catch me again!*

"Mrs Marsh is coming!" I cried impulsively and saw the malice in the child's face turn to terror before she disappeared.

Incensed, Isobel flew into the air to call her charges to her.

I didn't have to look down into the seating area to know that people were losing strength. How long could they hold out against an enemy that never tired?

We were distracted by the sound of running feet heading toward us. I tensed, but it was only Mr Helton and his students, holding several large plastic bags of salt along with all the shakers they could carry from the cafeteria tables.

"Good work," Alex said, and Mr Helton looked chuffed by the praise. "Now distribute them among your cast."

Some of the actors looked reluctant to take the salt, but Alex spoke encouragingly to them. "I know you are all frightened, but you must be strong for just a while longer. I need you to fight back against the ghosts so your families and friends can get to safety. Throw salt on the wraiths and that will deter them for a time. Are you up to the task?"

I was worried the students would refuse, but Alex's words seemed to fire them up. First Banquo nodded, then Lady Macbeth and Duncan were by his side in a show of solidarity.

Once each student was armed, Mr Helton let out a heroic battle cry, which in other circumstances might have been funny, and led the way into the seating area. We watched the newly formed army long enough to see that the strategy was working. As soon as a wraith came into contact with the salt, it hissed like steam before disintegrating. It only vanished for a minute or so before reappearing in a different location, but it was long enough to allow more people to take cover.

I strained my eyes to catch a glimpse of Rory and Dad but still couldn't spot them. I couldn't help wondering where Zac was too. He should have been here by now and we could really use his help. Had he arrived too late and been barred from entering? I just hoped he hadn't gotten into a wreck speeding over here.

Even though the salt was slowing things down, the ghosts were still attacking the remaining people in the auditorium and I wondered if this nightmare would ever end.

Then an idea sprang into my mind with such conviction that it stopped me in my tracks. Perhaps we hadn't exhausted all avenues yet. Perhaps there was one person left who could help us.

Alex could read me like an open book. "What are you thinking?" he asked.

"We have to summon the spirit of Agatha Marsh."

CHAPTER NINETEEN

It felt crazy even thinking it, let alone saying it out loud. The last thing we needed was to summon another spirit we might not be able to control. Although there'd been no evidence so far to suggest Mrs Marsh was also under Isobel's influence, conjuring her was risky. But what other choice did we have?

I saw the doubt in Alex's eyes. "I am not sure, Chloe, it is extremely dangerous. You have no idea how her spirit will react. How can we be sure she will not do more harm than good?"

He had a valid point, but we didn't have time for sitting down and hashing out the pros and cons of my idea. Right now there were people fighting for their lives in here.

"I've seen her twice now, so chances are she's still hanging around," I said.

"Did you not hear anything I just said?"

"Yes, I did, but those ghosts are hurting people as we speak. No one can get in here to help us and we're running out of time. This woman might be the only thing those kids will answer to and our only hope of putting a stop to this. So unless you have a better idea …"

The seconds that passed as I watched Alex try to come up with a less risky alternative were possibly the longest of my life.

He let out a groan of frustration and slammed his fist into his hand. "Alright! But there is no time to conduct a seance. Besides, we do not have the right tools at our disposal."

"There has to be another way," I said, and then it came to me. "An invocation!"

Alex said the same thing right at the same time. "We make a good team," he added, and winked at me.

Even with all the havoc around us I could still look into his blue eyes and feel myself melt. *Now is not the time, Chloe*, I reminded myself. After all this was over we'd have time to enjoy a moment of intimacy together, like we had at Grange Hall. I'd never been surer that what Alex and I had was timeless, and no one, living or dead, was going to tamper with it.

Alex followed me back onto the stage, where I thought about how I was going to summon Agatha Marsh. Instinct told me I'd have to appeal to her desire for control. I had seen a coldness in her ghost's eyes that suggested she was a hard woman, and Amelia Alcott had been terrified of her. *Don't let her catch me*, she'd said. Yes, I'd bet money that Agatha Marsh was the sort of person who enjoyed enforcing discipline a little too much.

"Mrs Marsh!" I called out. "The children are out of control! They're wreaking havoc and you're the only one who can restore order. They're running wild without you here to stop them. You must come and punish them."

"How else will they ever learn their lesson?" Alex called, getting in on the act.

"They're wicked, insubordinate children!" I yelled. "So come and stop them! Come and —"

I broke off as a voice hissed from the nearby shadows: "*Ungrateful!*"

A woman stood on the steps leading up to the stage. She was draped in a black shawl and had dark hair scraped into the tightest bun I'd ever seen. It pulled her eyes into narrow slits, giving her the look of a lizard. She stared into the audience with an expression like thunder, and I saw that her lips were quivering with rage, making her look all the more terrifying.

Luckily, we weren't her target. With a wild screech that made both Alex and me jump, she flew down the steps and into the seating area. The ghost children stopped dead in their tracks and immediately released their victims. A few even dropped their weapons in a flimsy attempt to hide their guilt.

"I can't believe it worked," I whispered to Alex.

Some of the orphans tried to run, but most stayed rooted to the spot with terror as Mrs Marsh swept over them like a tidal wave.

"You rotten little ingrates!" She grabbed the boy who'd been the first ghost to appear and slapped him so hard it left him reeling. "After everything I've done for you this is how you repay me!"

"I'm sorry, Mrs Marsh," he stammered and I almost felt pity for him.

"Not as sorry as you will be," she snarled. "The shame you have brought on this institution!"

She seized the ear of another child and pulled him into line with the first. They stood there trembling while she moved on to her next victim, looming over the little girl like a predatory bird. She only had to motion with her bony finger for the rest of the children to fall mutely in line.

The people still in the auditorium couldn't believe what they were seeing and clung to one another for support. One person actually passed out from shock. When two worlds collided this violently there were bound to be repercussions; I wondered how many of them would never get over this.

Just as Mrs Marsh had assembled her bedraggled charges into a single file, one of the exit doors swung open. People scrambled toward it, tripping over themselves in their eagerness to get out. Then, suddenly, the cluster of bodies stopped. A tall witch-like figure loomed in the doorway, blocking the light from the foyer. Isobel seemed to fill the entire space and nobody dared go near her. I should have known she wouldn't be so easily deterred. I should have known not to underestimate her.

At first I thought she was angry with us for thwarting her army of ghosts. But the look on her face wasn't defeat; it was defiance. That look could only mean one thing: Isobel had a new strategy. The idea filled me with dread.

With a devilish smile at me, she stood aside to let someone enter the auditorium. At first I assumed it would be her father and accomplice. Instead a tall guy wearing a balaclava, gloves and a long coat stepped into view. I didn't need to see his face to know who he was; I recognised him by the designer combat boots he wore to school every day. It was Zac.

He took a few steps forward, his movements slow and deliberate, and I saw that he was under some kind of spell. Isobel had turned my friend into her living breathing puppet. But why? What did she need him for?

Isobel trailed spidery fingers tenderly across Zac's exposed lips and tilted his face toward her. She kissed his mouth fervently, then bent to purr something into his ear.

"Zac, get away from her!" I screamed, but he was past hearing me.

He surveyed the crowd impassively. He may as well have been a sleepwalker, his steely eyes looking right through us. When his coat swung open, I caught sight of a gleam of metal and knew what Isobel's final act was to be.

"Oh my God, he's armed," I said.

"I see that," Alex said calmly.

"What do we do?"

"I will distract Isobel. You must break her spell on Zac before anyone else realises he has a gun."

I stood dumbstruck. "How do you propose I do that?"

"You must find a way. You are the only one who can stop him."

Things seemed to happen in slow motion after that. I knew I had to stay calm while I tried to talk to Zac. If any of the people still in the auditorium clued in to what was about to happen, mayhem would follow as they scrambled in all directions to get to safety.

I felt terrible knowing that all this chaos and horror was happening because of me. This wasn't just some assault on the school by some random maniac. If I hadn't fallen in love with Alex, Isobel wouldn't be here. I'd had the temerity to cross a line and love a ghost, a man who had once loved her, and in doing so I had incurred Isobel's eternal wrath. It was like she was taunting me: *Didn't you learn your lesson the first time, you stupid girl?* I didn't regret loving Alex for a minute, but now I had to take responsibility for the consequences. This was my mess and I was the only one who could clean it up.

Looking around the theatre, I could see some people had serious injuries and might not survive if help didn't come soon. I had to act now before their injuries turned into fatalities.

Again my thoughts flew to Dad and Rory. The idea of something happening to them was more than I could stand. But I reminded myself that I hadn't seen them at all since I'd arrived, so maybe they were someplace safe.

Just breathe, I told myself as I made my way toward Zac, trying to move slowly so as not to alarm people. It didn't even occur to me to consider my own safety, that he might try and hurt me.

A girl collided with me, our foreheads smacking painfully together. She looked a mess, with hair sticking to her face and mascara-stained cheeks.

"Chloe!" she cried, and it took me a second to recognise her.

"Sam! Are you alright? Where's Natalie?"

"She didn't want to come, and I'm glad she didn't now. Chloe, what's happening?"

Her voice came out as a whimper and I noticed that blood was seeping from a gash in her arm and soaking her sleeve.

"Okay, listen to me," I said. "Just get down and stay down, okay? Stay there until help comes."

She nodded gratefully. I was moving away when she grabbed me by the shoulders. "Wait!" she said. "I want to tell you something."

"Right now you just have to be safe," I said, trying to pull away but she wouldn't let go.

"Chloe, I don't want you thinking I'm angry with you because I'm not. We've been friends a long time and just because we're having some stupid fight doesn't mean I don't care about you."

"I know," I said gently. "And I care about you too. Now will you please do something for me?"

"Anything."

"Hide!"

She hugged me, then turned away to squeeze under a row of seats. When she was in place, she gave me a thumbs-up. In that second, everything we'd shared since fifth grade flashed through my mind. It had never occurred to me before how much of my life had been spent with Sam. And now she was looking to me to take charge and save her and everyone else stuck in this theatre. I determined not to let her down.

My fingers sticky with her blood, I moved closer to Zac. Isobel loomed behind him like a puppeteer, her movements a little jerky as she adjusted to having a physical form. Something told me she needed to stay close to Zac to maintain her control over him.

Alex must have realised that too because suddenly he appeared at her side. They circled each other like adversaries rather than past lovers. He was the first to pounce, grabbing Isobel and dragging her out into the foyer. Even though they were both ghosts, he was still stronger than her. I noticed that once their bodies made contact they lost some of their physicality, becoming a tangle of frenetic energy as they wrestled on the ground.

Alex was giving me the valuable minutes I needed to try and avert disaster. My legs turned to jelly. How was I going to pull this off? I was sure I was going to mess up. I would let everybody down and have to live with the guilt for the rest of my life.

A voice in my head snapped me to my senses. This wasn't about me. Whether I failed or not, I had to give it my best shot.

I stood directly in front of Zac and waited for him to notice me. He didn't move, just stood there transfixed. I wished I could see his face. It was creepy with only his eyes visible through the balaclava's slits. At least they'd lost some of their glassiness now that Alex had drawn Isobel away.

"Zac, it's me," I said. "Everything's going to be okay."

"I can't stop her."

His voice sounded resigned and I could tell he'd moved past fear to an unnatural calm.

"You can," I said. "You're stronger than you think."

He shook his head vehemently. "No one can stop her."

I hated hearing him sound so defeated. I knew Zac had a noble heart; he was the sort of kid who'd get himself hurt intervening in a fight that had nothing to do with him. That was the part of him I needed to get through to now.

"I can help you!" I said, and I took a step forward and held out my hands to him.

If he took them, I knew he'd have a chance of shaking off whatever spell Isobel had him under. I wasn't going to let her use Zac this way. If she succeeded, his entire life would be in ruins. This wasn't something he could ever come back from.

I saw him waver as memories filtered through the fog. Then his face changed.

"Get out of my way," he said, and the chilling voice was no longer his. I saw his hand slip under his coat, reaching for the gun I knew was hidden there.

I glanced quickly toward the empty foyer and knew Isobel had somehow got free. But where was Alex?

I looked back at Zac and he growled at me, his lips curling in a way I'd never seen before. I realised it was Isobel inside his skin now; she had taken possession of him.

"You have been a thorn in my side long enough, Chloe Kennedy."

Isobel uttered my name as if it were poison, but I ignored her and searched Zac's eyes for a sign that he was still in there somewhere. His pupils were massive, like he'd taken some kind of drug. His head twitched and he cocked it to one side as if struggling to recognise me.

"Hang on, Zac," I told him. "She can't do this to you. You have to fight back. If you don't, she'll destroy us all."

"You will have to do better than that!" Isobel jeered. "This boy is mine. You cannot always win, Chloe. You have taken from me the only person I loved. I am entitled to have some fun now."

I wondered why Isobel was bothering to talk to me when she had the power simply to tear me limb from limb. And then I realised the battle that was raging inside Zac. She had him in her clutches, but she didn't own him entirely. There was a part of him still putting up a fight. If I kept focused on him, there was a chance I'd get through.

"It's up to you!" I told him. "You have to fight her!"

A pleading look flashed across Zac's eyes, like he was asking me, *How?*

I had an answer; something my mom had taught me long ago. When I spoke, it was as if the words were coming from a deep well inside me.

"Order her to leave. Cast her out and claim your mind back. The dead have no dominion here."

But Isobel had created a wall around Zac's mind and I needed to do more to help him break through it. What else could I say?

An idea came to me. I had to reconnect him with his old self.

"Zac, when all this is over I can't wait to come over for a swim and have one of your gourmet breakfasts. Where did you learn to cook like that? Oh, that's right, your mom is Martha Stewart."

It was a lame joke, but it did the trick. A flicker of recognition came into his eyes and the hand that had reached for the gun dropped to his side, empty.

"Chloe, help me," he managed to croak out.

An instant later he was flying across the auditorium. He hit the brick wall with a thud, tumbled down some steps and landed in a heap like a broken toy.

I rushed to his side and lifted his head to remove the balaclava. He was breathing raggedly. As I scanned his face, he opened his eyes and I saw the demented stare was gone. The guy looking back at me was lost, confused and barely coherent, but just Zac.

I opened his coat, found the revolver and also a hunting knife, and hid both under the heavy velvet stage curtains out of harm's way.

"Stay here," I instructed him. "Don't try to move."

"Okay. Hey, Chloe?"

"Yeah?"

"I beat her, didn't I?"

"You did, Zac. You did great."

247

CHAPTER TWENTY

I finally saw Alex shepherding some of the injured out of the theatre. By now the phones were working again and people wasted no time calling for help. I signalled to Alex and he came over to where I was sitting with Zac, who had passed out after his ordeal with Isobel.

"How is he?" Alex asked me.

"I'm not sure. He just collapsed." Alex knelt to check Zac's pulse.

"It will take a few days, but he will be fine." A wave of relief flooded through me until I remembered that Zac being safe didn't mean things were over.

"What happened to Isobel?"

"She got away. I have been looking for her."

"You think she's gone?"

"No. She will be lurking somewhere. We have to find her."

"And when we do?" I was tired of fighting Isobel. It seemed like we'd never be free of her.

"Where is the gun?" Alex asked.

One look at his face told me the real fight was just beginning. His jaw was clenched and a vein in his temple throbbed.

"I hid it. I didn't want anyone to find it on Zac."

"That was good thinking, but we need it now."

"What for? It's not like we can use it against Isobel."

"We need it to kill Doctor Ritter."

For the first time in our entire relationship I found myself doubting Alex's judgment. "Are you crazy?"

"Where did you hide it?" he persisted.

I nodded in the direction of the heavy stage curtains. Without a word Alex retrieved the weapon and slipped it inside his jacket. My stomach was churning and Alex saw the revulsion on my face.

"We do not have a choice, Chloe. How many people have already been hurt? Ritter will not stop, and neither will Isobel. But if we destroy him, every spirit he has conjured will disappear with him."

"I can't kill anyone," I said, feeling ill.

"No one is asking you to."

"We don't even know where to find Doctor Ritter."

Alex looked down at Zac's inert form. "No, but he does."

"What do you mean? How would Zac know anything?"

"Zac and Isobel shared one mind for a brief time, which means Zac will know where Ritter is. We must prise that information out of him."

"Um … don't you think he's been through enough already?"

"Yes, I do. But I also think Zac would want to do everything in his power to help."

The events of the last week suddenly caught up with me. I felt on the point of breaking. "I just want to go home."

"I know, my darling. I need you to do this one last thing," Alex urged.

I knew why he needed me. Zac and I were friends; I was the person he trusted.

Without a clue what I was doing, I knelt beside Zac, took his hand and focused on transferring healing energy into him. He looked vulnerable and broken and I hated the idea of putting him under any more strain.

"Zac, can you hear me? I know you're not up to this right now, but I need to ask you something important."

A few tense moments passed before Zac's hand squeezed mine and I felt encouraged to continue.

"Alex and I need to stop Isobel before she does any more damage. In order to do that we need to find Doctor Ritter. You need to tell us where he's hiding."

Zac opened his eyes and gave me a vacant stare. He struggled to understand what I was asking. Then he moved his head as if to indicate he didn't have any answers.

"You do know," I pressed him. "Isobel's thoughts were linked with yours briefly. You have to access those memories now — don't block them."

Zac's face turned from white to red, like he was summoning every vestige of concentration in his overwrought brain. His eyes rolled back and he began to shake so much I thought he was suffering a seizure. He tried to speak, but the words weren't forming.

If I'd known this was going to cause Zac pain, I would never have agreed to it. I felt annoyed with Alex for not telling me.

"We have to stop this. We're making him worse," I said.

Alex nodded.

Just as I was trying to calm Zac, he croaked out two faint words. "Not here."

"Where?" Alex asked forcefully.

"Outside ... sheds."

I knew exactly where he meant. The only sheds on campus were the maintenance sheds behind the tennis courts. That's where Doctor Ritter must be hiding.

Zac must have fought hard to get that message out because the minute he did, his eyes lost focus and he slipped again into unconsciousness. I felt his pulse; it was erratic but still beating.

I'd never been so relieved to hear the sounds of sirens and screeching tyres as the emergency services arrived. Leaving Zac and the other injured to the paramedics, Alex and I slipped out a back exit before the police cordoned off the theatre building. We sprinted across the school grounds toward the maintenance sheds.

I wondered whether Alex had ever fired a gun; whether he'd actually be able to kill Doctor Ritter. The only time I'd ever held a gun was when I was about twelve years old and we visited my Uncle Jack in Idaho. He'd taken me and Rory to a shooting range for fun. The idea of actually using one on a person, no matter how sinister, made me feel faint.

One step at a time, I told myself. One thing I did know was that if we didn't stop Doctor Ritter now, there was no telling what he would do next. He must have committed his entire unnaturally long life to perfecting these dark arts. If he had finally succeeded in commanding the dead, he wasn't likely to give that up now.

The shed was a run-of-the-mill structure made of galvanised steel, the sort of place you wouldn't expect anything extraordinary to take place. The doors had dusty glass panes, some of which were broken, and were padlocked and chained. How were we going to break in without being heard?

I started when someone wearing workboots and overalls emerged from the gloom. Then I recognised him.

"Miguel! What on earth —" I began, but he tapped a finger to his lips to shush me. He nodded at Alex in acknowledgment and said, "Hurry. There isn't much time."

In his other hand he was holding a set of boltcutters. I watched in amazement as he used them to cut through the padlock and chain.

We slid one of the doors open just enough to slip through. I thought Miguel would follow us, but he stood back, like an actor whose part in a play is over.

There were no lights and I nearly crashed into a ride-on mower before my eyes adjusted to the gloom. We navigated our way carefully around the clutter of broken pots and rusty tools, and didn't see Doctor Ritter at first because he was hidden behind some metal shelves.

We crept toward him and I saw he was kneeling before a makeshift altar made from what appeared to be a packing crate with a white cloth over it. It was covered with lighted candles, as well as some statues of pagan deities and a collection of tiny bones that could have belonged to a small animal like a cat, or maybe … I chose not to finish that thought. There were also several glass vials, each containing a different-coloured liquid, and dried herbs burning pungently in shallow bowls.

Doctor Ritter was wearing a hooded robe like some ancient high priest instead of his usual three-piece suit and appeared to be in a deep trance. He hadn't noticed our arrival, which was lucky for us as I was sure we'd made a lot of noise. He was facing away from us, his silver hair loose, his body bent low in a position of supplication.

Alex watched him for a moment, eyes narrowed in fascination. "He is raising the dead right at this very moment," he whispered. Slowly he withdrew the handgun from inside his jacket. "We need to move closer."

I grabbed Alex's sleeve and tugged him back. There had to be another way to stop a necromancer other than murder. Maybe we could bargain with him. No matter how many crimes this old man had committed over the decades, wouldn't pulling the trigger make us no better than him?

Alex read the reluctance in my face. "Chloe, he is not a man. He is a fiend in the guise of a man."

Images of the attack in the theatre came back to me. I saw the blood-streaked faces of people whose names I didn't know but whose fear would remain with me forever. I heard the screams of pain and terror as if they were happening all over again. I tried to draw on those memories to reignite my rage, but instead I just felt flat. Doctor Ritter might deserve to die, but who were we to mete out that punishment? I didn't want that kind of power or responsibility.

Alex stroked my face. "Once this is over, Chloe, we can be together without fear. I hope you still want that?"

Of course I wanted it. I wanted it more than anything. I'd just stopped believing it was ever going to be possible. Our love had been under assault from the beginning; but without faith we didn't stand a chance. There was no way I was going to wimp out on Alex now, not after everything we'd been through. By way of answer, I took his hand, held it between my own and pressed it to my lips.

As I did, an inhuman shriek reverberated around the space as Isobel emerged from the gloom. I knew I was looking at a cold and heartless killer, twisted over the years by dark thoughts. Isobel would never change. She would never stop. Nothing would ever bring her peace, or stop her hating the living. Isobel and her father had violated a fundamental law of nature, but then again neither seemed to have much respect for laws. The realisation filled me with a sudden and overpowering exhaustion. I felt as if this fight would never end. Maybe Isobel *couldn't* be killed. How could we conquer such deep hatred?

When she rushed at me, I made no move to protect myself. She looked ready to tear me apart, but I felt strangely empty. Maybe the only way to end this was to give her what she wanted. Maybe that was the victory she had been seeking all along.

She was almost upon me when I heard a deafening sound. At first I thought part of the building behind us had collapsed until an acrid smell filled the air. It was only when I looked at Alex still pointing the gun at Doctor Ritter that I realised what had happened.

Isobel turned around with a crazed look then stumbled forward with her hands outstretched before letting out a strangled cry.

"Father, don't leave me!" The necromancer rocked back on his knees and his eyes flew open to stare at us. In that moment I could barely tell the difference between him and Isobel, as if they were one and the same. I supposed, when you thought about it, they were: a father who'd let his madness seep into his daughter until they were both twisted and knotted like the roots of an ancient tree.

Doctor Ritter's face was stiff with pain, but instead of crumpling to the ground like a regular person, he stayed upright and began to slowly shrivel like a piece of dried fruit. It seemed as if the flesh on his body was rapidly decaying, caving inwards around his bones. It was a disgusting sight, but I was unable to look away.

As the necromancer clawed at his own body, his eyes bulbous in his desiccated face, he wheezed a final threat at us. "You can never escape the past. It will always haunt you."

At the sight of her father reduced to a pile of smouldering robes, Isobel let out a savage scream that was half-pain, half-fury. But she had no opportunity to avenge herself on us as she also began to wither in front of our eyes. She whimpered like a wounded animal as she slowly disintegrated, but not for one second did her eyes leave Alex's face. Finally she was nothing more than a pile of ash on the ground alongside her father.

Suddenly I felt my knees give way from under me. Alex caught me in his arms just before I hit the cement floor.

"Is it really over?" I asked, and felt his arms wrap around me and his head come down to lean gently against mine.

"Yes, my love. It is over."

There was no sense of relief. Instead, a numbness crept over me. I willed myself to feel something, but it seemed as if someone had reached into my brain and switched off everything that made me Chloe Kennedy. All I was really aware of was one thing and that was how pivotal this moment was …

This was the moment every adversity had been leading to; the moment that would determine what the future held for me and those I loved. I couldn't believe it had taken so long for me to understand the truth. All this time I had been thinking my fight with Isobel was about revenge and vanity and the tragedies of the past. But now I saw that it was about me. It had always been about me.

From a young age I'd known I didn't fully belong to this world, and I had been right. At eighteen years of age here I was, still living a half-life, wavering on the fringe between life and death. Now the universe was telling me it was time to make a decision. *Choose, Chloe*, it seemed to say. *You know what to do.*

Faces flashed through my mind — so many of the ghosts I'd seen through my life. Isobel was there, and Alexander of course, and Becky Burns. My mom was there too. How had I become so tangled up in the world of the dead; tangled to the point I felt there was no way of extricating myself? Deep down, I wasn't sure I even wanted to.

Perhaps it was time to accept that I needed them. Perhaps it was time to stop fighting and embrace the destiny that seemed to have been chosen for me.

The siege at Sycamore High was all anyone talked about for a couple of weeks, but then, like all dramas, it died down. The FBI carried out an investigation, but it proved inconclusive. People's recollections of what had happened proved hazy. Some told the investigators about a crazed woman with long black hair and wearing a white gown, while others talked about child soldiers, but no evidence of either could be located despite extensive searches. Some people blamed it all on a gas leak or an electrical malfunction that had caused a mass hallucination. The incident looked like it would remain a mystery, and for my part I thought it was better that way.

Zac was the only exception; his memory of that night remained crystal clear. He disappeared off the face of the earth for a while and I figured he just needed space, but then I heard a rumour that his parents had shipped him off to some exclusive clinic in California. I was the first to visit him after his discharge. He looked tired and drawn. It was obvious he would need a period of rest and maybe some trauma therapy, but I knew he'd be okay, scarred but okay.

"I'm sorry for doubting you," he said as we sat by the pool, our legs dangling in the water. Zac's mom seemed to have snapped out of her alcohol-fuelled daze and kept bringing out snacks.

"And I'm sorry you got caught in the crossfire."

"That's not your fault." He gave me a wan smile. "It's hard to pick up where you left off, isn't it?"

"Yeah. But it gets easier. I say that from experience."

"Graduation's coming up. Doesn't seem real."

"I know." Not only did it feel unreal, it felt like an anticlimax.

"What will you do after that?"

"I haven't given it much thought. You?"

"Work on my music for a while."

"That sounds like a good idea. I might go hang out with my gran for a bit." The idea only took shape as it was being uttered.

"England?"

I nodded.

"I've heard the food sucks, not to mention the weather."

I smiled. It was comforting to see that even after everything he'd gone through, Zac hadn't lost his sense of humour.

"There's stuff I need to figure out," I elaborated.

"I get it. But you better stay in touch."

"Promise."

There were things other than Zac to be grateful for. After watching Isobel and her father violently depart this world, I wasn't up to walking or driving so Alex ended up carrying me most of the way home. I discovered that Dad and Rory hadn't made it inside the theatre at all that night. By a stroke of good luck, Dad's girlfriend Marcie (I no longer referred to her as *that woman*) had managed to get herself lost and wound up at the wrong school. She couldn't find her way back so Dad and Rory had to go pick her up before the play began. I couldn't begin to express my relief, and I supposed it meant I couldn't carry on hating her any more.

Dad took a few days off work and became attentive all of a sudden, frequently coming into my room bearing mugs of hot chocolate. It made me feel like a little kid in need of reassurance that there were no monsters lurking under my bed. But the monsters in my life had been real, and not so easily dispelled.

"Chloe, would you like to talk to someone about what happened?" he asked me a few days after the attack. "It doesn't have to be me. Perhaps a therapist or someone like that?"

"Thanks for the suggestion," I said. "But I don't think that's the answer for me."

"Okay," he said, obviously not wanting to press the issue. "But if there is anything you need, or anything I can do, you will tell me, won't you?"

"Sure." I took a sip from the foaming mug. It had been my favourite mug as a kid and had a big cheerful snowman on the front.

"I'm so sorry you had to go through that alone."

"I wasn't alone," I replied, glancing at the figure in the cane chair by my window, his long legs crossed at the ankles, a book of Elizabethan sonnets on his lap. "And believe me, I'm glad you and Rory weren't there."

"We're all okay, that's the important thing," Dad said, attempting a smile.

I wasn't sure how okay I really was but nodded anyway.

He crossed the room to look out the window onto our street. "You know, your mom and I had a pact."

These days it was rare for him to offer up any personal information so I wasn't about to let this opportunity slip.

"Yeah? What kind of pact?"

He turned to look at me and I saw that his eyes were glassy. He took a minute before answering. "We promised each other that if anything happened to one of us, the other wouldn't go through life alone."

"That's weird," I said, unsure what else to say or how I felt. Why was he telling me this now? Was he trying to justify moving on from Mom so quickly? Or seeking my permission to date Marcie?

Dad patted my hand and suddenly I could see the strain of the past six months permanently recorded in his greying temples and the lines around his mouth.

"No, honey," he said. "That's love."

My father's words stayed with me long after he'd gone to bed. I might be in love with a phantom, but love was love, wasn't it? You didn't choose a particular path; you just found yourself on it. I knew that if Alex had to leave this world, I couldn't forget him. I knew I couldn't be like my dad and find someone new to love.

Alex and I both knew he couldn't stick around much longer. We knew it, but hadn't talked about it, because the thought of being apart was too unfathomable. I wanted to believe that wherever Alex went, he would find me again. And wherever he was, I would be there too. It was as simple as that. Life hadn't been very accommodating to us, so why settle for its parameters when we could roam the universe freely and together?

As Alex hadn't been conjured by Doctor Ritter, he didn't disappear along with the necromancer and Isobel. But soon after that night, I sensed him beginning to fade. Every time he appeared to me was shorter than the last, and I often caught him watching me with a strange expression as if trying to commit my features, my voice, my every movement, to memory. And who could blame him? Neither of us knew when we'd see each other again so we had to make every moment count.

When it came to our last night, I had imagined us tearing each other's clothes off like in some romance drama. Instead, we lay on my bed facing each other, our hands entwined and our eyes locked. We didn't talk about the future. We didn't want what little time we had left to be sullied by doubts and questions we couldn't answer. As Alex nuzzled my neck, I took his hand and placed it over my heart as if I could meld us together. But something had changed. Alex already felt different under my touch, like he wasn't completely present. Even the tip of his finger felt cold as it traced around my face. His paleness and marble stillness reminded me of a beautiful statue — trapped in time, neither living nor dead. After a while I noticed I could no longer hear him breathing. It made me wonder how amazing it would have been to have known Alex when he was alive. That was the one thing I envied Becky; she had known the living, breathing person.

All I knew was that I couldn't lose him a second time. I had to find a way for us to stay connected. Even if I had my life to live, I couldn't imagine doing it without Alex by my side. I didn't want to. As I couldn't exactly abandon the mortal world, I had to find another way. My abilities had been bestowed on me for a reason. While once upon a time I would have done anything to be rid of them and feel normal, I now found myself wanting to know more. The dead no longer frightened me; in some ways I felt more connected to them than to the living. If Becky had been able to communicate with me through dream sequences, then maybe that was where I'd meet Alex. It wasn't exactly ideal, but for now it might have to do.

As usual, he read my thoughts. "If there is a way back, I will find it. I will never stop trying," he murmured.

I believed him. I just didn't know how I was going to fill the time while I waited. I knew everything life had to offer would be humdrum without Alex to share it with me.

"It's okay if it's weeks," I said, "but what if it's years or longer before I see you again?"

"You cannot think that way, Chloe. It will torment you."

"How should I think of it then?"

"Think of it as only time."

I should have felt a crushing sadness. Instead, a calm descended over me like I'd never felt before. As I slept, our spirits flew together through the universe, laughing and soaring and tumbling through time as if we knew no boundaries.

In the middle of the night I woke to find myself alone.

I opened my eyes to see a figure shrouded in mist standing right outside my window, looking at me while I slept. At first I thought it was Alex come to say goodbye, but as my vision cleared there was no mistaking the freckled girl in the starched apron with stray auburn curls falling from under her cap. It was Rebecca Burns. Her eyes travelled from my face to the drawer of my nightstand where I'd wrapped the brooch in a scarf and tucked it away. I knew what she wanted then; she had come to finish her story.

Becky stood there waiting until I pulled open the drawer and unwrapped the brooch for what would be my very last vision. I didn't fight the drowsiness and as I stared into Becky's eyes I let myself be transported back into her memories. Before I lay down, I saw myself standing outside the window beside her, even though I knew my body was still there in my bed. She took my hand, entwining her little cold fingers in mine, and I finally knew what bound us together. We had both loved Alexander Reade. Becky had only wanted to help him but instead had failed him. That sense of failure had tormented her into the afterlife. Now it was my turn. She was handing that responsibility over to me.

A gravel path opened in front of us with looming iron gates ahead. Hand in hand, we walked toward them together …

It has been many months since I've come anywhere near this house. I've been drawn to it many times before, but only today do I find the courage to venture onto the grounds …

It has been locked up ever since that horrible day, the servants all dismissed as there is no one for them to wait upon now. The garden has fallen into disrepair, the path choked with weeds. I feel like an interloper, trespassing on a site that no longer recognises me. Perhaps I am the first person to set foot here since it happened. An air of tragedy still hangs about Grange Hall as if it remembers all those young lives cut down in their prime. Who could have imagined it would end in so much heartache?

To my surprise the iron gates are not locked and give way easily when I push against them. I suppose there is no need to lock them these days. Nobody sets foot here willingly any more. I slip inside and walk along the once-familiar path until the house comes into view. It is like seeing an old friend who is much changed through hard times. To think it once intimidated me. Now it only looks cold and grey.

The villagers have talked of little else since the events of that day were revealed and with a scandal of this magnitude I believe they will talk of it for years to come. No one imagines I had any part to play and they will not believe me if I tell them. But I am more than content to live in the shadows. It has been six months and only now has the stabbing guilt begun to lessen. I tell myself things would have come unstuck with or without my involvement. After all, it was never about me to start with.

Even though the entire Reade family is now dead, it will never feel like they are truly gone. Some of the womenfolk in Wistings, coming home at eventide after working in the fields, claim to have witnessed sightings. Beatrice Barker told everyone she saw a dark-haired woman roaming the woods clutching a bundle of rags to her chest while Susanna Cummings saw a young cloaked gentleman keeping watch behind the gates.

I was fortunate enough to find a new situation and thus did not have to leave Wistings and work in the factories two towns over. The vicar and his wife are a young and kindly couple whose previous housemaid left them to marry a local farmer. It was

Mrs Baxter who put in a good word for me although since leaving Grange Hall, I do not know what has become of her. Some say she went to live with her cousin by the seaside. I know how much she cared for this house and it would break her heart to see it now.

Due to my history, the vicar is very gentle and patient with me. He never raises his voice or scolds me when I'm caught distracted. His wife, Anna, is just the same. She is quite an accomplished woman and kind enough to have begun teaching me French. But despite the generosity, I can see the pity in both their eyes. In an attempt to help me, they even called the doctor in to see if he could ease the shock, but he said this sort of thing can only be healed with time.

At least while working here, I am able to visit my family more often. This household is not nearly as strict. The cottage is modest compared to Grange Hall but warm and welcoming nonetheless. I try to devote myself to my duties, but the crack of a pistol and the blue lips of a dead infant still haunt my dreams ...

I think now that Alexander and Isobel Reade were doomed from the start. I will never quite be able to shake the blame that follows me, but in hindsight, what could I, a mere child unaccustomed to the ways of the world, have done to help them? I must not fixate on what cannot be changed. I refuse to let myself dwell on memories from that night. I prefer to remember the happier hours. When I think of Alexander, I shall think of him in the garden reading a book with threads of gold in his hair where the sunlight touches it. Or I shall picture him at his easel with a paintbrush between his teeth, face upturned and blinking at the sky to determine where the light might fall.

Just like the angel in the painting, Alexander looks unhurried, as if he has all the time in the world ...